"Sounds like your date's here."

"Cut it out," Cullen said, dismissing his brother's insinuation. "The lady needed a friend and I happened to be in the right place at the right moment."

"Yeah, well just watch your step or you'll have a ready-made family on your hands."

A ready-made family...

A knock on the door resounded in the entry hall. Rocket began to bark in earnest and giggly girls squealed in response on the front porch. The tranquility of his home was about to be shattered, for the day at least, and he had no one to blame but himself.

A ready-made family?

Perish the thought!

Dear Reader,

Welcome back to East Texas and life with the Temple
Brothers, whose stories are unfolding Deep in the Heart.
In *Fatherhood 101* you're going to fall for Cullen Temple,
named for Texas oilman and philanthropist Roy Cullen.
Cullen's life seems to be an open book, but in truth it's
more like a confidential file. When an abandoned pup, a
young widow and three little girls invade his quiet life,
Cullen must decide which is his greater fear: risking
the best thing that's ever happened to him or risking his
grip on reality. In true Lone Star State fashion, Cullen
will sweep you off your high heel boots and along with
him on his search for happiness.

Before the year is out, you're also going to get to know
Joiner Temple through the eyes of my new writing
partner, Gwen Ford Faulkenberry. Gwen is a high
school coach's wife, English teacher and a busy mother
of four who knows firsthand the joys and dramas of a
big family. Gwen will take Joiner on a wild ride as the
polo-playing Temple brother learns how to be a real
cowboy.

Until we meet again, let your light shine!

Mae Nunn

HARLEQUIN HEARTWARMING

Mae Nunn

Fatherhood 101

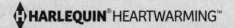

HARLEQUIN® HEARTWARMING™

Recycling programs for this product may not exist in your area.

ISBN-13: 978-0-373-36681-1

FATHERHOOD 101

Copyright © 2014 by Harlequin Books S.A.

The publisher acknowledges the copyright holders of the individual works as follows:

FATHERHOOD 101
Copyright © 2014 by Mae Nunn

FINDERS KEEPERS
Copyright © 2013 by Harlequin Books S.A.

Printed in U.S.A.

H HARLEQUIN®
™ www.Harlequin.com

CONTENTS

MAE NUNN

grew up in Houston and graduated from the University
of Texas with a degree in communications. When she
fell for a transplanted Englishman living in Atlanta, she
moved to Georgia and made an effort to behave like a
Southern belle. But when she found that her husband
was quite agreeable to life as a born-again Texan, Mae
happily returned to her cowgirl roots and cowboy boots!
In 2008 Mae retired from thirty years of corporate life to
focus on her career as a full-time author.

Other books by Mae Nunn

HARLEQUIN HEARTWARMING

COWBOY IN THE KITCHEN*
MORE ROOM FOR LOVE
HER LOVE NEXT DOOR

*Deep in the Heart

Mae Nunn

Fatherhood 101

"All that I am, or hope to be, I owe to my angel mother." –Abraham Lincoln

This book is dedicated to you, Mama.
You were my spiritual guide, my champion, my conscience and my example of a Proverbs 31 woman.
I miss you so very much.

Wilma Ruth Holliday

February 6, 1929–September 18, 2003

CHAPTER ONE

"CULLEN, IT'S TIME you stopped being the Texas version of Peter Pan and accepted some grown-up responsibility," Dr. Blair Mastal insisted.

"I take umbrage with that statement," Cullen Temple responded with an upward tilt of his chin that probably needed a shave, as usual.

Blair was a popular professor who'd been Cullen's mentor and friend throughout his college career. And after several degrees in history, college truly had become Cullen's career.

Blair was making a familiar point and it just happened to be shared by Cullen's three brothers and everybody else who felt compelled to express an opinion on his obsession with higher education.

"Well, you can take umbrage all you want to as long as you take over my classes for the summer term."

"I'm not a teacher," Cullen protested. The

very thought of being the one accountable for whether or not the students learned all the material in the syllabus caused goose-flesh to prickle the skin beneath his favorite flannel shirt. "I can't replace you in the classroom, Blair."

"That's hogwash. You've stood in for me a hundred times over the past dozen or so years."

"Standing in for a few days and stepping in for you forever are completely different. Besides, I don't have a teaching degree—I'm not qualified."

"The university wants a subject matter expert, not an educator. In that respect you are *over*qualified, but they'll turn a blind eye if you'll accept the contract, even on a trial basis."

"My life is sublime just the way it is, thank you very much. Why would I complicate perfection?"

"How about the fact that you're stuck in a rut about as low as a snake's belly in a wagon wheel track? This building has been your home away from home for a dozen years. You've run out of degrees to earn. Consider shaking things up a bit."

"I happen to enjoy being a student of history."

"I'm not suggesting that you stop learning, but how about studying somebody alive for a change?"

"No way." Cullen shook his head. "Folks who've been dead for hundreds of years are dependable, predictable. They're not likely to up and leave you just when you start appreciating their company."

"They're also not going to keep you warm at night, or watch the Rangers game with you."

Blair swatted the bill of Cullen's baseball cap and it flopped down over his eyes. He ducked the fake punch his mentor always threatened to land on his jaw and adjusted his cap.

"Seriously, my friend," Blair continued. "For a man of your advanced years you're sorta one-dimensional."

"Hey, I'm only thirty-four years old. I have my whole life ahead of me," Cullen insisted.

"But when your daddy was thirty-four, his life was already half-over. If he were still alive I have a hunch he'd suggest that you give fewer hours to the people in our textbooks and more to the living, breathing folks right here on this campus."

Much as the idea of teaching scared the heck out of Cullen, Blair's guidance had always been sound. "I'll sleep on it," Cullen agreed finally.

"With your life experience, you'd be a good fit over in Longview Hall. You could help some people, give back to the community."

"I see where this is headed. You're pimping for the psychology department to assuage your guilt over taking away their senior counselor."

"There's some truth in that, but my wife wants the change of scenery as much as I do."

"What's really behind this sudden desire you have to move to Europe? Have you stopped paying your taxes? Are you leading a double life? How come you have to hightail it out of town with hardly any notice?"

"I've had an offer to be an exchange-student liaison at our embassy in Rome, and it's too perfect to resist. Ailean and I haven't ever lived outside of Texas."

"And most Texans are quite happy to keep it that way."

"For my first sixty years on this earth, I shared that opinion. But the two of us have been talking for the past few years about an extended stay in Europe. My health scare last winter made us realize if we're going to make it happen, it has to be now. Life is short and fragile. We've been offered a gift horse, and we're not going to look it in the mouth. Ambassador Phillips wants us there in three weeks and we don't plan to disappoint him."

Cullen was practical by nature. What Blair said made sense, and as one who'd been afforded the ability to pursue his interests, Cullen wouldn't begrudge his friend the right to do the same.

"Okay, I can accept that you and Ailean are pulling up stakes, but that doesn't make me the right choice for your position here at the university."

The respected history teacher lifted a box and shoved it into his reluctant protégé's arms.

"These are my lecture notes for the class that starts next week. Take them home and go over them tonight. I believe the temptation to reorganize my thoughts will have you so excited, you won't be able to sleep. But if I'm wrong, drop them off tomorrow and I'll go back to the drawing board for another recommendation."

"Is there any chance at all that you'll change your mind about leaving?" Cullen was hopeful. Mastal was not only Cullen's mentor, he'd become a stand-in for the father Cullen had lost in his teens.

"None, whatsoever. My better half has already listed our house with a Realtor and hired an estate sale coordinator."

"Estate sale? You're not dying, you're taking a sabbatical. You'll be home in a few months."

"We don't plan to return to Kilgore, Cullen."

"Ever?"

"For a visit, sure. But not permanently. Our boys are in Denver and Phoenix. We're going to enjoy Italy for as long as it lasts and then we'll figure out where to go next. If we don't make a new home in one of the cities where our kids live, then we're going to check out Barcelona or Prague."

Cullen nodded and moved toward the door. There was no point in arguing against what he'd have done himself if the situation was reversed.

"Then you'll take a gander at my notes and consider teaching the class?"

"I'd rather go to Italy with you, but it seems Ailean has spoken for that position so I'll consider accepting this one."

Blair placed a warm hand on Cullen's shoulder. "This is tailor-made for you, just as the Italy job is for me. Have faith in yourself."

With the box of notes balanced in one hand, the brass knob clutched in the other, Cullen swung the office door wide and paused before crossing the threshold.

"Is there anything else?" Dr. Mastal asked.

"Yes, and it's important. I should speak up before I lose my nerve."

"What is it, son?" The older man's voice was quiet, patient.

"Can I call dibs on those bookcases in your den, the ones with the glass doors?"

"I'll tell Ailean they've been spoken for." He chuckled. "But I warn you they come with all her psychology textbooks."

"And unless you're donating it to the university library, can I have your resource collection, too?"

"Don't press your luck."

Blair pushed Cullen through the door and closed it on his heels, and Cullen was pretty sure he heard his friend throw the lock.

SARAH EASON WAS a goose in a new world. The wide halls of the university administration building had seemed exciting when she was fresh out of high school, but all these years later the arched ceilings and granite floors felt foreign and forbidding.

"I can do this," she muttered to herself as she swept the red hair she'd inherited from her daddy out of her eyes. "I'm a thirty-nine-year-old woman, for crying out loud. I've survived the birth of three daughters and the death of my husband. I won't be intimidated by an old woman who got up on the wrong side of the bed."

Besides, there was little reason to believe the grouch who'd answered the phone in the office of admissions that morning would still be on duty all these hours later. But Sarah stiffened her spine in case there was a battle to be waged. She'd promised herself she'd register for classes today, and come hell or high water, by golly she would do it!

That is, if she could find the office.

Where on earth were they hiding room 104B? She glanced down at the directions she'd scribbled that morning while packing sandwiches and chips for the girls and a Lean Cuisine meal for herself. Maybe she'd written it down wrong. Maybe the grouch had intentionally given her bad information. Or maybe God had sent the old biddy as a sign that going back to school wasn't such a hot idea.

"Can I help you?" a voice rumbled above her head.

Sarah raised her eyes and tipped her head up to see who'd made the kind offer. Familiar gray eyes waited for her response.

"Have we met?" she asked, unable to recall where she'd seen the lazy grin that was set in a handsome face dusted with a couple days of stubble. Dark curls poked out from beneath the Texas Rangers baseball cap that was molded to his head.

"Probably not, but I have a little brother you might know if you watch those cookin' competitions on TV."

She snapped her fingers and pointed in understanding. He mirrored her action.

"The Cowboy Chef," they said in unison.

"He's your brother?" Sarah enjoyed watching the Food Network with her girls; there was zero chance the competing chefs would take their clothes off or use filthy language on camera, so it was something they could do together.

"Hunt's my twin actually." The guy shifted the bulky box he was holding to one hand and extended the other. "Cullen Temple." He offered his hand.

"Pleased to meet you, Cullen Temple. I'm Sarah Eason." She slipped her palm into his grip. It was warm and smooth so she felt certain he didn't cut down trees for a living, despite the plaid lumberjack shirt he sported on an afternoon in May.

"Did I hear an offer of help?" she reminded him.

"Yes, ma'am. What can I do for you?"

"I called to get directions to the office of admissions this morning and I believe a crabby old lady gave me the wrong room number."

Cullen leaned his face toward the ceiling and laughed out loud, displaying white, even teeth that had probably been wrangled into braces during his teen years. After a moment of enjoying her accusation he shook his head, his eyes filled with amused compassion for her experience.

"Sounds as if you've had your first encounter with Miss Nancy Norment, lovingly known as the University Torment. Her job for more than fifty years has been to scare off fainthearted freshmen before they waste their parents' tuition money."

"Well, she deserves high marks for her efforts. If I wasn't so determined to pick up registration forms today, I might have climbed back into bed and pulled the covers over my head after I spoke with her."

"Oh, Miss Norment means well and she's probably saved families millions over the course of her career. You'll know her when you run across her."

"Does she pull her hair into a bun and wear Granny Clampett boots?"

"In a new millennium sorta way. You'll see," he teased.

"If you'd be kind enough to point me in the right direction, I'll take my chances."

Cullen put two fingertips gently on Sarah's shoulder and guided her toward the office that was less than three feet away.

"There's no number on the door," she insisted.

He pointed above the doorframe where a brass placard identified the Office of Admissions.

She closed her eyes and ducked her chin, hiding her face from the man who must believe she was an airhead.

"Another one of Miss Norment's attempts to cull the weakest from the herd. She doesn't bother to mention that there's no room number, or that you have to search up high for the sign."

"Thanks to you, her trick didn't work today."

He raised his wrist to check the time, and then glanced toward the door.

"It's still early. Miss Nancy could scare off three or four more applicants before the office closes at six."

Sarah's eyes followed his gaze.

"You don't think she's still in there, do

you? It's been almost eight hours since I spoke to her."

"She works a split shift. For years she's had an apartment over in the village section of the campus where she also acts as a dorm adviser."

"My goodness. She's either very committed to the university or has no life at all."

"A little of both. She's as much a part of this university as the bell tower. Miss Nancy is feared and revered by one and all."

"You have me intrigued and scared in equal parts. Maybe I should return on her day off."

"Nonsense. There's no time like the present." He reached for the door, pulled it wide and swept his palm outward for her to take the lead. As she stepped across the threshold she heard him call into the office. "Miss Nancy, take care of Sarah for me, will ya? She's a friend of mine."

Sarah glanced behind her to see Cullen Temple smile and wave just as the door slid closed between them.

"That Temple boy has been a thorn in my side for more years than I care to count. If you're a friend of his, then you're either a double dose of trouble or a few fries short of a Happy Meal."

Facing the interior of the office and the source of the comment, Sarah came eyeball to eyeball with a spiky-haired senior citizen in a scrubs top, camo pants and Chuck Taylor All Stars.

"You must be Miss Nancy Norment," Sarah said in her most charming tone.

"And you must be somebody's mama," the University Torment snapped. "'Cause you're certainly no spring chicken."

Knowing her fortieth birthday was just around the corner, Sarah couldn't disagree. Maybe she should have gone back to bed, after all.

CHAPTER TWO

THE AUBURN-HAIRED beauty was sitting alone in the student center with her back to the wall and her face just a few inches above the paperwork spread across the table. Over the years Cullen had come to recognize that posture as the sign of someone who expected they wouldn't fit in, who believed they didn't belong.

He wondered why on earth the lovely woman he'd met earlier in the administration building might be insecure. But then sending a child off to college could be a very unsettling period of life. Though they'd only spoken for a few minutes, Cullen had learned that her name was Sarah and she had daughters.

She'd seemed too bright to fall into the helicopter-parent trap, always hovering overhead and ready to swoop down and save the day. Still, this wouldn't be the first time a smart adult did all the paperwork to ensure their completely capable kid had no excuse for not showing up on the first day of class.

As Cullen passed through the beverage line he was jostled intentionally by several upper-classmen who smiled and greeted him. Those with unfamiliar faces ignored Cullen, leaving him to presume they were freshmen.

The kids who attended the summer semester were made up of two groups: those who were getting ahead and those who were catching up. As he moved toward the woman alone at her table he wondered whether her daughter would be at the top or the bottom of the freshman class.

"Forgive me for guessing instead of asking if you take your coffee black, but you seem more of a 'decaf with cream and sugar' lady to me," Cullen explained as he placed two mugs of coffee on the table. The blue eyes that met his opened wide with surprise and then squinted in good-humored gratitude.

"Make that sugar substitute and you're right on the money." She swept an area clear of paperwork to give him room to share the table.

Cullen dumped the contents of the small sack he'd also been carrying into the empty spot. Servings of flavored creamer and packets of sweetener rolled and fluttered about.

"Take your pick. Yellow, pink or blue."

"You're not just a pretty face, no matter what Miss Norment says about you," Sarah teased as she reached for a single serving container of French vanilla creamer.

"Miss Nancy calls me a number of things but I'd lay odds that *pretty face* isn't on the list."

"She did mutter something about you being the dullest knife in the butcher block."

"That sounds about right." He tore open three packets of brown sugar and dumped the crystals into his mug. "She's never taken much of a shine to me, even though I'm in there several times a week to see the dean."

"You get called in to see the dean *that* frequently, huh?"

"Occasionally he calls me, but just as often it's the other way around. We play racquetball, then grab some lunch."

"That's a novel way to keep an eye on your child's progress at school." She bobbed her head as if she approved.

"My child?"

"Sorry, I meant your son or daughter. I forget that young people want to be considered adults, not children. My Carrie certainly does."

"I don't have any children." He held up his

hand to show her that there was no wedding ring on his finger, not that the age-old symbol of commitment meant much to some people these days. "Not even married."

Cullen noted that her ring finger was bare but she fiddled with a gold band on her right thumb.

"So you hang around here because…" She waited for him to finish. Surely the lady didn't believe he was trolling for dates among the students?

"I hang around here because I'm getting an education." She continued to stare so he elaborated. "Actually, I've gotten several educations since I first enrolled right out of high school. I don't have plans to leave anytime soon, even though Miss Nancy has tried to kick me out into the real world on more occasions than you can shake a stick at. My brothers call me a professional student, and at this point it's useless for me to deny it."

"So you're a *student* and not a parent? That's cool," she said. Her smile and the tilt of her head said she was interested in his story.

"Finally!" He exaggerated the word. "Somebody who appreciates the idea that higher education isn't just what kids do while they wait for the best job or the right mate to come along."

"I'd enjoy hearing more, but I've got to finish completing these forms and get over to our apartment before the girls get home."

"Do you need any help? I know my way around a class registration fairly well by now. What is your daughter interested in studying? The curriculum is a bit limited during the summer sessions."

Sarah's smile was back. She relaxed against the folding chair and dropped her pencil on the form.

"I suppose I had that coming."

"What?" Cullen was confused.

"My oldest daughter is only thirteen and the primary subject that interests her is the ever threatening world of zombies and vampires."

Embarrassment warmed Cullen's neck. Assuming a woman was old enough to have a kid in college was up there with assuming a lady's rounded figure meant she was pregnant.

"I'm sorry." He struggled to apologize. "I didn't mean to insinuate you were old. I mean, there's nothing wrong with being old, you're just not *that* old."

She held a palm outward to stop the flow of words.

"I'm not insulted. Really, I'm not. I made the same assumption about you. What do you say we call it even?"

"It's a deal." Cullen extended his hand and he was very grateful when she accepted his shake and his apology.

SARAH CAUGHT THE gleam in Cullen's eye and the spark in his touch. For the first time in the three years since Joe's death, physical contact with a man had made her insides quiver. She'd figured that magical sensation was gone forever.

"So, whose application are you filling out, if I may be bold enough to ask?" He tucked his chin to his chest in a gun-shy but teasing posture.

It's for me," Sarah answered softly, still afraid to admit it out loud.

"Beg pardon?"

"Me!" she insisted more boldly. "The application is for me."

He stared at her with eyes the color of wet slate. The man was a ringer for that famous British soccer player who'd moved with his Spice Girl wife from London to Beverly Hills. Sarah's seven-year-old could probably recite their names, but there was zero allowance for pop culture in a single mother's life. Bearing the load alone was heavy, but not more than she could manage.

During the last moments of her husband's battle with leukemia, she'd held Joe in her arms and encouraged him to let go of this life, promising him that their girls would be okay. And that was mostly true. Today Carrie, Meg and Hope had *what* they needed, they just didn't have *who* they needed. And now Sarah was going to spend more hours away from them to finish the degree that had once meant so much to her. Some people would say her plan was selfish, but her employer had offered to pay the tuition—how could a widow turn that down?

"I'm going to complete my undergraduate."

"That's wonderful," Cullen said encouragingly.

"Really? You don't think I'm a bit…mature?"

He held his arms out in a "look at me" posture.

"Sarah, now that we've taken turns accusing each other of being over the hill, my guess is we're probably about the same age. Ninety percent of the people on this campus expect that I'm a teacher because I've been studying here for so long. But trust me when I say I'm not the only individual over thirty— or even forty—who's sitting on the observation side of the lectern. We actually have a sophomore in her seventies named Ruthie George. After Ruthie's husband passed away, she decided to get her master's."

"Good for her," Sarah said, voicing her approval over the older woman's decision to keep moving forward with her life.

But Ruthie had probably shared many decades with her husband, while Sarah had been cheated of so many precious years. Life had short-changed her young family and her heart would forever bear a tender bruise from the loss.

Somehow life went on, the girls outgrew their shoes and Sarah outgrew her fears. She'd put one foot in front of the other and pressed ahead for the sake of her daughters. And if she wanted to advance any further with the law firm and get her paralegal licensing, she had to complete her education.

"I think I'd enjoy meeting Ruthie. She sounds like a role model I could use in my circle of friends right now."

Sarah was grateful for her mother's unfailing help with the girls, but Margaret Callaghan had never had professional ambitions, and she'd never worked outside their family home.

"Ruthie says that it's her time to fly," Cullen explained. "For fifty years she put her family before her education and now that she's alone again, she's going to do whatever it takes to fulfill the dream she put on hold the moment her first child was born."

"Your friend and I have a lot in common, in spite of our thirty-year-age difference."

"You've been a stay-at-home mom, too?"

"Only when the girls were little. As soon as my youngest was out of diapers I went to work with a law firm. But now, if I want to advance any further I have to get my paralegal certification. I can't do that without an undergraduate degree, and since they're willing to pay for it, here I am."

There was a ruckus a few tables away as young people who were playing cards broke into laughter. Sarah supposed there had been a day when she'd been so carefree but it had been so long ago it was nothing more than a distant memory. Their smiling faces reminded her of her daughters and she glanced at the wall clock above the exit door.

"Let me get out of here so you can finish." Cullen gathered up the bits of trash from their coffee and swept the table clean with a napkin. "I'm sorry I interrupted your efforts," he apologized.

"I don't mean to run you off, but I have to get this to your Miss Nancy before the office closes."

"By next week she'll be *your* Miss Nancy, too."

"Oh, gosh, I hadn't thought of that."

"There are probably a lot of things you haven't thought of yet. When you want a class recommendation or even a cup of coffee with your new friend, Cullen Temple, just give me a holler."

"Do I holler at any particular corner of the campus?"

"I can generally be found in the history department, Heath-Harwick Hall. But if you don't spot me over there just leave a message with Miss Nancy."

"And she'll see that you get it?"

"Probably not, but it's worth a try."

Cullen tilted his handsome head in a gesture of respect, took his coffee mug and made his way toward the exit, stopping every few tables to speak to someone he knew. Sarah wouldn't be hanging out in the student center often enough to have acquaintances on campus like Cullen did. But she had made one new friend—though if she didn't finish the

enrollment form soon she wouldn't even get
another chance to speak to him.

"My new friend, Cullen Temple," she said
only loud enough so that she could hear the
words. "I like the way that sounds."

CHAPTER THREE

CULLEN FIGURED A week of preparation for his first class was enough.

He'd figured wrong.

Standing before the small group in Blair's lecture hall on Monday afternoon, he felt like a poor substitute for the professor the students had expected to hear. After he began to rush through the talking points, only one person bothered to make eye contact, and having that person's blue eyes fixed on Cullen's every move only made things more nerve-racking.

Twenty minutes short of the ninety-minute class he closed Blair's carefully prepared notes and dismissed the group. He turned about-face as they hurried toward the exit as if their stand-in instructor might call them back for another hour of boredom on European civilization.

"The sign on the lecture hall door claims you're Dr. Cullen Temple but you didn't sound anything like the smooth talker I had coffee with last week."

Cullen looked around to find Sarah Eason standing in front of him. She'd tried to be helpful by signaling him a couple of times during his lecture to slow his delivery down, without success.

"Was that awful, or what?" he asked, already well aware of the answer.

"I wouldn't say *awful*. Awful is a dried-up, day-old hot dog. That was more of a cold, greasy onion ring. If you just warm it up there may still be potential."

"I'm sorry you witnessed that debacle." He slumped against the white board on the wall behind him. "I shouldn't have agreed to take over this class. It's one thing to be a guest lecturer on a subject of my own choosing and quite another to pick up where a tenured professor has left off."

"So Dr. Mastal really was supposed to be teaching this class, as it says on the syllabus? I thought maybe I'd wandered into the wrong lecture hall, but when I saw it was you I decided to hang around. I'm only auditing this semester so it's not as if anybody was expecting me."

"I hope my performance tonight doesn't stop you from sitting in on the class again.

I'm really gonna have to cram so I can re-
deem myself on Wednesday. Otherwise, your
husband's going to complain that your time
away from the family is being wasted."

She took a seat in the front row, settled her
notebook and purse on the adjacent chair and
crossed one bare leg over the other beneath
the full skirt of her faded yellow sundress.

"Come, sit," she encouraged, probably in
the same patient voice she used with her children.

He did as instructed, sitting two seats away
with her things in between them.

"I'm a widow." Her voice was soft but matter-of-fact.

Before he could stammer out condolences
she reached across the vacant seat and placed
a hand on his arm.

"Don't say anything. It's been three years
and the girls and I are adjusting to our new
normal."

"How…" Cullen wanted to ask, not at all
sure he should.

"Joe was diagnosed with leukemia right
after we learned I was pregnant with our
third daughter, Hope. He'd suspected something was terribly wrong for months but kept
it to himself because he didn't want to worry
me. We were told from the start it was ter-

minal but we'd have a few years. I don't pretend it wasn't devastating to our lives or that everybody's fine now. We get through it one day at a time and treasure every blessing."

"I'm so sorry," he said softly. "I can't imagine losing a spouse. When I was in high school, both of my parents were killed in a private plane crash, so I understand a little of what your daughters are going through."

"It's tough for my girls. I try to meet all their emotional needs but nothing can take the place of a daddy, as you well know. And I'm sorry you had a tragic loss at such a young age."

"Thank you." Cullen released a sigh. He was a bonehead, making too much of one failed lecture when the woman beside him was struggling with problems that might eventually get better but would never completely go away. Something else he was well acquainted with.

After his parents' deaths, he'd suffered terrifying anxiety attacks, and while they'd subsided years ago, the dread of their return never left him. He'd only ever told Blair and Alma, the woman who'd stepped in to care for the Temple brothers, of his fears.

Hoping to get them past these sad subjects, he said, "Do you have to rush home, or can

I buy you a bite to eat? I'm suddenly starving and the grill in the student center makes great cheeseburgers. I'll even spring for some onion rings so the evening won't be a total loss." He smiled to lift the mood.

"Could I get a rain check? Tonight I'm meeting my mother and the girls for pizza. It's one of those family places where kids can stay busy with arcade games for hours. Mom gives them each a roll of quarters and then she's free to sit and read her romance novel. That should keep everyone occupied for a while, but I should head over soon."

"You say it's a family place?"

"Yeah, it's the one out on the loop, near the mall."

"Oh, I know the one you're taking about. They have a nice buffet. What could be better than all the pepperoni pizza you can eat?"

"Would you care to join us?"

He shook his head. He hadn't meant to fish for an invitation. But Blair's words about giving less attention to the people in books and more to the living had stuck in Cullen's mind like bubble gum on hot pavement.

"Oh, I wouldn't horn in on your family evening. Besides, how would your mother and girls react if a man you just met showed up to share the table?"

"It's going to take them about thirty seconds to recognize your face and then they'll be all up in your business asking questions about your famous twin."

Cullen leaned away from the comment. "Hey, I wouldn't exactly say Hunt's famous, at least not for anything other than being my little brother. I will give him credit for being a great chef, though. And he still does some appearances on television when he's not working with his fiancée over at Temple Territory."

"Oh, that mansion in Kilgore that's become a hotel? I hear it's quite an historical landmark."

"I can arrange for your daughters to get a tour of the estate if they'd be interested. Our grandfather built the place and it comes with lots of interesting stories and legends."

"That's a great idea for an outing this summer," she agreed. "But please join us tonight. There's probably a whole pepperoni pizza over there with your name on it."

The mental picture of rising dough swimming in golden grease from cheese and sausage caused his mouth to water like Pavlov's dog. He did an inward double take at his very predictable reaction. Maybe he was a natural for the study of human behavior, after all.

"Only if you're sure nobody will object."

"With five women at the table somebody is always bound to object. It just comes with the territory. So don't take it personally, it's a family female thing," Sarah assured him.

A family female thing was uncharted water for Cullen. But how hard could it be to share a casual meal with three generations of women? He might even learn something from the experience if he carried some gestures of kindness to soothe the savage breast.

SARAH WASN'T NEARLY as confident as she tried to sound for Cullen's sake. While she could trust her mother to be hospitable, the girls were another matter. Carrie was in the throes of a Goth stage and Meg was forever wrestling with some imagined worry. Hope lived in la-la land, inventing superhero memories of her daddy to replace the fragile flesh-and-blood truth.

Thank goodness Sarah had a thirty-minute head start before Cullen arrived at the pizza place. He'd said he had personal business to attend to and then he'd join them. She'd have to set the scene carefully, to say the least.

"What do you mean a friend from the university is meeting us for dinner?" Meg questioned. "Who is she and how well do you know her?"

"I was about to ask the same thing," Sarah's mother added.

"My friend is actually a guy and he's teaching the European history class I'm auditing. He was going to eat dinner alone so I invited him to have pizza with us. You might even recognize him."

"He's not that old high school boyfriend of yours, is he? That Bobby Whatshisname?" asked her mother.

"Of course not."

"Good. I was always suspicious of that kid."

"Mom, Bobby got married right after we graduated, he was a torpedo man on a navy guided-missile destroyer and he has a Ph.D. in agricultural economics. I'd say he's done pretty well for himself. You can let go of those qualms."

"Well, I've read how women are hooking up with their old flames these days and I don't want any surprises when this stranger shows up."

"He's nobody from my ancient past, but he does have a face you might have seen before."

"Like on an FBI Most Wanted poster?

What if he's a bank robber or a mass murderer?" Meg chewed the tip of a plastic straw.

"Honey, this guy has spent his entire life in Kilgore, he's well respected at the university and I'm pretty sure he's been too busy studying and teaching to dispose of bodies."

"So, is this the way college women behave? Will there be a different man in your life every week now?" Carrie's snide question was inappropriate, but at least she was talking.

"No, dear," Sarah said with restraint. At home she'd have lectured her daughter on being disrespectful, but tonight reassurance was more important than manners. "Cullen is the only person on campus who's even spoken to me, if you don't count the grouchy woman in the administration office."

"Oh, Nancy Norment is still over there? So the University Torment is alive and well. She must be up into her eighties by now."

"She might be too mean to die."

"I'm glad to hear Miss Nancy is on the job. The town honored her years ago for her service to the community. You'd better pray she lives twenty more years so she'll be there when your girls go to college."

"Right now I'm praying that I can stick around for two years to finish my degree, but

I'll add Miss Nancy's continued health to the bottom of my lengthy prayer list."

"Don't look now, but a suspicious man just spotted us and he's walking this way." Meg's words were muffled behind her hand.

Sarah watched Cullen approach. He seemed much more relaxed than he had in the lecture hall. In one hand he clutched a bunch of flowers and with the other he gripped the handles of an oversize canvas bag stamped with a recycle emblem. When he stopped at the head of their table, Sarah stood to make introductions.

"Cullen Temple, this is my mother, Margaret Callaghan, and my daughters Carrie, Meg and Hope. Ladies, this is my instructor, Dr. Cullen Temple."

There was silence except for a nod from her mother.

Sarah stamped her foot, a not-so-covert sign for her daughters to use their manners.

"Pleased to meet you, sir," the girls responded politely as they'd been instructed all their lives.

"I appreciate your mama inviting me. I love a pizza buffet."

NOT FEELING OVERLY WELCOME, Cullen decided to go straight for the peace offerings, hoping the atmosphere would warm up. He set the canvas bag on the tabletop and handed the flowers to Sarah's mother.

"These are for you, Mrs. Callaghan. My mama taught me that you never go to a woman's dinner table empty-handed, not the first visit, anyway."

Next he made a production of poking around in the bag, which seemed to get the girls' attention.

"I had to shop fast and I only have brothers so I hope I did okay," he apologized as he withdrew a trinket for each of the sisters. For Carrie, whose hair was…*purple*…there was a paperback volume of *Vampire Academy*, the first in a popular young adult series. He presented Meg with a silver-tone bracelet that had a dangling smiley face charm inscribed Don't Worry, Be Happy. And for Sara's youngest, who was missing her front two teeth, there was a fluffy stuffed bear holding a velvet heart that read Faith, Hope and Love.

"I think this was meant just for you," Cullen said as he handed over the teddy.

"What did you bring for Mommy?" Hope asked.

"The best gift of all," he answered as he rubbed his palms together.

He reached to the bottom of the bag and then pulled out a thick, gray volume. Black letters on the spine read *European Civilization*. It was the very expensive textbook for his class.

"I can't accept this, Cullen."

He waved away her concern. "Dr. Mastal kept a stack in his office for loaners. When the semester is over you can return it and I'll use it to bless another unsuspecting victim."

"Hey!" Carrie had glanced up from her novel and was studying Cullen through squinted eyes, her index finger pointing a silent accusation his way.

Margaret nodded her head. "I was just about to say the same thing."

"What?" Meg slid the bracelet over her hand and rejoined the conversation.

"You look just like the Cowboy Chef!" Carrie insisted.

"Actually, I'm the older twin, so he looks just like me."

"You're brothers with the cutest chef on food television? Awesome sauce!" Meg exclaimed.

"Why don't we go fill our plates and you can hear all about it while we eat," Margaret suggested. She took charge and herded the girls toward the buffet line.

"Thank you for everything, Cullen. You really shouldn't have gone to all this trouble and expense."

"It's only one evening of my life and it's the least I can do for your family. If I never meet your girls again they'll have a personal reminder of a Temple brother—even if they forget about me and only remember the Cowboy Chef."

He smiled, not the least bit bothered by the shadow his twin cast.

"Shall we?" Sarah suggested.

"After you." Cullen stepped aside to let her take the lead.

He smiled as he watched the family of women load their plates, but inwardly he shuddered over what the atmosphere must be like in their home. The noise, the bickering, the demands, the drama—all the stuff he did his best to keep out of his life. Anything short of peace and quiet might tempt his old nemesis, anxiety.

What he'd said to Sarah was true. Giving up one evening was an easy gesture to make, especially for one of his students. But a steady diet of this bunch would not simply have him under the covers, it would have him under the bed!

CHAPTER FOUR

TWENTY STEPS OUTSIDE the pizza parlor door, Hope dug her heels into the sidewalk and pointed toward a maintenance alley beside the restaurant.

"Mama, look!" she insisted.

All heads turned at the urgency in her voice. By the entrance to the alley, a small life shivered, barely noticeable, cowering in the shadow of a Dumpster.

"It's a puppy!" Hope squealed, and tugged harder on Sarah's hand in an effort to get closer. "Let's go get it!"

"Wait!" Meg cried even louder. "It could be rabid."

"Its ears are too short to be a rabbit."

"Rabid, not rabbit, you stupid baby," Meg chided.

"Mona Margaret, what have I told you about name-calling?"

"That it's ugly, inappropriate and indicates a weak vocabulary," she said, repeating what Sarah said to her daughters at least twice a day. "But she *is* a stupid baby sometimes." Meg always had to have the last word.

The whimper of the animal echoed in the alley.

"Do something!" Hope pleaded.

"Stay put and let me check things out," Cullen instructed, handing his to-go box of pizza to Sarah.

He made his way cautiously, stopped several feet away and knelt to the dirty concrete. The shaggy thing stood, unfolding long wobbly legs. Cullen rested one hand atop his knee, palm down to allow the puppy to make the first move. Even from a distance Sarah could hear soft murmuring as Cullen appealed to the frightened pup. It slowly crept forward, sniffed cautiously, then retreated behind the safety of the Dumpster.

"Don't leave him there!" Hope broke the quiet that had enveloped their group, startling everyone.

"Will you shush, please?" Carrie reprimanded her sister, who complied for once in her life.

Cullen crept down the alley and slipped out of sight in the direction the dog had gone. Long moments later he returned, a wad of blond fur enfolded in his arms.

"I thought his mama might be in there, too,

but he was all alone," Cullen explained, keeping his voice low as he got closer.

Sarah kept a tight grip on her youngest daughter, certain Hope's excitement would spook the already-frightened animal. Cullen moved underneath the glare of the parking lot lights and they could see the puppy, long legs dangling, curly fur in need of a bath, its muzzle shyly tucked beneath Cullen's elbow.

"Poor thing. He must be lost from his family." Hope reached up to softly stroke an ear that flopped over Cullen's arm.

"It's more likely he was left here on purpose in the hope that someone leaving the restaurant would give him a home," Sarah's mother spoke up.

"That's us!"

"Honey, we can't take in a dog. We don't have the room or the money for a pet." Sarah had to be reasonable, though her heart broke for the animal.

"Grandma?" Hope moved anxious eyes to her grandmother. "Can't you take it home for us? I'll give you my allowance to buy it food."

"Baby girl, we can't have pets because of your grandfather's allergies. You wouldn't want your grandpa to be sneezy and itchy, would you?"

"I guess not." Her eyes were downcast

with sadness. "But if we leave it here it might starve to death."

"Or get eaten by wolves," Meg added, to her little sister's horror.

"Yeah, packs of wolves in mall parking lots are really a hazard in Longview this year," Carrie deadpanned.

"I suppose I could take it home with me." Cullen's suggestion was halfhearted at best.

"For reals?" Hope's face lit with gratitude as her frown flipped into a smile, exposing the gap in her teeth. She tugged her hand free from Sarah's and launched her body at Cullen, wrapping her arms fiercely around his legs. "My hero," she mumbled against his jeans.

Sarah's eyes sought Cullen's and she mouthed, "You don't have to do this." He gave an affirmative nod and jostled the puppy's face free so they could get a glimpse of the long snout and huge eyes.

"Judging by the size of his feet, this boy's gonna require a big house and a fenced yard. I have the room and I'm home a lot so I can't imagine why not."

"Can we come visit him whenever we want?"

"Hope, it's not polite to invite yourself over

to somebody else's home," Sarah corrected her child.

By now Cullen was probably wishing he'd had his dinner on a TV tray, alone. All three of her girls had become outspoken and unpredictable, and it seemed she was forever apologizing for their words or behaviors.

"Cullen, please excuse my daughter for being so forward. Just because we enjoy having Hope around, she assumes everybody else will instantly welcome her, too."

"I don't enjoy her, she's always poking through my side of the bedroom," Meg chimed in.

"Yeah, she's a pest, always into our stuff," Carrie added. "So if you've got a big house, you can take Hope home with you, too."

"That's enough, ladies," Sarah admonished, cringing inwardly that a respected new friend was being put in such an awkward position.

"Actually, you're all welcome to come see the puppy once I get him settled. I haven't had a dog since I was a kid and I'm going to need lots of help. Especially teaching him to swim so he'll be safe around my pool."

"You have a pool?" Carrie brightened.

For months she'd been complaining that their apartments didn't offer a swimming pool for the residents. The complex was small and old but it was in a safe neighborhood near the girls' schools and that was more important to Sarah. It was bad enough that they'd had to sell their family home. Sarah wasn't going to make them move away from their friends, as well.

"Yes, I do. It's nothing fancy but it keeps me cool in the summertime."

"Backyard pools can be dangerous. A person can drown in a thimble of water."

"Safety is always a priority at my house, Meg. And I promise to teach the puppy to swim right away."

"Okay, now that we have that all settled," Sarah's mother cut in, "I should be getting home to your father before it gets any later."

"Thanks for everything, Mom." Sarah leaned into her mother's hug as best she could while still holding Cullen's pizza box. "You're still available to hang out with the girls on Wednesday evening?"

"I wouldn't miss it."

Carrie huffed and rolled her eyes. "I'm too old for a babysitter."

"Well, that's good because babysitters expect to be paid and I only expect for you to let me win at Crazy Eights. At least occasionally," Margaret teased.

She kissed each of the girls, handed their shopping bag full of Cullen's thoughtful gifts over to Carrie, thanked their guest again for the flowers and then headed toward the practical minivan she kept just for transporting her three grandkids.

"Where are you parked, Cullen? We'll follow you to your car so I can give you the pizza."

"My Explorer is just over there, but how about if you take the pizza home with you instead? I'm not sure how safe it will be with a hungry puppy on the loose."

"You should go straight to that pet shop down the street for a doggy seat-belt thingy," Meg reminded him. "It's not safe for him in your backseat otherwise. And you'll want some food, and a collar, too."

"Meg, lighten up on the lectures, please," Sarah insisted.

"Actually, that's an excellent suggestion. Are you ladies in a hurry or could you come with me to pick out a few things?"

Cheers erupted from the younger girls, and though Carrie didn't officially agree, there was an expression of mild interest on her face.

"Are you sure?" Sarah asked. "Haven't you had enough of my zoo crew for one evening?"

"Meg's right, I should get some things for this little guy. We can't take too long because they'll be closing soon. I'd appreciate the help since I don't have the first clue what to get."

"It's the least we can do." Sarah swept her palm for him to lead the way. Hope bobbed up and down as she skipped beside Cullen across the parking spaces to a shiny, clean SUV that probably didn't have a back seat filled with hair bows, pink sneakers, and empty Yoo-hoo bottles.

HALF AN HOUR and two hundred dollars later, Cullen was on his way home. The puppy they'd dubbed Rocket was shivering quietly in the backseat, held securely by his pet restraint. Who knew a dog wasn't supposed to ride with its head hanging out the car window anymore? But according to Meg, Sarah's little worrywart, allowing pets to do that was dangerous and really should be illegal.

Cullen yawned as he pulled onto the highway for the twenty-minute ride home. It was only a little after 9:00 p.m., but he was pooped from a roller-coaster ride of a Monday. Sleep had eluded him the night before and he'd been anxious all day over his first lecture of Blair's class.

And rightly so. It had been a disaster.

"Rocket, a very smart man named Einstein once said that the definition of insanity was doing the same thing over and over and expecting different results. Tomorrow you've gotta help me figure out another way to approach Western Civilization. The mere fact that you're in my car at this moment is proof that I'm capable of change when the situation demands it, so I'm bound to be able to make adjustments."

Now that he considered it, the past few hours had called for a lot of flexibility and he'd done fairly well. He'd left the classroom without obsessing too much over his dreadful performance, made a whirlwind shopping effort for virtual strangers, bought dinner for a gaggle of girls and rescued a helpless critter from a pack of wolves. Well, maybe that last part was a bit extreme, but if Meg was willing to give him props he'd take them. Not that there had been any danger of him leaving the puppy on the street. He'd taken one look at the orphaned dog and sworn he would give him a secure, loving home.

"Rocket, my little buddy." Cullen glanced at the weary, wide eyes behind him. "We've both had a tough break, losing our parents when we needed them most. Only a couple of people know this about me and now I'm going to tell you and trust that you'll keep this between us."

The dog yawned and settled his belly on the leather seat, but kept his eyes trained toward his new master.

"So, here's the deal. I was diagnosed over a dozen years ago with post traumatic stress disorder. Dr. Dermer said my pounding heart and sweaty, shaky hands were symptoms of anxiety. I just called it *the creeps* when the attacks came on during my junior year in high school. I hated the hours I spent with my head under the covers praying for that sensation to go away. Whatever you label the condition, it was awful and I never want to revisit those days. So now I do everything I can to avoid getting overstressed. You'll like our home. It's a quiet oasis in a noisy world and I'll do my best to make it a sanctuary for you, too."

As soon as they got to the house Cullen began to make good on his promise. As he ran a warm, soapy bath for Rocket, he tuned the radio on the bathroom counter to a classic country channel. While the pup soaked and enjoyed the gentle massage, Cullen hummed along with the soft music he found so much more appealing than the hard rock his friends had preferred growing up. His daddy said it was "racket" and Cullen couldn't disagree.

In his college years he'd stayed away from the loud fraternity parties that were sure to set off his anxiety. So he kept the music low and comforting for himself as well as Rocket.

An hour later the puppy was towel-dried and fed and lay snuggled beside Cullen in the big sleigh bed. His nose was poked into his master's armpit, as if burying his head and hiding his face would stave off night terrors. It was an attempt at self-soothing that Cullen knew well from many, many efforts of his own to sleep away the pain of loss.

Deep into the night, he suddenly woke to find Rocket kicking and whining in a way Alma would call "chasing rabbits." As the thrashing became more frantic, the little dog's cries grew into howls of despair that tore at Cullen's heart.

"It's okay, buddy." He gave Rocket a little shake to ease him from his dreams.

Huge eyes stared upward, pleading for mercy from the man who was still a stranger. The pup shivered with fear of an unfamiliar place.

"I understand," Cullen crooned as he stroked the long nose and silky ears. He scooped the animal close to his heart, kissed the head that smelled of shampoo and kibbles and wondered why it had never occurred to him that calming the worries of another creature could be so comforting.

He continued to stroke the puppy and the tremors through Rocket's body grew less frequent and his breathing grew deeper. Cullen slipped his hand around the thin body and cupped the soft tummy.

"I'm gonna fatten you up so you forget what hunger feels like and love you so much that all you remember is being wanted. You won't suffer through another night alone, not if I have anything to say about it."

Cullen pulled the blanket close to warm his body and the puppy closer to warm his soul.

CHAPTER FIVE

"I REALLY APPRECIATE your time, Dr. Temple," an attractive young woman thanked Cullen for answering her questions after class.

"It's not necessary for you to be formal, Trish," he insisted. "Call me Cullen."

Sarah waited patiently off to the side and listened while several students engaged their handsome instructor with questions. Everything about this evening's class had been so different from the first that Sarah had been compelled to stick around and compliment him. Evidently, others felt the same since a line had formed as soon as the lesson concluded.

"Well, I see you brought your 'A' game tonight," Sarah teased once everyone else had gone.

"Nobody's more amazed than I am," Cullen admitted.

"How did you prepare differently this time?"

"I simply followed my mentor's orders

and applied the process that's always worked for me."

A relieved grin that would melt any woman's heart spread across Cullen's face. It was such an endearing sight, especially after the worry in his gray eyes a few days before.

"Blair had suggested that I study his notes and then reorganize them into my own words. I didn't have the sense to heed his advice for the first class, and you saw how well that worked out for me. So this time around, instead of teaching directly from what he'd written, I reviewed the chapters and then, based on what I'd learned about the subject myself years ago, I just shot from the hip. When you're dealing with ancient civilizations, there's a pretty fair chance nothing's changed much since you last checked the facts."

"Well, you certainly bring the time period to life. I was watching the faces of your students and they were completely engaged."

"When you have fellas like Charlemagne and Genghis Khan to work with you don't have to dig too deep to find a story that will keep the listeners tuned in for ninety minutes."

"Don't sell yourself short, Cullen. You're vying with the sci-fi network, the Kardashians and Grand Theft Auto for the attention of these young people, and I'd say holding their focus for an hour and a half is quite an accomplishment. You're a natural."

"Aw, shucks, ma'am, 'tweren't nothin'." He lowered his chin in a show of false shyness. "You'll blow an old country boy's head up so big his Stetson won't fit."

"Just accept the compliment," Sarah insisted as she gave Cullen's bicep a light punch. Her knuckles connected with solid arm beneath the long sleeve he seemed to favor, even in the heat. The lightweight flannel obviously shielded a muscular build, and for some reason, Sarah was glad he wore modest clothing around all these young women. Whether or not it was by design, it was probably a smart defense against inappropriate attention.

"The bottom line, Dr. Temple, is you gave an excellent lecture and I can't wait to dive into the Crusades with you this semester."

"You, my dear, are a rare find indeed. Any student excited to spend her summer recalling bloody battles is a woman after my own heart."

"Aw, shucks, sir," she mirrored his silly comment and drawl. "You'll turn a simple girl's head with such purty words."

"How about if you two take your mutual

admiration society meeting outside so Merle can mop this floor?" a voice growled from the doorway.

"Evening, Miss Nancy!" Cullen called as he gathered his notes and shoved them into a well-worn backpack. "Sorry to hold up the operation. We'll be out of here in three minutes."

"She's *still* here?" Sarah asked. "Is she the night watchman, too?"

Cullen chuckled. "She and Merle have been keeping company for years, but he can't join her for wine coolers and Skip-Bo until the floors are dry."

Sarah shifted the carryall that contained the loaner textbook and her legal pads and walked alongside Cullen to the exit of the lecture room.

"How are things going with the puppy?"

"Rocket has been a revelation."

"Meaning?"

"Meaning, I expected he'd be a lot of trouble and under my feet constantly. Which he is, but in a nice way. I figured Alma would be disgusted to find rawhide chews and dog hair in my bed, but she just shook out my sheets and brushed off my favorite quilt without a complaint and sidestepped the water bowl on the bathroom floor."

"Alma?" Sarah repeated the name carefully to cover the sinking in her spirit. Some woman was hanging out in her new friend's bedroom and somehow that seemed wrong. "She shakes out your sheets, huh?"

Well, what do you expect at his age, Sarah Elizabeth, that he's still an altar boy?

"Sorry. That didn't exactly sound complimentary to the most important woman in my life, did it?"

"You're a grown man and how you categorize a consenting relationship is your private business."

"You're right, Sarah. And after all these years I really should call her *mi amorcito*— Lord knows she's earned the title of sweetheart."

"Wait." She halted their forward motion. "Who is this Alma to you?"

"She's the woman who raised me and my three brothers when our parents were killed. She and her husband, Felix, stepped in and became our surrogate parents. They kept us on the straight and narrow to make sure none of us ended up in prison like our grandfather."

"Your grandfather served time in prison?"

"That's East Texas lore for another evening." Cullen waved away the question. "I'll be glad to share it with you over a glass of wine one night but Pap Temple's story is old news that I'd rather not get into right this minute."

The knowledge that Cullen's grandfather had gone to prison took Sarah by surprise. She ought to do a little research or talk to her parents. Surely they'd remember the story of a man named Pap Temple if it was a part of the local history, as Cullen claimed.

"So, you were updating me on Rocket."

Cullen's exhausted smile said this was a more pleasant subject.

"The past two nights have been a challenge, but we're managing. The poor little fella whimpers and kicks in his dreams, but I can survive a few weeks without REM sleep if lullabies and snuggles help him adjust. How could any man resist such a call to adventure."

And how could any woman resist such a heartwarming image?

As he pushed the heavy security door open and held it wide for Sarah to exit the building, Cullen could only imagine what terrors might invade a puppy's subconscious mind. But he had a sneaking suspicion they were akin to his own fears and hurts that had kept him from resting as a teen. Spooning Rocket close, rubbing his tummy and murmuring soft sounds every couple of hours seemed to give them both peace, and that was a fair trade for the whole pot of coffee he'd have to consume in the morning to keep himself awake.

"It was so kind of you to rescue that puppy, Cullen. You're Hope's new hero."

"Speaking of your girls, how about bringing them to my house for a barbecue this weekend?"

A crease formed between her auburn brows as she answered. "You're so kind to offer, and I'm tempted to accept. I'm just not sure that's such a great idea."

"What concerns you about a picnic?"

"How much time do you have?"

"As much as you want, my friend."

They stepped out into the muggy evening that was still lit by the waning summer sun. He sunk down on a nearby marble bench and Sarah joined him.

Her blue eyes searched his face, maybe for a clue about how much to say.

"So talk," he encouraged. The woman carried a lot on her slender shoulders and it didn't come as a surprise that she had to consider emotional burdens carefully.

"Each of my girls is a needy mess."

"Aren't all kids?"

"By nature, yes. But losing their daddy and then our home—"

"Wait." He placed a hand on the small of her back, the touch intended to be comforting and nothing more. "You lost your home?"

She nodded, a sad smile curving her lips.

"There was a mountain of medical bills and most of Joe's life insurance went to cover that obligation. There was no chance I could manage the mortgage on my salary, so we sold the house and moved into an apartment. We're comfortable, but there's nothing cushy about our lifestyle."

"From what I've observed, your girls are part of a loving family and that's more valuable than stuff."

"Thirty-somethings understand that, but try to explain to a tween that not owning an iPad builds character."

"So how does that translate into a barbecue at Chez Cullen being a bad idea?"

"Oh, it's a wonderful idea! I didn't mean to sound ungrateful."

"Then what?"

"That's the question that worries me."

Cullen scrunched his brow and exaggerated a squint to show his confusion.

"If we come for an afternoon, *then what?* My girls have all learned to compartmentalize their emotions, but it's not been easy. One afternoon of fun at a male friend's house could create expectations on their part. It's not fair to ask you to deal with the fallout."

He moved his hand from her back to her shoulder and gave it a squeeze.

"How about if you let me handle the *fallout,* as you call it. Growing up in a house with four rambunctious boys has made me fairly resilient."

"I'm just warning you, young females are different animals. They think and react in unexpected ways."

"So having three of them is sorta like Forrest Gump's box of chocolates?"

"Exactly," she agreed.

"You never know what you're gonna get," they replied in unison.

He held up a three-fingered Boy Scout salute.

"I solemnly pledge to accept all responsibility for the outcome of a pool party."

"That's a grave oath you just made, Dr. Temple. When you say your prayers tonight you'd best ask for a special layer of protection for your life and property."

"Come on," he chided. "How much damage can little girls do?"

"And as long as you're already on your knees, ask for protection for your heart, too."

She was trying to make light of the situation, but she'd done her best to spell it out and give him fair warning. Well, he'd keep that in mind.

But for now he and Rocket had a barbecue to plan. He needed to test the waters, find out if he would sink or swim in a chaotic environment, even if he found he was already in over his head.

CHAPTER SIX

"WHAT ON EARTH was I thinking, Rocket?"

Cullen moved from room to room in a last-ditch effort to tidy up his cluttered home before his company arrived.

His brothers had been teasing him for years that his house looked like one of those ancient bookmobiles had pulled through the front door and exploded. Volumes of every conceivable genre and subject were crammed into shelves and stacked in corners. Each room in the rambling, ranch-style home smelled of printed words bound by glue, cardboard and stitching. The aroma was reverent to Cullen, something most people, and certainly his obnoxious brothers, would never understand.

Well, that wasn't entirely true. Hunt had displayed a love of cooking at an early age and the kitchen had long been his sanctuary. Their older brother Joiner loved all things equine. The inside of a barn, smelling of horse sweat and leather tack, was his place of solace. And then there was the oldest, Mc-Carthy, a natural bean counter whose blood pressure was kept steady by frequent immersion in spreadsheets and 401(k) statements.

As much grief as they'd always given Cullen over his obsession for education, the four Temple brothers shared a bond when it came to having a passion. And each man's passion seemed to come from deep inside and wouldn't be snuffed out or denied.

Alma said their parents had been no different, and from Cullen's earliest memories, he had to agree. Their father was a surgeon who'd given countless hours to the hospital and the community it served. And their mother had had an incredible green thumb and knack for growing things. The constant cycle of fertilizing, planting, nurturing, weeding, pruning and picking had been what she'd adored, second only to the five men in her family.

Yep, no doubt about it, they were all destined to obsess, just as their patriarch had once done over striking it rich in the East Texas oil fields. That thought reminded Cullen that he'd offered to tell Sarah about his grandfather. Maybe he'd get that chore over with today since it was best to let the old skeleton out of the closet early and be finished with him. Even so, being endowed with the Temple name in these parts would never completely allow Cullen to bury Pap's notorious legacy.

"Anybody home?"

"In here," Cullen shouted. Rocket growled, a sound too small and endearing to be threatening.

"Hey, little brother!" Joiner's voice boomed from the front entryway.

"I've gotta start locking my door," Cullen called from the den that served as his study.

"Yeah, as if anybody with a lick of sense would want to steal a stack of old books."

Rocket scurried to investigate the newcomer, skidding to a stop as he was confronted by cowboy boots and jean-clad legs.

"Whoa! Who's this?"

Joiner squatted, held open his arms and Rocket went into the embrace as if his longlost friend had come home from the war.

"As I said, I should start locking the door because it seems my new watchdog isn't gonna keep out the riffraff."

"Since when do you have an animal in your home?" Joiner gathered Rocket's long limbs and stood, reminding Cullen of a cowpoke holding a rescued calf.

"Since that one wandered out from behind

a Dumpster at the pizza restaurant begging for a handout."

"You took in a stray?" Joiner seemed incredulous, and rightly so. Cullen had always been too focused on his studies to make room for an animal in his life, much less in his home.

"How could I resist that face?"

"Looks like your boy's got a lot of golden retriever in him," Joiner noted.

"That's what the vet said when I took Rocket in to get him checked out and vaccinated."

Cullen watched his brother tenderly cradle the pup, stroking his blond coat and floppy ears while Rocket poked his curious nose at Joiner's shirt pocket.

"Can he have a peppermint?" Joiner fished out a striped candy.

"Just this once. But if he throws it up, the mess belongs to you."

Joiner settled Rocket on the rug, tore open the small cellophane packet and offered the treat. The puppy sniffed it and turned uncertain eyes to his master. Warmth shot through Cullen's heart at Rocket's request for approval.

"It's okay, you can have it," Cullen assured his new buddy.

Rocket scooped up the candy with a swipe of his pink tongue and crunched it between puppy teeth as sharp as carpet tacks.

"How many years have you been carrying Life Savers in your pocket, Joiner?"

"As many as I've been coaxing and training horses. They all seem to cooperate a little better if you sweeten the deal." He stood but kept an eye on Rocket as the puppy enjoyed the treat.

"Think that principle applies to girls and cookies?" Cullen had purchased an assortment of baked goods, hoping to win favor with Carrie, Meg and Hope. And maybe Sarah.

"Sugar and females have gone hand in hand since the Garden of Eden. I personally think the forbidden fruit was a Moon-Pie instead of an apple.. I can't imagine why it would be any different today," Joiner replied. "Why do you ask?"

"I have company on the way."

"If you already have plans, why'd you ask me to come by?" Joiner slanted a questioning glance at Cullen.

"I figured it might be nice to invite my brother over for a swim and some lunch." Cullen tried to sound offended by Joiner's suspicion.

"My, aren't you domestic all of the sudden."

"A new friend from the university is bringing her three daughters over to use the pool."

Joiner's head snapped back, his eyes wide.

"A new friend? Anybody I might recognize?"

"It's always a possibility in a town this small. Her name's Sarah Eason."

"Joe Eason's widow?" Joiner asked, his brows drawing together.

"You knew her husband?"

"I met him at the gym years ago and we played racquetball a handful of times before he got too sick. Nice guy. I'd heard he passed away a while ago." Joiner gave a sad shake of his head.

"Did you ever meet his wife?"

"No, never did. I was aware that Joe was married with kids, but guys don't do much more than point and grunt within the perimeter of the gym. Where'd you meet her?"

"Sarah's auditing the lecture I took over for Blair this semester."

"Yeah, what's up with that? McCarthy mentioned you were teaching a class of your own now. Aren't you worried responsibility might cramp your style?"

"That's the pot callin' the kettle black,"

Cullen scoffed. "You've never been responsible for more than shoveling horse manure in your life."

"Hey, that's not true. Ninety percent of my time off the polo field is spent fundraising."

"How's that working out for your own checkbook?"

Joiner held a palm outward. "Enough. Nobody has to remind me how much time and money I've exhausted in the past ten years when I could hardly afford either. Now I've gotta figure out how to invest what I've got left once the ponies are sold."

"You gonna sell Pistol, too?"

"No way. He's the smartest investment I ever made. I'm going to stud him out for as long as he's interested in fraternizing with Texas fillies."

"How long is Render willing to put you up at his ranch?"

"He's agreed to trade his foreman's cabin for my services until I can find the right place or he hires a permanent manager."

Car doors slammed and high-pitched female voices announced the arrival of Cullen's guests. Rocket's head angled toward the sounds. He woofed softly and ambled down the hallway to the front entrance.

"Sounds like your date's here."

"Cut it out. Alma's coming over too so it's strictly on the up and up." Cullen dismissed his brother's insinuation. "The lady could use a friend and I happened to be in the right place at the right moment. And between you and me, Blair suggested I try something completely different, stretch my legs a bit. So I've enrolled in a psychology class for the fall semester. I figured observing some kids who have lost their daddy, kind of like we did, might be helpful to me in the class."

"Yeah, well, just watch your step or you'll have a ready-made family on your hands."

A ready-made family…

A knock on the door resounded in the entry hall. Rocket began to bark in earnest and giggly girls squealed in response on the front porch. The tranquility of his home was about to be shattered, for the day at least, and he had no one to blame but himself.

A ready-made family?

Perish the thought!

"Want me to get it?" Joiner said, offering to greet Cullen's guests.

"I'll go. But you can keep an eye on Rocket for a minute." He took a leash from the peg by the door, attached it to the puppy's collar and handed it to Joiner.

The two moved toward the kitchen to

let Cullen pass and he inhaled a final deep breath of calm air before letting hurricane Eason into the house.

"Greetings!" He pulled the door wide, expecting Sarah's girls to be lined up like little soldiers waiting for instructions. Boy, howdy, had he been wrong. The force of being crowded and squeezed by three pairs of arms as young bodies crushed against his midsection nearly knocked that final calm breath out of him.

"Ladies, we agreed to show some restraint today, remember?" Sarah coached her exuberant brood. "Sorry, Cullen, but Meg and Hope have been watching the clock since their Cheerios went mushy at 6:00 a.m. If they'd had their way we'd have been here hours ago."

"Yeah," Hope mumbled, her face pressed against Cullen's pant leg. "Even Carrie got out of bed without griping for a change."

At the mention of her name, Carrie dropped away from the group hug, a mask of indifference replacing the smile she'd been wearing. "MYOB, Runtzilla. It's not exactly front page news when a person gets up early on a Saturday morning."

"By early she means ten o'clock," Meg explained with an unsympathetic roll of her eyes—eyes the same lovely color as her mother's. "I wanted to come sooner to enjoy the clear weather. It's a documented fact that spending time in the sunshine is the only reliable way to create vitamin D in your skin, and studies show the lack of it can lead to schizophrenia."

"Well, then, Dr. Jekyll, you'd better get outside quick before Miss Hyde makes her first appearance of the day," Carrie snapped.

"Where's Rocket?" Hope looked past Cullen and into the house.

"He's inside with my brother."

"The Cowboy Chef's here?" Carrie's question was almost breathless, her eyes all kinds of dreamy.

"I'm sorry to disappoint you but it's my older brother Joiner. Hunt's working today. His fiancée owns Temple Territory and they have their own pool event going on over there this afternoon."

"Oh." Carrie's face fell. "I hadn't heard he was engaged."

"What did you expect, that he'd wait on you for ten more years?" Meg taunted.

"No, but I was at least hoping to see him while he was still available. The Cowboy Chef is a hottie patottie."

"Hey! He's my identical twin so I assume

that makes me hot, too, huh?" Cullen held his arms wide, waiting for a compliment.

"I meant hot in a television sort of way. Your look is more…" Carrie paused, not wanting to dig the hole deeper.

"Rustic?"

"Exactly!"

"Gee, thanks."

"Your word, not mine."

"I wanna see Rocket!" Hope danced with excitement, the ruffles on her swimsuit cover-up jiggling to her imagined beat.

"Let him loose, Joiner!" Cullen called down the hallway.

Seconds later the golden-haired pup came flying through the doorway, skinny legs a flurry of speed, mouth wide in a doggy grin as he hit Hope with big front paws and knocked her to the ground.

"He remembers me!" she shouted, and then burst into shrieks of laughter, assuring Cullen she'd survived the impact. Meg and Carrie joined the calamity on the ground, rolling in the warm, summer grass, taking turns letting Rocket plant wet, joyful kisses on their faces.

Cullen watched, fascinated by the moment of sweet innocence and pure play, trying to remember a day when he'd been so young, so unafraid.

Trying to remember what life had felt like before PTSD.

Before he started cutting himself.

CHAPTER SEVEN

SARAH STRUGGLED TO concentrate on what Cullen was saying about his lecture plans for the coming week. Between watching her girls splashing in the pool and worrying whether she should be helping Alma and Joiner in the kitchen, she was far too distracted to dive into subjects of historical importance with Cullen.

What Sarah really wanted to do was dive into the cool depths, but her host seemed content to sit in the shade. So when Cullen and Rocket went inside for a pitcher of lemonade, she quickly slipped off her Bermuda shorts, perched near the Gunite steps and let her feet dangle in the blue, blue water.

"Get in with us, Mama," Hope coaxed from the shallows, safe in her Pretty Princess swim vest.

"This is enough for now, maybe later."

It didn't seem appropriate to take off her T-shirt and get in when Cullen showed no interest, even with the girls taunting him. The puppy stayed hot on his master's heels and was also quite content to stay clear of the water, his pink belly exposed as he stretched out, napping in the short grass.

"But we should have four people for games and races."

"Will I do?"

Heads turned as Joiner stepped out onto the patio wearing surfer-style, knee-length trunks. The loud, floral print so popular in decades past was making a comeback, and on Joiner's trim body Sarah could certainly see the appeal of the low-riding garment.

"You're on my team!" Hope called.

"We should toss a coin to decide whose team he's on," Meg insisted.

"How about if we just toss you on your pointed head instead?" Carrie cupped her hand and splashed her sister.

"Now, now, ladies. There's no need to fight over me when you can take turns instead," Joiner teased as he closed the door behind him and then walked the perimeter of the pool before stepping up onto the diving board. "I have enough energy for several rounds of competition, if you're up to it."

"Make a big splash!" Hope screamed, delighted with the new development.

Joiner bounced twice, the board bending

beneath his weight as he balanced on the balls of his feet. Finally he took a high leap and gracefully folded at the waist in the classic jackknife position. But instead of stretching his body to make a clean entry, he tucked into a tight ball and slammed into the water cannonball style, the impact sending sprays arching in every direction.

The girls shrieked and shielded their faces from the unexpected soaking.

"Was that splash big enough for you?" Joiner asked after he surfaced next to Hope.

Her playful response was to kick water in his face.

When he karate-chopped the surface with the edge of his hand in reply, the battle began in earnest—three sisters against Cullen's brother in a contest for who could launch the strongest torrent in the other's direction. The girls held their own quite well.

Sarah jumped to her feet and retreated to the table just out of reach of the wet madness.

The glass patio door slid wide once more and Cullen stepped through carrying a tray of plastic cups, a tall pitcher and a bowl over-flowing with snack mix.

"Let me guess." He settled the tray on the tabletop. "Joiner did his special dive for them?"

"It was extremely impressive." Sarah filled the cups of ice with the tart drink she'd seen Alma lovingly squeeze from fresh lemons.

"And extremely effective—if your intention is to empty half the pool in one motion. There goes my water bill."

Rocket wandered over to retrieve a bit of pretzel that had found its way to the grass.

"Ladies, how about taking a break?" she called.

Hope climbed the steps, deposited her Pretty Princess vest beside the pool and dripped her way to the table.

"Look, Mama." She held her palm outward. "My fingers are all raisiny."

"That happens when they get waterlogged. Catch your breath and have a snack and they'll plump up again in no time."

Meg and Carrie joined the table while Joiner began to swim laps, his body slicing through the water in sure, confident motions.

"If you hadn't noticed, Joiner's the swimmer in the family."

"Did you have a pool when you were a kid?" Meg asked over a mouthful of the salty snack mix.

"No, but we had a membership to the YMCA. We all had lessons, but Joiner was the only one who really took to the water.

Hunt and I prefer the baseball diamond, and for Mac it's the golf course."

"My mom says golf is a waste of time and money invented for the purpose of keeping a husband away from his wife's honey-do list," Sarah shared.

"I continue to be impressed with your mother's wisdom." Cullen smiled and raised his red Solo cup in salute.

"Do you cover up because your skin burns really badly?" Meg pointed to Cullen's light-weight khakis and long sleeve T-shirt on such a perfect summer day.

"He fries worse than bacon on a hot skillet and he's really hairy and gross underneath his clothes," Joiner answered as he approached the table. He stood next to Hope and, to her delight, shook like a dog, flinging drops of water in every direction.

"You wanna learn to swim without that floatie thing?"

"Can I?" Hope turned wide eyes to her mother for permission.

"Joiner, you're kind to offer but we can't trouble two Temple men this weekend."

"Let him do it, Sarah. Joiner's very patient with kids and animals, which is why he's going to teach Rocket to swim, too."

"Are you sure?"

"We're here and we're wet," Joiner pointed out the obvious to Sarah. "I can teach her a lot in a half hour, as long as her sisters don't mind giving us the pool for a bit."

In response, Carrie and Meg tossed beach towels over a couple of lounge chairs, poked their earbuds into place and stretched out to sun and enjoy their music.

"Carrie, turn your iPod down. I can hear Def Leppard all the way over here," Sarah insisted.

"She's right." Meg thumped her sister to get her attention. "You'll blow your eardrums out."

"Do that again and I'll break your fingers," Carrie threatened.

"Let's go, kiddo." Joiner invited Hope with a wave of his hand and the two made a beeline for the pool.

Cullen cast a curious glance toward her surly daughter and then settled into a chair beside Sarah.

"I apologize for my oldest. She seems determined to make the awkward middle school years as tough as possible for all of us."

"No worries, Joiner used to speak to me the same way. It lasted a couple of years but he eventually grew some respect for me and cut the crap talk."

"Was there something in particular that made him change?"

"I shot up about six inches one summer and learned to swing a mean baseball bat."

They shared a laugh.

"I can't thank you enough for this break from the apartment today."

"No thanks necessary. It's nice to have some company besides my brothers. And Alma loves somebody to fuss over. She's in there right now singing away while she makes chicken salad. There haven't been any kids in this house since the previous owners moved out."

"How come such a handsome guy doesn't have a family of his own by now?"

"The Temple boys get asked that a lot. Not that handsome part, since the others are somewhat toady, but the marriage part because we're all still single. I expect it's because we witnessed an extraordinary relationship between our parents and none of us will be happy with anything less. When that kind of love comes along, we'll recognize it."

"I understand what you mean." Sarah glanced toward her older daughters, who drowsed in the sun a few feet away. "I'm grateful that my girls have my parents as role models of marriage, since they're growing up without a man in the house."

"Do you think you'll ever remarry?"

"Eventually, but I have the girls to concentrate on so that's not even on my radar. I enjoyed marriage and partnership, so I do hope that blessing comes around again."

"You have a nice outlook after the loss your family has experienced."

"Having my daughters makes all the difference, to me *and* my parents. They started hinting for babies at my wedding reception."

"I get that, too. Hunt's engaged now so that takes the pressure off the rest of us to give Alma and Felix grandchildren before they're too old to enjoy them, as if people in their fifties are old these days."

"Mom keeps telling me fifty is the new thirty."

"Yeah, well, Miss Nancy says seventy is the same drag it's always been."

"What's it like to have gone to college for so many years that you know everybody on campus?"

"It's the same as any other job after a dozen years or so, it's just that I pay them instead of them paying me. When I wouldn't go away after my first Ph.D., they started asking me to be a guest lecturer, and then to stand in when the history department needed short-term coverage. Doing those two things built my dubious reputation as a subject matter expert and allowed me to build a résumé. Now I can shop myself out to other universities when they have to fill some empty space in the curriculum and I want a free trip to visit a new city. I've got everybody fooled into thinking I know what I'm doing."

"Cullen, why do you sell yourself short by making light of your talent?"

"It's just easier to make a joke than to be one. I think it's the birth-order curse of being born number three of four."

"Well, kindly leave the doubts at home when you come to class, because the students believe you're number one."

"Including you?"

"Including me." Sarah touched his sleeve lightly, to ensure he took her seriously.

CULLEN'S GAZE FELL to her hand patting his arm, just as he'd seen her do with her girls.

What made you ask her that, dummy? Now Sarah will think you're as needy as one of her kids.

"If you're campaigning for teacher's pet, you've got my vote," he said, trying to cover his misstep.

"I can see there's no harnessing your self-deprecation, so I'll just enjoy your bad jokes instead of trying to get you to go easy on yourself."

"I'm not so hard on myself."

"Oh, sure you are, and probably more than you realize. Anybody with a hunger for knowledge that never lets up is bound to have a perfectionist streak a mile wide. You want to get everything right, and you beat on yourself when you don't, true?"

Cullen squinted up into the umbrella and then down under the picnic table as if searching for something.

"What are you doing?" Sarah laughed at his silly efforts.

"There must be a hidden camera and microphone around here somewhere. You've analyzed me so well that you're bound to be spying on me."

"As if I have the time," she teased. "Actually, I see some of Meg's behaviors in yours. She's my little perfectionist and that causes her to dwell over negative things most people wouldn't even notice."

"I've noticed. She's a walking, talking warning label."

Sarah leaned closer, concern shadowing her eyes as she kept her voice low.

"Meg was already headed in that direction, and her daddy's illness exacerbated her fears. We had to be so vigilant about his care, not exposing him to things that would stir up a respiratory infection or fever. Watching for hidden dangers became her self-imposed role in the family. Joe was stage four when he was diagnosed. He and I always knew he wouldn't be with us for long, but the girls were too little to understand that fact. And when the end came, Meg felt she'd failed him."

"Has she actually said that to you?" Cullen's stomach knotted at the idea of the sweet girl going down the same path he'd taken after losing his parents.

"Not in so many words, mostly because she wasn't old enough to articulate her feelings. But after Joe died, Meg continued to check the thermostat and close doors so there wouldn't be drafts, just as she did to keep the house comfortable for him. I'd hoped that behavior would stop when we moved to the apartment, but she does it there, too."

"Well, consider it this way—she's helping you keep your utility bills under control."

Sarah smiled, the tension in her face eased.

"There is that to be thankful for," she agreed.

It was his turn to lay a friendly hand on her shoulder.

"I didn't mean to make light of what you just told me, Sarah. You're smart to pay attention to her signals. A kid can develop all kinds of coping mechanisms when they're internalizing a loss, and some of them are unhealthy. Have you considered therapy?"

"Not lately. We went to family grief counseling at our church for a while but I think it was too soon for any of us to get much out of it. Maybe I should look into that again."

"The psychology department at the university has an excellent staff, and as a student you might qualify for free services. I can ask around for you if you'd be interested."

"Thanks, Cullen. That would be helpful. God was good to send me a thoughtful friend just when I needed one."

"Don't give me credit just yet. I may have ulterior motives."

"Such as?"

"Help with grading papers, doing research, cleaning blackboards. The usual teacher's pet chores."

He stopped short of admitting to Sarah that having her family around was a perfect study in childhood behavior, one of the topics in his upcoming psych class. That sounded a little too clinical, even for his taste.

"So the job is a go?" Her voice was hopeful.

"It's all yours if you want it."

"Then consider the position filled, Dr. Temple. I'll start right after class on Monday."

It was a tongue-in-cheek discussion but the idea of spending more time with Sarah Eason was appealing, even if he broke out into a cold sweat if he gave too much thought to the consequences.

"When are we eating?" Carrie complained.

"I'm hungry, too," Meg added. "And remember, you have to wait at least an hour before getting back into the pool or you'll get a cramp."

CHAPTER EIGHT

WITH THE EXCEPTION of Carrie's headphone squawking, the yard was blissfully quiet while everyone enjoyed the picnic Alma had laid out in the shade of the covered deck. The peaceful setting and the meal prepared by someone other than herself was a treat for Sarah.

"This is the best chicken salad that ever passed my lips," Joiner complimented Alma. "What's your secret, *mi dulce mami?*"

"It's Hunt's recipe, but I punch it up with cilantro and red onion."

"He probably charges ten bucks a plate for this in his restaurant at Temple Territory," Cullen mused.

"Eighteen," Alma corrected. "And he justifies that price with a teaspoon of Russian caviar in the cracker basket. I know, because I suggested it." Her Cheshire cat smile was proud.

"What's caviar?" Hope gazed up at Joiner.

"It's fish eggs."

"Eeeeew." She contorted her face into a Mr. Yuck grimace.

"It's an acquired taste," Joiner assured her. "You'll probably love it when you're all grown up and some guy is buying expensive dinners to impress you."

"I would *never* eat fish eggs," Hope insisted.

"But you'll suck the head off a boiled crawfish, so go figure that one out," Carrie said, apparently still able to hear their conversation over the music in her ears.

"That's different." Hope dismissed her sister.

"I have to agree with my little mermaid here when it comes to mud bugs."

Joiner and Hope exchanged new-friend grins and Sarah felt as if a vise squeezed her heart tightly. Her baby girl had found yet another hero.

"Crawfish are local critters and God intended them to be enjoyed right here in Texas, juicy heads and all," Joiner instructed. "But I'd be suspicious of anything stuffed in a can and shipped five thousand miles."

"If it was so yummy you'd think they'd keep it all over there," Hope reasoned over a mouth full of chicken salad.

"Exactly," Joiner agreed. "But they send

most of it to other countries and people pay prices higher than a cat's back just to get a teeny little bite."

"How did you get so smart?" Hope was all eyes and ears for Joiner.

"He got his smarts from sharing a room with me when we were about your age." Cullen jumped into the conversation. Like Carrie, he never missed a chance to poke fun at one of his siblings. "But you're right, my big brother does have pretty good sense, even if it's all horse sense."

"Don't forget about the nonsense," Joiner added.

"Yes, there's plenty of that to go around."

"You guys sound a lot like my girls. Don't you ever give each other any rest?" Sarah asked.

"Why would we want to do that?" Joiner gave Hope a look of confusion, as if her mama was missing the obvious. "Rest is for bedtime when everybody goes to his own corner."

"I agree." Cullen nodded. "It's not as though we're arguing, just conversing."

"With gusto," Joiner insisted.

Sarah turned pleading eyes to Alma for support.

"Don't drag me into this." Alma chuckled.

"I gave up trying to get my boys to make nice many years ago. It's how they communicate, and as long as they show up at the table with clean hands, that's the most any *anciana* can ask."

"You are *not* an old woman," Joiner and Cullen insisted.

"Not yet. But one of you had better get married and give me some *grand niños* before my hands are too gnarled from cooking and cleaning to change diapers."

"You and Felix have two daughters of your own to give you babies. You remember that, right?"

"And they are about as cooperative as my Temple boys. A woman of my age and experience should be bouncing little ones on her knee."

Hope got down from her chair, moved to Alma's side and slipped her slender arm around the older woman's shoulders.

"I may be too big to sit on your knee, but I can be your grandbaby if you want one."

Alma scooped Hope into her arms and then deposited the skinny seven-year-old on her lap.

"You're not too big at all, see? In fact, you're just perfect."

"That's what my Grandma Maggie says."

"Is that your mama?" Alma asked Sarah.

"Yes, and the girls also have Grandma Eason, but she lives out in Lubbock so we don't visit her very often."

"Well, in that case, I'd be honored to be your *gran madre*. I haven't had a *niña* in my house for many years, so you'll have to come and visit."

"Can I, really?"

"You can all come," Alma assured the three girls. "And I'll teach you how to wrap and steam tamales the way the ancient Mayans did thousands of years ago."

"Steam can be very dangerous, you know," Meg warned Alma.

"That's why you have to be trained correctly. And for dessert, I'll show you how to bake *pan dulce* stuffed with guava and vanilla cream."

"Better watch out, Alma, this bunch may take you up on that offer—and I might join them." Cullen winked.

"Tomorrow, then, after church. Bring the girls and leave them with me for a few hours. We'll have a cooking lesson and you two can study, or whatever it is you do at that university of yours."

Sarah surveyed the pleading faces of the group. Even Carrie seemed interested.

"Alma, are you sure you don't mind? Sunday should be a day of rest."

"Cooking rests my mind, it's only my hands that stay busy. Besides, Sunday afternoon is when I do the specialty baking for Temple Territory, so I'll be elbow-deep in a batch of dough, anyway."

"That's a bona fide offer, Sarah. Just say yes and give the girls a new experience. And you can get started in your new position," Cullen encouraged.

"Which new position is that?" Joiner asked.

"Teacher's pet," Cullen answered his nosy big brother with a grin.

CULLEN ORIGINALLY HAD no intention of putting Sarah to work. But if helping with his class preparation drew her into the subject matter, it would be well worth the effort. He remembered his early years of assisting Blair and how his mentor's assignments had transformed the boredom of a textbook into an adventure into the past.

More importantly, assigning Sarah tasks gave him an excuse to spend a few hours with the woman he found as appealing as her family was interesting. Though he'd decided to bring her to the classroom to keep his mind on strictly professional subjects.

"These maps are fascinating," Sarah muttered to herself for the tenth time that Sunday afternoon.

Cullen peered over his reading glasses and smiled at the picture she made sitting behind a scarred library table at the front of the lecture hall projecting images and facts about Mesopotamia onto the jumbo screen.

"There's an incredible amount of information here and most of it is new to me," she continued.

"It's called the Cradle of Civilization," he replied from his seat in the middle of the darkened auditorium that could accommodate a hundred students. "Historians began documenting the details of their culture about three thousand years before Christ, so you could study it endlessly and never cover everything. I know, I've tried. How do you think I got all this gray hair?"

She raised her face from the laptop computer that was feeding the overhead monitor. Her eyes gleamed with the interest every teacher aspires to instill in a pupil.

"I get your point, though I doubt you have the gray hairs to support it, Dr. Temple."

"Oh, I do!" He tipped his face forward, pulled off his Rangers cap and gestured toward the top of his head. "Come see for your-self."

He waited with his eyes down and his crown exposed as he heard the stool she'd been perched on scrape the surface of the lecture platform and her sandals slap the old wooden floor. Then Sarah's pretty red toe-nails entered his line of sight. She leaned in to study the top of his head and Cullen caught the light floral scent of her perfume.

The aroma was very appealing and oh-so-womanly, like Sarah herself.

The stirring thought caused him to lift his gaze, sweeping up her curvy legs, past mod-est denim shorts and a faded Dallas Cowboy's T-shirt, and coming to rest on intense blue eyes framed by auburn bangs. She squinted for a closer look at his so-called gray hair.

"Oh, baloney!" Sarah complained, and raised her hand to playfully swat at his head. "I have more than you do."

Cullen caught her hand, tugged her into the seat beside him and leaned close with her fingers clasped in his. Her eyes widened with surprise, but she didn't draw back.

"And here I figured it would be wiser to work at the university than alone at my house."

"Why is that?"

"I figured a public place would minimize my daydreams about kissing the teacher's pet. Seems I figured wrong."

Her response was to lean her forehead against his and close her eyes. Was it a sign of encouragement or surrender?

He gave her fingers a squeeze, then shifted away.

"Maybe we'd better return to the hilarity of history."

"Please don't," she whispered.

"Don't joke?"

"Don't move away from me. I've almost forgotten how nice a tender moment and a personal touch from a man could feel."

Cullen slid his arm around Sarah's shoulders and pulled her close, pressing her head to his chest. A sigh escaped her as she relaxed against him. Her hand sought his and she pulled his fingers to her lips where she placed a soft kiss. Of what? Gratitude? Longing?

Of course, she misses her husband.

Sarah raised her face and sucked in a breath, no doubt preparing to explain that very thing. There was no need for her to feel embarrassed, so he covered for her by saying, "Maybe we should get back to work."

"Maybe you should kiss me."

"Maybe you're confused."

"Maybe I'm thinking clearly."

"Maybe you're just lonely for the past."

"Maybe I'm very much in the present."

"Maybe you're cozying up to me for a good grade."

"I'm only auditing, remember?" She released his hand, slid hers behind his neck and pulled his mouth down to cover her lips.

The instant warmth of their kiss sizzled through him like a bolt of electricity. This was no sympathy kiss on his part, and if she was conjuring up the past it sure didn't seem that way to Cullen.

After long moments Sarah released her hold on him and put a few inches between them as she straightened in her chair.

"Would you mind telling me what that was all about?" Cullen asked as he tugged his cap into place again.

"I'm not sure I know myself, yet."

"Well, if you should decide you want to run through that exercise again to help you figure it out, you say the word and I'll be more than happy to oblige."

"You are a gentleman and a scholar."

"He wasn't lookin' like either one of those things to me a second ago," Miss Nancy observed, her voice craggy as always.

The overhead lights blazed to life.

"Sittin' here in the dark doesn't help, either," she added as she advanced down the aisle.

"Miss Nancy, the lights were out for a reason."

"Yes, I noticed." She stopped next to the row where they were seated. "You two are waaay past eighteen, so you can do whatever you want, but if you're gonna neck in public, you oughta do it in a movie theater like the rest of us."

"Thank you for that piece of advice, Miss Nancy. Was there a reason you dropped by on this fine Sunday afternoon?"

She fished into the pocket of her camo pants, pulled out a white envelope and handed it to Cullen.

"It's a special occasion so I'm delivering these personally."

"Dr. Cullen Temple and Date" was artfully written in calligrapher's ink.

"Go ahead, open it," she urged in a manner that was uncharacteristically shy.

Cullen removed the engraved card and a smile spread across his face as he silently read the invitation. He stood and wrapped the older woman in a hug, and for once she didn't resist. It was his day for cooperative women.

"Congratulations, Miss Nancy! You're finally going to make an honest man out of Merle."

"The old goat's been making noise about moving in with me, and campus housing won't approve it unless we make it legal."

"Well, I think it's superb."

"Then you'll come?"

"And I'll bring Sarah as my date if she's free to join me. You're kind of doing this on short notice." He glanced at the invitation again. "This isn't a shotgun wedding, is it?"

Miss Nancy let loose with a loud snort.

"Now, that's an idea! Maybe we'll have the preacher hold my daddy's double barrel Winchester just to get Merle's attention."

"Miss Nancy, you could have can-can girls dancing on the tabletops and Merle would only have eyes for you."

The older woman turned to Sarah.

"You watch out for this one, you hear me?" She pointed a finger of accusation at Cullen. "He pretends he's not marriage material, but he'll be a keeper for some lucky lady—if he ever stops learning and starts living," Miss Nancy warned.

In response to the observation, Cullen's cheeks flushed.

"You might be right," Sarah said, agreeing with Miss Nancy.

Suddenly, Cullen's pulse picked up and his hands began to tremble ever so slightly—the classic signs that a panic attack was threatening.

CHAPTER NINE

ALMA'S KITCHEN HAD been clean as a whistle when Sarah had said goodbye to her girls earlier that day. Now, several hours later, it looked like a sack of flour had exploded.

"Mama, we just met the Cowboy Chef!" Hope shouted from her position at the head of the enormous farmhouse-style table where the girls and Alma were rolling out dough and shaping small loaves. Hope's cheeks and hands were dusted with the white powder and a fingerprint dotted the tip of her nose. Her auburn hair had been caught up in a blue bandanna, making her appear for all the world like somebody's granny on baking day.

"You really did meet him?" Sarah responded to her daughter's excitement. "How cool!"

"And what's so cool about an introduction to my twin?" Cullen pretended to be insulted. "Hunt has the same face that I do. He puts his Wranglers on one leg at a time, the same way I do. He throws a split finger fastball the same way I do, though not as well. He thumps the steering wheel and sings off key in the car the same way I do. He even drools in his sleep and wakes up with bad breath the same way I do. Wait, that's Rocket I'm thinking about, not Hunt, which is an insult to my dog. Anyway, I don't get it. Can somebody please let me in on what's so special about my little brother?"

"I've been asking the same thing since the day you started high school and I quit being Mac Temple and started being Cullen's brother."

A man Sarah hadn't noticed before pulled his head from inside the refrigerator and came to stand beside the table.

"Hey, bro!" Cullen slung his arms around the guy she judged to be closer to her age and, from the resemblance, was obviously another Temple brother.

Sarah watched the two embrace, awed by their open expression of love. And then awed some more by yet another drop-dead, good-lookin' Temple. Wow, their parents had done a stellar job of populating East Texas with handsome men.

"What a nice surprise to find you here, you sorry sack of s—"

"Cullen, watch your mouth," Alma cautioned.

"I was only gonna say 'sack of sugar.' You sorry sack of sugar."

"He does call me that a lot, Alma."

"Maybe to your face, but it's a little different behind your back." She snickered.

"Sarah, this is my oldest brother, McCarthy. Mac, this is Sarah Eason."

Mac took her hand in his, held it fast and pierced her with a kind, brown stare. "I was acquainted with your husband from our Rotary Club meetings. Joe was a stand-up guy and we miss him in the service community."

"Thank you," she murmured, an instant fan of McCarthy Temple. Most people ignored the fact she was a widow, as if Joe had never existed. As if he'd hadn't been the center of her world only a few years ago.

"You knew my dad?" Carrie spoke up.

"Yes, ma'am, I did, and with those pretty hazel eyes you are his spittin' image. Except of course for the purple hair," he teased.

Carrie tucked her chin but not quick enough to hide her pleasure at the compliment.

"Great shirt, by the way." Mac nodded to the face of Ozzy Osbourne on a faded red background.

"Black Sabbath was one of Dad's favorite bands and he bought this himself at a concert. Mom let me have it because she said it clashed with her hair."

"Well, it certainly sets off that lovely shade of purple you've chosen to distinguish yourself," Mac agreed.

"I had to do *something* to stand out in this redheaded family."

"Did you know that red hair and blue eyes are the result of recessive genes?" Meg joined the conversation.

"Is that a fact?" Mac switched his attention to Meg, who was also doused in self-rising flour.

"Oh, yes, Carrie got all the dominant genes in the family. The rest of us got stuck with Grandpa Callaghan's awful features."

"I beg your pardon, but my daddy would not appreciate hearing that his granddaughters 'got stuck' with his beautiful Irish traits."

"And his freckles!" Hope reminded Meg.

"Yeah, don't forget his freckles," Carrie agreed. "If these two didn't have freckles they'd be as white as Casper the Friendly Ghost."

Meg slung her hand toward Carrie and the flour on her fingers flew through the air and showered Carrie's head.

"Now who's as white as Casper?" Hope crowed.

Sarah knew she should discipline her unruly brood, but why throw a wet blanket on their fun?

"Momento de la limpieza," Alma announced.

"Huh?" the three chorused.

Alma clapped her hands together and a swirl of flour filled the air, to the little girls' delight.

"We need to clean up and get these last baking sheets into the oven while your *madre* samples the delicious tamales you made today."

"I have to agree with Alma. With the extra help from you girls, this batch of pork tamales may be Alma's best ever," said McCarthy.

"How do you know how the tamales taste?" Cullen asked. His eyes narrowed with jealousy.

"Because I already had a few," Mac taunted.

"You let him eat before I got here?" Cullen spun to Alma.

"Hunt came to pick up the *polvorón* and *cremas de fresas* for Temple Territory and since he let everyone taste the pastries I agreed to share the tamales even though you weren't here. *Forgive me, mi querido muchacho?*"

MAE NUNN   111

"Nana Alma said it was a special exception since we're company, but after today we're family." Hope's eyes were wide with the seriousness of the subject.

"*Nana Alma,* is it, then?" Cullen angled his squint toward his mother figure and pretended to pout. "One afternoon with a bunch of giggly girls and I'm kicked to the curb?"

"*Usted sabe que está mi favorito.*" Alma held white hands out and opened her chubby arms to Cullen, who deftly sidestepped her offer of a flour-coated hug.

"Wait a minute, you always tell me *I'm* your favorite," Mac accused.

"Is that what she just said in Spanish? I heard her say that to the Cowboy Chef when he was here," Carrie announced.

"And I let Joiner think the same thing when he comes to see me. So what? It's been going on for years and everybody's happy," Alma insisted.

"She makes an excellent point," Mac agreed with an easy smile.

"Sarah, let's join in the sampling of these tamales that everyone says are so wonderful."

Cullen motioned for Sarah to follow him into the kitchen where Alma rinsed her hands and then peeled away the foil from a pan large enough to roast a turkey. The homemade tamales were piled high, steaming packets of corn husks tied up with string, resembling little gifts.

"Hot!" Alma warned when he reached toward the mother lode.

"I'm not a child." He pretended to be insulted.

"But you still act like one."

"That's so you'll still take care of me." Cullen tried to gather Alma in his arms but she swatted him away.

"These Temple boys are experts at turning on the charm when it suits them, so watch out for their ulterior motives," Alma warned Sarah.

Then she offered Cullen a pair of long-handled tongs, which he wisely accepted. Sarah watched as he put two packets on a small plate and unrolled them carefully, wisps of steam escaping. He took a fork from a kitchen drawer, portioned off a bite and then scooped up the tamale. He turned and offered her the first taste. An almost forgotten feeling of excitement inside her said this moment would be memorable.

CULLEN SENSED SOMETHING special was taking place. Offering a woman her first taste of Alma's tamale was right up there with feeding a bride her first bite of wedding cake. He watched as Sarah closed her eyes and gave her full attention to savoring the pork loin cooked for hours in a Dutch oven, then shredded and seasoned before being rolled in corn husks spread with lovingly prepared *masa*. The process was a centuries-old tradition of Hispanic cooking that not everyone would appreciate.

Cullen recalled the scene from *Pretty Woman* when Edward observed Vivian's reaction to opera. He'd told her, "If people love it, they will always love it. If they don't, they may learn to appreciate it—but it will never become part of their soul."

Only this was not a video that Alma had watched a thousand times in their home. This was real life. If Sarah loved the flavor of the simple food, it would be part of her forever. If not, then her meals with the Temple Brothers would probably be limited.

Sarah chewed quietly, her eyes still closed, shielding her first impression and blocking Cullen's ability to guess. Only a couple of seconds passed, but the suspense was killing him.

"How does it taste, Mama?" Hope broke the spell.

"I need something." Sarah had everyone's attention.

"Water?" Hope asked.

"Hot sauce?" Alma guessed.

"Salt?" Carrie wondered.

"More!" Sarah teased them all. "More tamales and my own plate. These are amazing! You all did a wonderful job!"

Cullen released the breath he'd been holding, handed over his serving and relinquished control of the fork. The question was answered. He wasn't sure why it mattered so much, but it did. Sarah and her girls were fitting into his life with the comfort of a beloved old pair of Lucchese boots. Comfy and welcoming, though they sometimes rubbed you raw and smelled a bit.

That's the way his family had felt before his parents were lost to him forever. Then Alma and Felix stepped in and restored the comforting and welcoming part, while his brothers still supplied the painful and stinky part. If the Eason ladies kept this up there was no end to the potential.

As the revelation sunk into his brain and the noisy conversation continued around him, Cullen's armpits trickled sweat beneath his shirt. He'd managed to quell the earlier threat of an attack by practicing deep-breathing techniques he'd learned in therapy. But with these new symptoms, perhaps he'd just delayed the inevitable.

Only in addition to the clammy discomfort, an appealing pulse of warmth surged outward from his chest and through his veins.

Maybe this upset to his orderly life was worth the cost.

Then Cullen's scalp began to prickle, an edgy sensation he hated.

Maybe not.

How was he going to manage his nerves and still be around this family that was slowly but surely finding a way into his heart?

CHAPTER TEN

"MOM, YOU WON'T be offended if the girls hang out with Alma this week, will you?"

The Sunday sun was still high in the evening sky, streaming light into the kitchen where Margaret Callaghan was stewing homegrown tomatoes to be put up for the winter.

"Heavens, no," she said, allaying Sarah's worry. "My granddaughters are welcome here with me and your daddy anytime, but backup help is always welcome. It's nice for them to have a different cultural perspective since they're a whole lot more likely to encounter Hispanics than Irishmen in East Texas."

"I hadn't thought of it that way, but you make an excellent point."

"And from what Meg tells me, the Temple brothers are frequent visitors there, too."

"They're more family than visitors. The guys show up without notice at Alma and Felix's house the same way I do here."

"If memory serves me, only one of the four is spoken for, so that makes three eligible bachelors who are all pretty easy on the eyes."

"Mom," Sarah warned.

"You could do worse than a Temple boy, my dear, even considering their colorful family history—which we won't bring up in front of your opinionated daddy. Decades ago he swallowed the story hook, line and sinker that Pap Temple was nothin' but a liar and a thief."

"Cullen gave me the *Reader's Digest* version of his grandfather's conviction. Was it really that big of a deal?"

Margaret squinted hard at her daughter as if she'd just uttered a curse.

"Clearly I've failed as a mother and as a Texan to properly educate my only child on the importance of black gold in these parts."

"Well, it's not as if I didn't realize this is oil country."

"*Oil country* is an understatement. We live on top of one of the world's largest reserves. When the Daisy Bradford No. 3 struck oil in 1930, it made the California gold rush look like a sack race. Major companies and wildcatters came from all over the globe, and at the height of the rush, Kilgore had over a thousand active wells, making it the densest oil discovery in history."

"So if all that happened in the '30s how did Cullen's grandfather get into trouble in the '60s?"

"Mason Dixon Temple has the dubious distinction of being the only man convicted of drilling a slanted well in order to steal oil from a lease that didn't belong to him. Plenty of others were guilty, but Pap Temple was the one who took the fall for the practice."

"Cullen seemed to think I would already have heard the gossip about his family."

"I'm not surprised. It was a huge story all those years ago, and those of us who were around remember it the same way your generation will remember the O. J. Simpson trial."

"Cullen said he and his brothers feel that they still live in the shadow of Pap's crime."

"As I said, it was a big deal, and people have long memories. In another hundred years it'll be forgotten, but for now it's still something of a dark blot on the name."

"Well, other than that, I believe the Temple men are quite happy with life as they know it today."

"And how about you?"

"Busy." Sarah pretended to miss the intent of her mother's question.

"I'm well aware that you're busy. But are you happy?"

"Reasonably, considering the circumstances."

"Honey, you've been on your own for over three years. And for a long while before Joe died, you were as much his caregiver as you were his wife. Nobody expects you to live for the girls' sake alone. It's okay to let a man into your life."

"In my head I realize that's true, but my heart is still confused on the subject. It's not just loyalty. My own husband held out on me for months about his diagnosis. How can I ever completely trust a man again?"

"Joe was just trying to spare you for as long as possible."

"But maybe things would have been different if he'd started treatment sooner. If he'd only shared the truth with me."

Sarah had never fully understood or forgiven Joe for keeping that devastating news to himself, denying her the right to help search for other options.

"It wouldn't have made a bit of difference, Sarah Elizabeth. Your husband was a smart man. He knew his circumstances, and he chose to do what was right for himself and his family in the months he had left. You have to accept that and try not to hold Joe's decision against every other man you meet."

Sarah nodded, wanting to accept her mother's perspective.

"And the girls are all at an age where they need an example of how a man and a woman share a healthy relationship. Only you can give that to them, honey."

"I worry they won't handle it well, Mom. Each one has her own little psychosis going on. Carrie's eaten up with that Goth business, Meg's a class-A worrywart and Hope sees every man she meets through rose-colored glasses. My hands are too full wrestling their issues to sort through my own."

"Exactly my point. If divine providence orchestrates the opportunity for you to go with the flow and enjoy the company of a man, there's no shame in that. Do you think it was pure chance that you went back to college and the first friend you made was a nice, single fella?"

"Mom, the stars have not aligned for my benefit, if that's what you're insinuating."

"But if they have, don't be a martyr, clinging to the belief that being a widow is your lot in life. It's not, and I'm certain there is happiness in the future for you and the girls."

"I'll keep that in mind."

"It's actually something your dad said last night. He'd like to see you with a husband again someday, too."

"Don't you two have anything better to talk about other than my lack of a love life?"

"Actually, no. That's the way it is when you only have one child. The common topics for discussion are somewhat limited. But with those three live wires of yours, you will never have a lack of funny anecdotes to share with the handsome man across from you at the dinner table."

Sarah went to her mother's kitchen window and peeked through the blinds.

"Just as I suspected, no line of men around the house hoping to date a woman with a passel of kids."

"Are you saying you're ready and there are just no candidates?" Her mother's voice was hopeful.

"I'm not sure what I'm saying, Mom."

"Well, what about Cullen? You've been together quite a bit lately. Is there any chemistry between you two?"

"I like Cullen, maybe even more than I'm ready to admit to myself. But he's reluctant to drop his guard too low. Maybe it's because I'm one of his students, even if I'm not in his class for a grade. For now I'm enjoying his company and the preparation for his lectures, which I find fascinating, by the way. We'll have to see how things go after the semester is over and we don't have any class-related reason to hang out."

"Well, it sounds as if your mind is open to romance, and that's all I can ask."

"But the door to my open mind can slam shut a dozen times a day depending on what's going on with my daughters."

"They say you can only be as happy as your most miserable child."

"And since one of mine is always in the dumps, I can't plan my joy too far in advance."

"You know, you weren't exactly a happy-go-lucky kid yourself."

"I wasn't?" Sarah was surprised by her mother's comment.

"Oh, heck, no. There was a string of about six years in there when you didn't go two days in a row without a crisis."

"At least I didn't argue with you constantly the way Carrie does with me."

"Of course you did." Sarah's mother smiled at the memory. "But you didn't consider it arguing, you were simply expressing your opinion, and it generally disagreed with mine."

"That's strange because I don't remember you making a big deal out of me behaving that way."

"Honey, when you raise a child to think for herself, you can't hold it against her when she does it."

"You're the best mother in the world." Sarah took comfort in her mother's soft embrace. "The girls and I would be lost if we didn't have you and Daddy."

Margaret held Sarah for several moments and then patted her shoulder gently before returning to a sink full of tomatoes.

"How are my granddaughters around Cullen?"

"Amazingly relaxed. But I expect it's because they don't sense anything physical between the two of us, so they don't perceive him as a threat to their daddy."

"Then just continue to take things slowly and let the good Lord work out your life in His time."

"So far the good Lord's timing has been pretty hard on me."

"Baby girl, gold is refined by fire."

"Well, when He's finished with me, I should be twenty-four carat for sure."

"Mama, are you and Cullen getting married?" Hope asked over a mouthful of corn dog, a smear of mustard on her cheek.

"Not as far as I am aware. Why do you ask?"

"Because she's stupid," Carrie insisted.

"Stupid is as stupid does," Hope reminded her sister.

"I didn't bring you girls to the Dairy Dream for dinner so you could be ugly to one another."

"I'm not sure we should be eating here, anyway," Meg said. "Did you see their health department rating on the wall over there?" She pointed to a posting beside the restaurant's entrance. "It's down a percent since we were here last month."

Hope glared with suspicion at her meal on a stick.

"Ignore what Meg just said, baby," Sarah cautioned. "A rating drop from ninety-nine to ninety-eight is not exactly a reason to call in the food police."

Hope scrunched up her nose and mouth at Meg, who returned the *"so there"* face.

"Now to your question, Hope."

"Nana Alma said when you and Cullen go to your wedding, we can stay at her house."

"She means that the two of us are attending the wedding of a couple who work at the university. Cullen's been friends with them both for a long time, and since I'm a student there now, and most of the people at the wedding will be his colleagues, he thought I'd enjoy meeting everyone."

"Well, it's okay with me if you do marry him."

"Me, too," Meg agreed.

"It's nice to have your blessing, girls, but Cullen and I are just friends. He's my teacher and there's nothing more to our relationship."

"I already explained that, but you know how childish they can be." Carrie rolled her eyes skyward over her sisters' immaturity.

"But what about S-E-X." Meg spelled out the word.

"Mona Margaret!" Sarah had no idea where this conversation had come from or where it was headed, only that they should change the subject.

"Carrie says that's why people get married, so they can have S-E-X. She said her friend's parents are getting divorced because they don't want to have S-E-X anymore."

"Stop saying that, please."

Sarah jerked her head toward Hope, who

was presumably engrossed in her corn dog but was taking in every word.

"Well, is she right?" Meg persisted.

"She is correct in the sense that married people are free to enjoy relationships differently than unmarried people. But she was wrong to discuss it with you, and you are wrong to be asking me such personal questions. When I'm ready for a serious relationship, I will discuss it with all three of you. However, it will not involve intimate details. Do we understand one another?"

"Jeez, Mom, you've always said we could ask you anything."

Sarah reached across the table and took Meg's hand.

"That's still true, sweetie. I'm sorry if I overreacted just now, but that subject is very personal and if you have questions we should discuss them privately and at home, not in a crowded restaurant."

"So when we get to the apartment you'll tell us more about S-E-X?" Hope asked.

Carrie choked on a curly fry and Meg spewed Coke through her nose as both girls fell into a fit of laughter. Sarah covered her mouth with her hand to hide her smile.

Hope stared, openmouthed. "What?"

"Finish your meals, please. I can see we need to go home for some girl talk."

CHAPTER ELEVEN

"CULLEN, I'M NOT at all certain what's going on between us is healthy for my family." Sarah spoke quietly into the phone in her bedroom to keep their exchange private.

"That raises two questions."

"Okay."

"First, how would you describe what is going on between us?"

"I'm not sure."

"I'm not positive, either, but it might be called dating."

"But we've never been on a date."

"Then may I suggest we change that situation. How about dinner Friday night, just the two of us? Alma can watch the girls and I'll take you to Temple Territory. I'm fairly sure I can get that big-shot chef over there to whip us up something special."

Sarah's heart thumped. This wasn't what she'd expected. She'd role-played this phone call in her head before dialing his number, and in her mind she'd efficiently ended any future contact between Cullen, herself and her girls.

This was not going as planned.

It was going much worse. Or was it?

She sucked in a deep breath while she studied the hot-pink polish she and the girls had applied earlier to one another's toenails while they shared a very personal conversation. Her daughters had questions she wasn't prepared to answer, but they deserved honesty. Things were moving fast between Sarah and Cullen and she either had to pull the hand brake or grab hold for dear life. Both choices came with heavy consequences.

"Sarah? Are you still there?"

"Yes, of course."

"Well, what do you think?"

"I think I need to hear the second question."

"Why would our relationship, however we classify it, be unhealthy for your family? I'm certainly inexperienced in this field but your daughters seem to be enjoying themselves when I'm around."

"They are, Cullen, and that's what worries me."

"Then you worry too much. Trust me, I'm an expert at blowing things out of proportion and letting youthful angst get the best of me. When we lost our folks, I went into a quiet tailspin. Even my twin didn't realize how bad it was for me. Instead of dealing with the pain in a healthy way, I did the 'guy thing' and bottled up my emotions. It took years before I faced them head-on, but in the meantime I worried myself sick over what-ifs that never occurred. I have some idea what you and your girls are going through, and I promise I'll do my best to make your lives better and not worse."

"Thanks for sharing that with me," Sarah murmured into the receiver. "This is a new season in our lives. It's as if we've come through a long, cold winter and spring is trying to break through."

"That's a fitting metaphor, so keep it in mind. Change is inevitable in every life. Most of it will be positive, though sometimes it can be extremely painful. Your girls can be a bit quirky but they all seem resilient and strong, like their beautiful mother."

"Thanks for the kind words, Cullen." Sarah let the personal compliment pass but her cheeks warmed with pleasure. "I wish my daughters had led sheltered lives up till now, instead of having to face facts so early on, but our situation is what it is and we've survived."

"So, what about Friday night?"

Sarah's heart pounded even harder now that she was about to make a decision. Saying yes meant intentionally moving ahead with her life and the lives of her daughters, as well. Answering no would keep her on the fast track she'd only recently begun to travel. It was stressful enough being a single parent, back in college and preparing to move up in her workplace. The sensible thing to do would be to decline Cullen's tempting invitation and keep her mind on matters within her control. She had responsibilities. She had people depending on her. She had to be careful and cautious. One wrong move could set off a chain reaction Sarah would regret.

"Thank you for your offer but…" She hesitated.

"But what?"

Oh, what the heck. She'd tip-toe over that bridge when she came to it. Today she'd enjoy life.

"But Saturday would be better for me since I've already agreed to attend a partner's meeting at the firm on Friday evening."

"Then Saturday it will be. I'll make our dinner reservation for seven, if that works for you."

"Cullen, won't your department head frown on you dating a student?"

"You're not technically my student, and they're only concerned if the student is under eighteen."

"Then you're definitely safe with me. As Miss Nancy has already pointed out, I'm no spring chicken."

"Speaking of Nancy, did you mark her wedding on your calendar so you can be my date? I believe Alma's already asked the girls to sleep over at her house that night, as long as it's okay with you."

"Yes, tonight at dinner Hope mentioned the invitation…and in the same breath she asked if you and I are getting married so we can have S-E-X."

Sarah was fairly sure she heard Cullen gasp on the other end of the phone line.

"So *that's* what brought on this business of our friendship being unhealthy for your family."

"Now do you understand why I'm reluctant do anything that would give them the wrong impression?"

"Maybe you're overanalyzing this situation. Can't we just take it a day at a time and see how things go?"

"Cullen, that approach may work on grown

women and college students, but with little girls you have to stay one step ahead of them or their imaginations will go hog wild."

"Good point. My lack of parenting experience is showing, isn't it?"

"Just barely. You've been understanding and generous with the girls and they like you a lot. But I can't let them get the impression that you're auditioning to be their new daddy."

There, that was enough to scare him away. Wasn't it?

CULLEN PULLED HIS heels off the ottoman where his stocking feet had been propped up and let them fall to the floor. He needed solid ground beneath him to make sure his world hadn't just tilted on its axis in the opposite direction.

New daddy?

Rocket raised questioning eyes from his spot on the leather sofa and then rested his paw on Cullen's thigh, as if sensing his master could suddenly use comfort.

I knew better, Cullen berated himself.

When he'd invited Sarah and her girls to his home, he'd considered there might be a chance they'd imagine it to be more than a kind gesture. But new daddy? Cullen was reminded of the saying *No good deed ever goes unpunished*. Was this the fallout for being a nice guy? Couldn't he simply commit random acts of kindness without becoming a candidate for fatherhood?

"You've gone quiet on me, Cullen. Did you faint, or has the cat got your tongue?"

"Sorry, it took me a moment to digest what you said. I've put you in this pickle with your daughters and I apologize for that."

"Life in a houseful of women is constantly a gallon jar of gherkins." Then she chuckled low in her throat, a sultry sound he'd come to enjoy. "Listen, Cullen, you didn't contribute anything I wouldn't have had to deal with sooner or later, anyway, so no apology is necessary. However, now that you have a bit more food for thought, nobody would blame you if you wanted to reconsider our date."

"Don't even try to weasel out on me, pretty lady, it's full steam ahead. I'll bear in mind that what's going on between us doesn't just affect you and me. This isn't a one-act play, it's a family circus."

"Thank you for saying that, Cullen." She chuckled at his silly effort to get them past a tough moment. "But if you reach a point when we become more than you bargained for, you can say so and I'll completely understand."

"I'm fairly certain that comes with dating in general, and the road runs both ways, you realize. I'm not exactly a prize catch and I want to knock a knot on each of my brothers' heads at least once a month. The only thing that stops me is Alma, God bless her, and she's probably saved all our hides on more occasions than we can count."

"Then it's a date for this weekend. If Alma's free to watch the girls on Saturday night, I'll take her up on her offer. Would she mind if I asked her to steer the conversation away from the two of us if it comes up in her presence?"

Cullen smiled, leaned against his leather sofa, returned his feet to the top of his favorite old ottoman and stroked Rocket's silky head.

"She won't mind a bit. She's been keeping the peace between Temple boys for so many years that it's second nature. Running interference with a group of girls will be right up her alley."

Thumps and shrieks could be heard on Sarah's end of the line.

"Can you hold on a moment?" she asked.

"Sure."

The mouthpiece was muffled, probably by Sarah's hand, but he could make out the sounds of a mother refereeing an argument between her children.

If he was true to what he'd just said to her, this decision to date Sarah was also a decision to accept that there may be a family in his future.

And much sooner than he'd ever imagined. Could he deal with that kind of change in his life?

As the female voices continued to squabble, Cullen stretched out his bare arm, palm facing the floor, and studied his hand. It was steady. He brought his palm to his face and stared. Dry as a West Texas summer. He pressed his hand to his chest and felt the thumping of his heart—regular and even.

Glancing down he saw the spiderweb of fine lines that marred the skin covering his bicep.

Fading scars from the dark days of cutting.

Thin slices to release the pain, just deep enough to free the blood and the scream inside. The relief and the shame of the act equally awesome.

He'd come so far. Did he dare to risk his recovery? Sinking into the abyss of despair could never again be an option.

"Cullen, I'm sorry, but I've gotta go settle a disagreement before it turns into pistols at dawn. I'll see you at class tomorrow night, okay?"

"Sure thing."

Cullen pressed the off key on the portable phone and tossed it to the end of the sofa. He reached for Rocket with both hands, gathered the pup's warm body to his chest and buried his face in the silky softness that smelled of kibbles and rawhide chews.

The house was silent except for the low hum of the cable television in the kitchen. All was quiet and calm.

Just the way his life had to stay if he expected to keep his PTSD under control.

CHAPTER TWELVE

"Folks, I always try to hang around after class to take your questions. However, as I mentioned earlier, I have a commitment tonight so forgive me if I slip out during the video. Make notes and we'll talk about the film on Thursday."

Sarah watched Cullen signal the guy in the A/V booth to start the DVD. It was a documentary on the reign of Charlemagne that she'd unearthed for him last week in the resource library.

Funny that he hadn't mentioned anything to her about leaving early, but then she'd arrived a few minutes late for Cullen's lecture and he hadn't had a chance to speak to her privately. But neither had he acknowledged her apologetic wave when she'd taken her usual seat by the aisle. Could he possibly be angry over her tardiness? He was the teacher, after all, and had every right to expect the students in his class to arrive on time. She made a mental note to be early for the next lecture and bring him a shiny apple to make him smile.

"Dr. Temple seems a little under the weather," the young woman who often occupied the next seat whispered to Sarah. "Almost like that first night when he bombed." The cute brunette with the pierced eyebrow, whose name was Kimmy, snickered at the memory.

Sarah scrutinized him more closely and noticed Cullen's cheeks were flushed. He was either irritated or feverish, but either way he seemed distracted as Kimmy had noted. Maybe he wasn't well. That could explain why he hadn't glanced her way all evening.

And now he was leaving without a word, without a note. She reached into the side pocket of her purse for her cell to check for a text.

Nothing.

"Did he mention why he had to hurry off?" Sarah quizzed the student.

She felt silly, probing a college kid for information like they were two schoolgirls riding the bus together.

"No, ma'am."

Sarah winced at being called *ma'am* in this setting. Clearly they were not peers from Kimmy's perspective; they were one young schoolgirl and one almost forty-year-old widow.

"I've already watched this video so I'm going to slip out, too. See you Thursday."

"Yes, ma'am." Kimmy continued to show the proper respect for her elder, as any young lady reared in Texas should.

Sarah gathered her belongings and moved quietly toward the exit as the story of the medieval European emperor began to unfold on the jumbo screen.

The door closed softly behind her as she stepped into the quiet hallway. She glanced left and right for some sign of Cullen, but the corridor was deserted. She felt her phone vibrate through the side pocket of her purse and she smiled as she touched the screen without bothering to check the caller ID.

"You caught me ducking out on the DVD," she confessed, expecting Cullen to be on the line.

"That's a relief," her mother answered. "I didn't expect you to answer."

"Is something wrong, Mom?"

"Carrie's been in the bathroom most of the evening and she's more surly than usual. I'm guessing she's experiencing womanhood issues."

"Oh, I meant to warn you she's PMSing

big-time and I suspected this was coming. She's prepared, and we've discussed it thoroughly, but it's still new territory."

"Well, I recognized the signs so I've kept the other two busy so she could have her privacy. Is it okay if I give her a couple aspirin?"

"Hold off, Mom. I'm leaving the campus now and I can be there in fifteen minutes."

"I hate for you to leave early."

"I was headed to the car, anyway. The class is watching a film I've already seen so I'm not missing anything important."

"Cullen won't mind?"

"Actually, Cullen mentioned he had someplace to be and he's been gone for a few minutes himself."

"Then we'll expect you shortly."

"Yes, ma'am."

Sarah immediately remembered Kimmy saying the same thing and wondered if the girl thought it was odd that a woman older than the teacher was in a sophomore lecture class. In spite of Cullen's efforts to draw her into the college atmosphere, Sarah was little more than a visitor on the campus where he was completely at home. Maybe she'd never have the ease he had with the kids who were two decades younger.

But what should that matter? She was only

here for the short-term, while Cullen was in it for the long haul. Her goals were very different from his, and in that respect they had little in common. She wondered again if there was any future in their relationship. Saturday night would be a perfect litmus test for whether or not they could move to the dating level or should simply remain friends.

The quiver in her stomach confirmed she was hoping for the former, but something in Cullen's odd behavior tonight said he may be regretting inviting her out for dinner.

The headlights on her sedan flashed as she clicked the door locks open and she also had a flash of insight. Saturday night she'd steer clear of relationship issues. Maybe she'd guide the conversation to the family history her mother had mentioned and keep Cullen on familiar ground.

That's what she'd do, keep it light. Stay away from the constant narration of single parenthood. She could hardly blame him if he was tiring of her circumstances. But if that was the case, shouldn't she find out now and not mask the situation with empty chatter designed to distract him from the truth of her life?

"It shouldn't have to be this complicated," she muttered as she shifted into drive and headed for her mother's house and the demands waiting for her there.

CULLEN SAT BEHIND the wheel of his SUV and watched Sarah's sensible family sedan pull out of the student parking lot. He'd lied so he'd have a reason to leave class without talking to her. She hadn't even been there when he'd set up the excuse, announcing he had something important to do and couldn't hang around as usual. Then she'd taken her seat and his mind had gone blank. Whether the cause was her nearness or the lie, it didn't matter. The rush of blood to his brain had caused a pounding headache and now he was truly glad he was free to go home and climb under the covers with Rocket.

Her vehicle was out of sight but Cullen remained beneath the dark coverage of the live oak trees, letting the engine idle before he hightailed it to the house like a coward. *Some role model you are, Dr. Temple.* Lying, sneaking away, hiding in the shadows, running in the opposite direction, and from whom?

Sarah. Undoubtedly the bravest woman he'd ever met. Beautiful in every possible way.

"So why are you acting like a fool, Temple?"

He could imagine his mentor posing the question.

And Cullen should be smart enough to figure out the answer. He was deliberate by nature. He rarely did anything without re-searching it to death first. So when Sarah had said it was best for her girls if she pulled away from their friendship, why had he rashly in-sisted that they make a date? He should have accepted her wisdom, trusted she was mak-ing the right decision for her family.

But nooo, he couldn't leave well enough alone—he had to force the issue and give dat-ing a go. And in response his gut had become a roiling mess. And it was only Tuesday! He had to make it through the week and an-other night of class on Thursday before they could get this relationship experiment over with and he could score himself a big fat *F* on the exam.

He rested his throbbing head on the steer-ing wheel, sucked deep breaths in through his nose and let the air whoosh past his lips. It was a relaxation technique he'd learned years ago when he'd realized clenching his fists and holding his breath only made the attacks worse.

"This is ridiculous," he muttered into the dashboard. "It was only after we made our plans that I began to have second thoughts and get panicky. I was doing great while Sarah and I were talking on the phone, sure of myself and of her. So why now do I worry that the situation might spin out of control?

"All I have to do is ease up, go with the flow and accept the things I cannot change," he quoted his old mantra, and took more cleansing breaths.

The words he spoke aloud swarmed in the Explorer around his head. *Ease up. Go with the flow. Accept the things I cannot change.* A man with his IQ and credentials should be able to do those things, shouldn't he? And a family of females was not exactly Homer's sirens, calling him to crash into the cliffs, were they?

Cullen needed answers to his rhetorical questions, a sounding board, impartial guidance.

He glanced at his wristwatch. Rome was seven hours ahead. Blair and Ailean had always been night owls but it was late even by their standards. Hopefully Blair wouldn't mind a wakeup call from his protégé. At least it was only to ask for advice and not cash for beer or bail.

CHAPTER THIRTEEN

CULLEN'S FIRST DATE in high school had been a disaster. He'd shown up early and been made to wait in the living room while Tammy Sue Lancer's daddy grilled him like a steak over hot coals. Then his car had run out of gas, which Tammy Sue had insisted through an irritated twist of her lips was the oldest trick in the book.

Some trick—he'd sweated through his dress shirt while he'd tramped eight blocks to the Exxon station and back again, the can of gas sloshing on his trendy, acid-washed jeans when he poured it into the tank. Tammy Sue kept her distance the rest of the evening, leaning away from him at the Wagon Wheel restaurant and again at the movies. He couldn't blame her, knowing he smelled of male armpit and unleaded high octane. There was no second date, and blessedly there was no social media back then so the details only spread as far as the baseball field where Cullen took a vicious ribbing from his teammates. And his brothers.

As all historians worth their salt were aware, if we don't learn from our history we are doomed to repeat it. So on Saturday night, Cullen had made sure the tank was full, he'd dabbed on the expensive cologne he saved for special occasions and he was on schedule to leave his house exactly as planned. Satisfied with his image in the bathroom mirror, he checked his cell for any sign of a cancellation message from Sarah. There was just the one text she'd sent on Thursday afternoon.

"Cullen, I can't make it to class tonight. Carrie's been under the weather all week and I should stay home this evening. See you on Saturday."

Otherwise, they hadn't spoken all week. It wasn't as if they were boyfriend and girlfriend and talked on the phone every day, but this was the longest they'd gone without communicating since he and Sarah had met. Cullen told himself she was simply tied up with work and family, but with a woman it was hard to be sure.

When he'd woken Blair and Ailean on Tuesday night, after assuring them nobody had died, Cullen confessed he was in need of relationship counseling. Blair had advised him to take a chill pill but not before he'd laughed at Cullen's worries. Laughed! A man cries out for help in the middle of the night and instead of showing grave concern, his mentor thinks it's a hoot.

But to Ailean's credit, she suggested he dig through the boxes of books they'd left behind and find a psychology text she highly recommended that focused on blended family dynamics.

"Treat this the same way you do everything else, Cullen. Study the subject, analyze the facts, apply what's useful and document your findings. But by all means, ignore what Blair said. He's a Neanderthal, and being this close to the source of his ancestry has him reverting to his genetic roots."

Cullen had gone to bed that night grateful for Ailean's guidance. It fit in with the class he was going to take and his own thoughts when he'd first met Sarah's family.

And given Blair's reaction he was doubly glad he hadn't called any of his brothers for advice. They wouldn't be able to relate to his circumstances. Hunt was still goggle-eyed over his engagement to Gillian, Joiner was busy searching for some ranch property to call his own and Mac was planning a trip overseas to take a break from his business for a while.

Cullen could trust his brothers with his life without question. But his love life was another matter altogether.

He hadn't confided in Alma, either. She was too crazy about Sarah and her girls to be impartial, and women always seemed to stick together. In this situation Cullen was on his own.

Alone in no-man's-land. A barren and frightening place, a minefield of emotion.

He burst into laughter. Maybe tomorrow after church he'd pick up one of those romance novels Alma was always reading. He could use something touchy-feely to counter the effects of studying thousands of years of war on planet Earth. Or better yet, he'd invest a couple of hours into reading up on blended families and ways to relate with stepchildren.

Yep, tomorrow he'd get comfortable under the pool umbrella and make some notes from Ailean's psychology text, and maybe later in the afternoon he'd invite Sarah and the girls to come for a swim.

Whoa, Temple! First things first. Get through this evening before you start making new plans.

His daddy used to say, "Son, tomorrow has enough worries of its own, so don't get a jump on it tonight."

"HE'S HEEEEEERE," HER girls singsonged in a silly chorus. Three pairs of flip-flops beat a path to the door.

Sarah was in her bedroom applying lip gloss for the third time in an effort to keep her shaking hands busy. She glanced toward her bedside clock and smiled at his punctuality.

Her gaze moved to rest on a family photo, their last before Joe's decline began. His left arm was around Sarah's shoulders, a protective shield from the cares of the world. His right hand cupped Carrie's elbow, Hope perched on his lap and Meg wedged between her parents, squeezing close to her daddy. The girls framed Joe perfectly, as if unconsciously closing ranks against the disease that lay dormant in his body.

Sarah wondered if her daughters noticed the same photo and remembered their daddy full of life instead of the way he'd become at the end, thin and frail, every breath a struggle. She stayed clear of reminders of his illness for fear of robbing them of the sweet memories. One day they'd bring it up, when they were ready, and together they'd deal with it.

But today, she was dealing with a new chapter in her life and the girls seemed to approve. Especially since the two younger ones had already given their blessing to a wedding. Now Carrie, she would be a tougher nut to crack, but if things ever progressed that far, Sarah hoped she could count on her oldest child to be supportive. Since the day Sarah had come home from work and neither fainted nor pitched a fit when she'd found her thirteen-year-old with purple hair, Carrie had been amazingly cooperative.

Would Carrie be so agreeable if Cullen was still around when the hair dye had washed out?

"Mama, Cullen brought you flowers!" Hope called.

"They're the kind that drop pollen all over the place," Meg pointed out. "I hope my summer allergies don't flare up."

Sarah stepped into the cluttered family room to find Cullen clutching a bunch of orange and yellow lilies wrapped in green florist's paper. He grinned sheepishly and held them out like a peace offering. Maybe she hadn't imagined that he'd been avoiding her this week, after all.

"Thank you, sir. They're lovely." Sarah accepted the large bouquet and headed to the kitchen. "Give me a minute to put them in water."

The lilies would be amazing in the crystal vase she'd been given as a wedding gift, but it was in storage with most of their household items. She searched the cabinets for a suitable alternative and came up with a huge jar that had once held a year's supply of pickles from the warehouse store.

"It's not Waterford but it'll do the trick," she apologized as she set the arrangement on their dining room table, which was strewn with puzzles and macaroni crafts.

"What a thoughtful thing to do," Sarah murmured as she accepted his side hug.

"I'm glad I got the chance to see the girls. I assumed they'd already be at Alma's house."

She caught his unasked question about why the three were still at the apartment.

"Nana Alma's coming here tonight," Hope announced.

"Do you mind if we wait a bit, Cullen? She phoned a few minutes ago to say she was on her way."

"And she's bringing a surprise for dinner," Meg added.

"For your sake, I hope it's not some of Felix's hog's head cheese, or that year-old fruit cake she's always trying to get rid of." Cullen made a face and fake shuddered.

The girls grimaced and then giggled. Having already sampled Alma's cooking, they knew better than to fall for Cullen's joke.

"And she's going to teach them to make tortillas from scratch."

Cullen shielded his response to Sarah behind his hand as if to hide it from the girls.

"Even wrapped in Alma's homemade tortillas that head cheese is still nasty."

Sarah socked him on the shoulder.

"Stop that, Cullen, or they'll believe you."

"Just in case, how about bringing us some dessert?" Carrie asked. "I read a review online and it said the Cowboy Chef's cheesecake is to die for."

"Yes! Cheesecake!" Hope and Meg cheered in agreement.

"That's a tall order, but I'm familiar with the restaurant owner so I believe I can swing a to-go box," Cullen assured the girls.

A knock at the door announced Alma's arrival. After hugs all around and Alma's observation that Cullen smelled nice for a change, he swept Sarah out of the apartment and away from the concerns of her life for a few hours.

"So, THIS IS the charming mother of Hope, Meg and Carrie," Hunt said as he reached for Sarah's hand.

Sarah stared, as starstruck as her daughters had been the day they'd met the Cowboy Chef. Hunt Temple was Cullen's identical twin, so everything about him was familiar. But standing there in his white chef's coat, it was as if he'd stepped from the pages of a celebrity cookbook.

"Oh, don't tell me you've been rendered speechless by this pepper mill pusher, too." Cullen shook his head in mock despair, disbelief in his voice.

"Of course she is, brother dear. It's not every day a woman gets both halves of this picture in a single frame. Good twin, evil twin." Hunt gestured back and forth between himself and his brother. "Handsome twin, ugly twin. Average but practical twin, brilliant but useless twin. Professional twin, can't seem to get out of school twin. On and on it goes."

"Could you send for the owner, please?" Cullen asked. "I want to register a complaint about the staff in this establishment."

"Who said the word *complaint* in my hotel?" A blonde dressed in a vintage Chanel wrap dress approached and slipped her arm around Hunt's waist.

She was the kind of tall, willowy, fair complexioned blonde that made Sarah—at five feet three inches and one hundred and forty pounds—feel like a fire hydrant by comparison. Sarah sat a little straighter and sucked in her tummy, but there was nothing she could do about her freckled nose and cap of copper-colored locks.

"Ma'am, your short order cook here is being testy with us this evening," Cullen addressed the beauty.

"Let me guess, you asked for ketchup with your chateaubriand? That sends him over the edge every time. These creative types can be temperamental when you mess with their idea of perfection," she responded.

"Especially when they get to be his age and set in their ways."

"If hospital records are to be believed, you came into this world three minutes ahead of me, so save that observation for one of your other brothers," Hunt insisted.

"Can we move past the subject of age, please? I'm pretty sure I outrank all three of you," Sarah teased, but couldn't help feeling every bit the *older woman* at the table.

"Certainly," Hunt agreed with a bow.

"Allow me to introduce my fiancée, Gillian Moore, owner of Temple Territory. Gillian, this is Sarah Eason. She's a friend of Cullen's but try not to make any judgments based on that association. Sarah has three adorable daughters, she works for a law firm in Longview and she's recently gone back to school to complete her degree."

"How do you know so much about Cullen's date?" Gillian arched a brow at her fiancé.

"Alma," he said simply.

Gillian shrugged at Sarah.

"Well, there you go. If that woman approves of you, nothing more matters to the Temple boys."

"And she definitely approves." Cullen settled his hand over Sarah's and let it rest there, as if it were the most natural gesture in the world. Her skin tingled at the warmth of his touch.

Gillian turned to Hunt. "Honey, please send over a bottle of your 2009 Chateau St. Jean Reserve Chardonnay, compliments of the house."

"You need to hurry up and marry this woman while she's still generous with the key to that wine room," Cullen said.

"I'm doing my best, but her mama claims you can't rush wedding plans." Hunt brushed a kiss against his beloved's cheek and then gave the guests his attention again. "Your goat cheese tarts and steamed mussels will be out shortly along with that bottle of Chardonnay, and I'll personally handle your carryout dessert request."

"Would you mind signing the top of the pastry box?" Sarah remembered to ask.

"Yeah, Meg thinks she can sell it on eBay—as long as she can clean out all the crumbs so there's no deadly mold growing inside." Cullen snickered at the idea.

"How about one box for the cheesecake and a second for the budding entrepreneur?"

"Hunt, you're a generous man, just like your brother."

"It's our Southern upbringing and has nothing to do with sibling influence."

"Could you influence some activity in the kitchen and leave us to our quiet evening?"

"Yes, sir, Dr. Temple, sir." Hunt squared his shoulders and clicked his heels together smartly in reply.

Gillian tugged at his sleeve.

"Let's get back to work, darlin', and give these two some privacy." Then to her guests she said, "Enjoy your meal and let me know if there's anything you need."

Hunt disappeared toward the kitchen.

Sarah watched as Gillian glided across the dining room to greet another table of diners.

"She's stunning."

Cullen squeezed her hand. "So are you, Sarah."

Her heart quickened. When was the last time a man had paid her a compliment? A warm flush began to creep up her collarbone and spread over her throat. Her face would be in full blush at any moment, so she lowered her chin and dipped her gaze, causing him to cover her hand with his again.

"Too much?" he asked, somehow understanding.

"Just what I needed actually." Her voice was suddenly thick. She raised her eyes, knowing they held a grateful glimmer.

His smile slipped for a moment as if he were deciding how to respond. She prayed her rush of emotions wouldn't scare him away.

"I hear there will be live music on the patio tonight. After our meal, how about the nickel tour of Pap's old place and a chocolate martini by the pool?"

"I can't imagine a nicer plan for the evening."

"I've got a few other plans up my sleeve

for the summer if you and your daughters will allow me to intrude on you some more."

"Cullen, are you sure?"

"I've been remembering my folks a lot lately. My daddy used to say, 'You can only be sure of two things—death and taxes.'"

"Well, you can be sure that I think you've been a godsend."

"You might want to hear what I have in mind before you start thanking God."

She scrunched her brows. "Maybe you'd better give me an example."

He grinned, as mischievous as Hope caught with her hand in the M&M jar before dinner.

"I hear the Texas SkyScreamer over at Six Flags is all the rage, and I happen to have free passes for Wednesday if you can get a day off in the middle of the week."

Their waiter approached the table with their mouthwatering appetizers and the perfectly chilled bottle of wine Gillian had chosen. Conversation ceased for a few minutes while Sarah savored the food and considered Cullen's invitation.

"Did I mention Meg's afraid of heights?"

"Meg's afraid of everything." He laughed. "I used to be the same way and look at me today."

He spread his arms so she could appreciate the view.

And she did appreciate what she saw in Cullen Temple.

She really did.

CHAPTER FOURTEEN

HAVING SURVIVED A painful loss and then finding a new relationship, the temptation can often be to rush into a blended family without first laying a solid foundation. By spending time together you give everyone a chance to get used to one another. Find ways to experience real life.

Cullen started his to-do notes by copying the book's advice on the top lines of his legal pad and enumerating with a "1" beside it. Then he tossed his pen on the table beside his pool chaise and smiled.

"You're on the right track with this Six Flags invitation, Temple," he congratulated himself. "What's more real life than a theme park with overpriced treats, giant Looney Tunes characters and death-defying roller coasters designed to make the passengers upchuck their cotton candy?"

His smile slipped at the image of dear little Hope getting nauseous after her third trip through Runaway Mountain, clutching her belly with one hand and her dripping ice cream cone with the other.

He grabbed the pen and made another note. *Monitor sugar intake.*

Rocket jumped to his feet, rambled through the open patio slider and stopped in the front entry with his nose pressed to the door. Female voices sent him into a fit of woofing, which caused the little girls on the porch to carry on even louder as they pounded to announce their arrival.

"I'm coming!" Cullen called, scrambling to drag his shirt over his bare arms and pushing the cuffs to his elbows.

He pulled the door wide and braced himself for the hugs he was beginning to enjoy so much. Hope and Meg never held back. They threw themselves at him with the kind of fearless emotion that only a child can display. Carrie came forward only after Cullen opened his arm to make room for her, but her affection was pure and unforced. Over the heads of the girls he saw the lovely Sarah walking toward him with plastic shopping bags in each hand. He swallowed down the lump in his throat that threatened to surge straight down to his heart and burst.

The book was right. He'd lost so much, so long ago. And he'd finally found a relationship that made him want to rush into unfamiliar territory. But first they should experience real life together.

Rocket led the way through the house and out the sliding glass doors where Meg headed straight for the steps of the pool while Carrie dutifully stopped to secure Hope's swim safety vest.

"It was so kind of you to invite us over, Cullen." Sarah deposited her bags on the kitchen island and began to unpack chips, ready-made sandwiches and boxed cookies from the bakery. Cullen reached for a snickerdoodle.

"Will you stop giving me credit I don't deserve?" He talked with his mouth full of crumbly goodness. "This kind invitation is my cover for a selfish effort to get you to help me read papers."

"After last evening, 'You had me at hello.'" Sarah quoted the line from *Jerry McGuire*. The tender curve of her lips said she was sincere.

Cullen glanced out the door to confirm the girls were safely occupied before stepping so close that Sarah couldn't possibly miss his intention. She leaned against his chest, snaked her arms around his waist and pressed her cheek to his heart. He smoothed the back of her T-shirt with his left hand and slipped the fingers of his right hand through her auburn waves to cradle her head. They stood for long moments simply enjoying the comfort of one heart close to another, beating at different rhythms but seeking to sync up.

When the splashing outside became too loud to ignore, Sarah let her arms drop and stepped away.

"Would you prefer turkey or roast beef with your European history, Dr. Temple?"

"Ladies first and I'll have whatever's left."

"Have you always been this easy?"

"As far as I remember, but a second opinion from Alma might be wise."

"How did Alma and Felix come into your lives?"

Cullen climbed on a stool beside his kitchen counter, resting his elbows on the tile while Sarah loaded plates of food for her family.

"When we were little boys they were both part of the maintenance staff at the hospital where our father was chief of surgery. Felix posted a notice on the bulletin board for extra work and Daddy offered them some gardening and babysitting. It was a perfect fit for our busy lifestyle and their family became part of our family. When they weren't at the hospital or home with their two girls, they were with us. It was only when our parents were killed that we learned Felix and Alma had agreed years before to be our legal guardians. Their daughters were already on their own at that point so Alma and Felix moved into our family home out near the airport. We lived with them until we were all out of high school and then we sold the house."

Sarah listened quietly. Though her hands kept busy, a shadow of sadness passed across her face.

"Sarah?"

"You've given me something important to consider."

"What's that?"

"Joe and I never made guardian arrangements for the girls. Now that it's just me, I have to take care of that, and the sooner, the better. My firm can handle it for me, but I've got to decide what's right for my daughters."

"I understand," Cullen softly assured her.

But he really didn't. How could an unmarried man truly empathize with the weight of single parenthood on a woman's shoulders? Especially one widowed at such a young age.

"Is there another couple the girls are especially close to?"

"Only my parents. I'm sure they'd accept

the responsibility, but it would be a great deal to ask of them at their age."

"What about close friends?"

She shook her head.

"Unfortunately, instead of leaning on friendships when Joe got sick we kind of turned in on ourselves and kept everything in the family. After he died I had to focus on the girls and making a living and I just never got back into hanging out with friends again. There are plenty of women I could call to meet me for a drink, but none I would ask to raise my daughters."

He left his spot on the bar stool, rounded the counter to stand before Sarah, rested his hands on either side of her face and angled her so they were eye to eye.

"It's not a decision you have to make right away. For today it's enough that you've started considering your options."

He leaned down, placed a light kiss on her upturned mouth and resisted the urge to allow the contact to last longer. He took a step back and then reached for the plates she'd prepared.

"Let me help you."

"You've already helped so much, Cullen. More than you can possibly realize."

ACTUALLY, *HELPED* WAS not the word Sarah wanted to use, but *rescued* seemed too intense, too needy. And she'd resolved not to scare Cullen away with the emotional demands of her family. Their date the night before had been amazingly easy on everyone. If they were to move forward as gracefully as they'd proceeded so far, she'd have to keep a tight rein on everyone so Cullen wouldn't have reason to reconsider a ready-made family.

That was a tall order, especially at mealtime.

"I didn't want pickles," Hope whined. "They make my nose itch."

"That's probably an indication of anaphylaxis," Meg warned as she popped a barbecue chip in her mouth.

"What's that?" Hope asked.

"It's when your throat swells shut and you die because you can't breathe," Meg said matter-of-factly as she licked her salty fingers.

Hope's face crumpled, she dumped her sandwich onto her plate and burst into loud sobs. "But I don't wanna die!"

"Mona Margaret." Sarah spoke through gritted teeth, a warning for her too-smart-for-her-own-good middle child.

"Oh, stop being a baby, Hope," Carrie

fussed at her little sister. "You've had pickles a hundred times. If they were gonna kill you, it would have happened way before now."

Hope's bawling stopped as she looked to her mama for comfort.

"Carrie has a point, honey. It's probably just the vinegar that tickles your nose."

"And that's why *pickle* rhymes with *tickle*," Cullen teased.

"A tickle in your throat is one of the warning signs of anaphylaxis, too." Meg wouldn't let it go.

"Mona Margaret!" Everyone in the shade of the pool umbrella chorused.

"Okay!" Meg grinned, loving the last word even if it was in agreement.

"So how does Six Flags on Wednesday sound?"

"Let me check my hectic schedule." Carrie pretended to hold a day timer in her hand, flipping through invisible pages and then running her finger to the date. "As I suspected, no plans at all." She slapped the imaginary book on the table with a sour glare toward her mother, who had her under house arrest because of the previous year's grades.

"Hey, your summer at home is your own fault. But if you want to go to the amusement park with your sisters this week, you may."

"Then I'm in," she grumbled, holding in a smile.

"Me, too!" Meg and Hope insisted.

"Can you get the day off, Sarah?"

"And if I can't? Will you take them by yourself since you've already extended the invitation?" Sarah challenged, fearful he might actually give it a try.

"Are you saying I'm not up to it?"

"I'm saying you might live to find out if you're not careful."

"Consider me all in, ladies." He glanced from girl to girl, his word his bond. "If your mama can't get the day off we'll get Alma or Joiner to go with us and we'll make a day of it."

"Don't overload your ability with your intentions, Cullen," Sarah warned.

"You keep forgetting that I'm one of four boys, my dear. I've survived three brothers for thirty-four years and I can certainly endure these three prissy britches for one day."

"Prissy britches?" Carrie cocked an eyebrow that she'd penciled on heavier than usual.

Though Carrie was grounded, Sarah had agreed that for the summer months she could experiment with makeup. Her technique was still a bit ghoulish.

"Forgive me, O Duchess of Darkness," Cullen corrected as the little girls giggled. "Does that title suit you better?"

"Indeed," she agreed before returning to her veggie sandwich.

"Mama, it's so hot I might faint," Meg complained. "Can I get in the pool now?"

"As long as you take Hope with you and stay close to the steps."

The two jumped down from the table, grabbed their new pool noodles and headed for the cool, aqua-blue water.

"I have some vacation days on the books. I suppose I can ask the boss to give me one on short notice."

"Attagirl!"

A smile of pleasure spread from one corner of Cullen's kissable lips to the other. He reached across the space between their two chairs, caught Sarah's hand and squeezed it. The gesture was filled with silent promise, even if it did only last a second or two.

"I saw that," Carrie grumbled.

"Good," Cullen responded. "Get used to it."

CHAPTER FIFTEEN

*DON'T EXPECT TO fall in love with your part-
ner's children overnight. Get to know them.
Love and affection take time to develop. Insist
on respect. You can't make people like each
other, but you can require that they treat one
another with respect.*

Judging from the second point on his list,
Cullen was holding his own. He was getting acquainted with the girls individually
and was confident that the affection between
them was the real deal. For the most part they
showed him respect but they sniped at one
another regularly, in spite of their mother's
warnings. The book said he shouldn't intrude
on Sarah's efforts to discipline her kids, but
it was hard to keep his mouth shut.

The trip to Six Flags today would be the
baseline test of how they might behave as a
family. Cullen pulled the Explorer to a stop
outside their apartment building, flipped
down the visor and checked his teeth for
signs of this morning's spinach omelet. Sat-

isfied he was looking his best, he tugged on his favorite old Texas Rangers baseball cap, blew out an anxious breath and loped up the path in comfy sneakers.

"Let's go!" Sarah's command reverberated from behind the closed door.

He checked his watch. Not quite seven o'clock in the morning and the shouting had already begun. But to be fair, their raised voices had nothing to do with anger and everything to do with being heard. It seemed in their family, the one who talked the loudest was the winner. Unlike the males he'd grown up with, who'd settled disputes with their bare knuckles, the weapon of choice for these females appeared to be the decibel level.

"Mama said, 'Let's go!'" Hope followed her mother's lead, calling her sisters at the top of her voice.

Cullen smiled, shrugged off the fight or flight instinct that threatened and knocked on the door, *hard* so they'd hear him.

"Good morning!" Hope greeted him with a grape-jelly-smeared smile and a sticky-fingered hug.

"Is everybody ready to go? We should get on the road."

"Carrie's being a butthead."

"Do you kiss your mama with that mouth?"

"Huh?"

"That's ugly language for such a pretty little girl. You shouldn't call your sister bad names."

"She calls me a stupid baby," Hope countered.

"Which is wrong since you're really a smart young lady."

"But she's really a butthead."

"Hope, watch your mouth," Sarah instructed her youngest as she pulled Hope out of the doorway to let Cullen enter.

"Difficult morning?" he asked as he stepped into the family room where a pizza box might have exploded the night before.

"Normal actually. Please excuse the mess. I worked late so I could take today off. Carrie ordered pizza delivery for dinner, and by the time I got home it was late and I was too tired to clean up."

"I wish you'd called me, Sarah. I was home at my desk all evening. I could have taken them for a bite to eat and brought some dinner by the office for you."

"I'll keep that in mind if you're still speaking to me after today."

Carrie and Meg appeared, but grudgingly so, eyes still half-closed. The family made their way to the SUV and the girls climbed in back.

"I'm tired," Carrie moaned.

"Me, too, and sleep deprivation has terrible effects on the cerebellum," Meg advised. "Research shows it causes death in lab animals."

"Since your cerebellum is about the size of a rat's, you should definitely be worried," Carrie sneered.

"You can all sleep during the drive over and when we get there this bellyaching comes to a grinding halt. Do I make myself clear? Otherwise, you're going to sit in the shade all day while Cullen and I enjoy the rides."

"Mama, how long will it take to get there?" Hope asked.

"A few hours so y'all should be rested and in a fine mood when we arrive at the park," Sarah replied.

"From your lips to God's ear," Cullen muttered.

"What does that mean?" Hope asked.

"It means lean your seat back and take a nap so your mama and I can visit."

Thankfully, all three were down for the count before Cullen made it to the interstate and pointed the Explorer toward Arlington. He adjusted his rearview mirror, checked for three pairs of closed eyes in the seat behind him and then reached across the console to take Sarah's hand. She laced her fingers with his as naturally as if they'd done it for years.

"Thanks for working this all out. I imagine it's not a simple matter to get away from an attorney's office in the middle of the week."

"I had to juggle a few things around, but otherwise it wasn't a big deal."

"I would have taken them by myself."

When she didn't respond he glanced over to see Sarah pressing her lips tightly to hold in a chuckle.

"You think that's funny, huh?" He squeezed her hand.

A sweet smile spread across her face, curving the freckles on her cheeks upward toward her eyes, which were the color of Texas bluebonnets this morning.

"I think it's brave that you'd offer to spend a day by yourself with my girls."

"I'd have found myself a bodyguard."

"I'm happy to fill that role."

"Do you mind if I turn the radio on?"

"Please do." She slanted her eyes to check the huddle of sleeping females behind them.

Cullen released Sarah's hand long enough to find George Strait on a classic country station, then resumed their handholding and enjoyed the trip with his favorite crooner and best girls along for the ride.

"ONE MORE ROLLER coaster and my eyeballs are gonna pop out of my head," Cullen insisted.

"That last one was a doozie," Sarah agreed.

"You said Meg was afraid of heights."

"I guess she's gotten over it because she hopped right onto Dive Bomber Alley as if she had good sense."

"I hopped on, too, but that guy at the end of the track had to pull me off. My legs were Jell-O."

He caught her hand but Sarah wasn't sure if it was to pull her close or to steady himself. She was fine with it either way. His low-key displays of affection had been steady throughout the day. Once the girls got past the giggling and pointing they didn't seem to mind.

"There was a time when my stamina was off the charts. An all-day baseball tournament was no hill for a stepper like me. Boy, that's changed."

He wagged his head at the memory. Dark curls in need of a trim poked from beneath the cap he wore in faithful support of his team.

"In those days I could play centerfield in

the heat for hours and still hit the dance floor that night."

"You dance?"

"Does a coyote howl at the moon? What boy from East Texas can't at least two-step?"

"Joe."

"How long since you've been on a dance floor?"

"My wedding day, and then it was only for a few painful minutes. Poor Joe was born with two left feet."

"Pretty lady, we're gonna fix that real soon. But for now—"

Cullen stepped back, stretched her hand above her head and twirled her until she fell dizzy and laughing into his arms.

"Just what I needed today, another head spin."

"Today seems to be what your girls needed, too."

"That's an accurate observation. It was nice for them to release all their bottled-up summer energy on something besides one another. I'm not used to all this sniping and name calling and it's wearing me out."

"So, that's not standard behavior at your house?"

"Heck, no!"

Did he believe she'd always allowed them

to talk to one another as if they were the Hatfields and McCoys?

"Now, don't get me wrong, they're sisters and the tongue of a sibling can cut deeper and faster than a Ginsu knife. You should understand that after growing up with three brothers."

"That wasn't my experience, though. We didn't settle our issues with insults and eye rolls. We took it to the boxing ring or the batting cage. Popping a jaw or a fast ball always makes a guy feel better."

"I like the sound of those options. Maybe I should get the girls into a gym and let them duke it out."

"Or sign them up for a softball league and let them battle it out with others their age on the diamond."

"Did I hear someone say diamond?" Carrie approached, catching the tail end of their conversation. "Holding hands is one thing but don't you think it's too soon for a diamond?"

"Baseball diamond," Cullen corrected.

"Why do they call it that?" Hope wanted to know.

"Baseball is played on a field that's called a diamond because of the way it's shaped."

"I like baseball," Meg chimed in.

"You do?" This was news to Sarah, but

then Meg was a constant source of news flashes.

"What makes you say that, Meg?" Cullen guided the conversation as Sarah steered them all to the next waiting line.

"There aren't as many contact injuries in baseball as there are in football and soccer."

"That's an excellent point," Cullen agreed.

"And the uniforms are really cute," Meg added with a grin.

"And all the guys hang out at the ballpark in the summer," Carrie mused.

"Would you girls be interested in playing ball?"

"Me, too?" Hope bounced up and down on her toes, reminding Cullen of Rocket at dinner time.

"You're too little and dumb." Carrie dismissed her baby sister.

"Am not!" Hope's heels dug into the ground to make her point, then turned pleading eyes to Cullen. "Can I play, too?"

"Of course you can. Carrie's yankin' your chain." Cullen glared at Carrie as he reassured Hope. "There's a game level for every age and the earlier you start the better."

"Could we really get on a team?" Meg's voice was hopeful.

"Sure. But you have to learn the basics

about the game first, and if you're willing to cooperate with me and with one another I can teach you."

"Mama, Cullen says he'll teach us." Hope was bouncing again.

"Under the condition that all three of you participate and that you show respect for one another. That's how athletes are expected to behave," Cullen said.

"What about the players on TV who get into big fights on the field?"

"Sometimes emotions get heated, but you have to understand that hundreds of games are played in a season and it's rare for a ruckus to break out."

They reached the front of the line for the next ride. The girls were herded into a half-moon-shaped vehicle, secured by a bar across their laps and reminded to keep their hands inside the car. Then off they flew out of sight, echoes of nervous squeals trailing behind them.

"Why don't we pass on this one and meet them at the other end?" Sarah offered.

Cullen was quick to step out of the line and allow the folks behind them to pass.

"I'm fine with that," he agreed, and pulled Sarah along toward the exit area for the Tilt-A-Whirl.

"Cullen, you just offered to take on a big commitment with the girls for the rest of the summer. Wouldn't you like a few days to think this over?"

"I admit it was a spur of the moment idea, but I have a lot of experience in the sport and it'll be fun for all of us."

"Are you sure you have the time and the patience for this project?"

"You let me worry about those things. Besides, the book says we should experience real life together, and playing on a team is more similar to real life than a day at an amusement park."

"What book?"

"Um, I'll fill you in on that some other day. Here come the girls, and your purple-haired daughter looks like she might hurl. How funny is that?"

CHAPTER SIXTEEN

Give as much one-on-one time, love and affection to your new partner's kids as possible. Consider it making small investments that may one day yield a lot of interest.

During their drive home from Six Flags, Cullen had considered that advice over and over again. There was a strong nudging in his spirit to invest a heavy dose of Temple male influence in Sarah's daughters.

She'd mentioned wanting a day on her own to shop and run errands. It was the perfect opportunity, so he'd offered to take the girls on Saturday.

She'd agreed, and here he was on a sweltering summer morning teaching Carrie, Meg and Hope about baseball with Rocket in tow while Sarah and her mother had a ladies' day together.

When it got entirely too hot outside, Cullen moved the girls to the indoor batting cages for some relief from the sun.

"Now, the most important thing to remember is to keep your eye on the ball. With practice you'll start to swing where you're looking and the bat will connect with the ball every time."

"I'm gonna knock one over the fence!" Hope insisted.

"Honey, that would be quite an accomplishment since you're in a cage, but you stay positive and you'll get plenty of chances during a real game."

"When will it be my turn?" Meg asked. Her patience had just about run out as she'd waited for him to get Carrie and then Hope set up with individual slow-pitch machines.

"Come with me and we'll get you into the next open spot."

She followed dutifully with Rocket at her heels. All three girls were tired and quiet from their morning of practicing the basics in the park before making the trip to the local hitting academy. Meg had a natural stance with a bat on her shoulder and Cullen was excited to see her take a few promising swings.

She'd just gotten into the rhythm of the mechanical pitcher when a male voice rumbled, "Is that you, Temple?"

"Depends on who's asking," Cullen responded, already certain of the answer.

"I'm not surprised you don't remember

since you haven't been in this place for about twenty years."

"Coach Uprichard, how the heck are you?"

The two grasped hands, stepped into a man-hug and did some serious backslapping. Coach had been exaggerating about how long it had been, but Cullen honestly couldn't remember the last time he'd made contact with a fast ball.

"I'm well," Coach answered. "Doing a little reconnaissance to make sure my team is keeping up with their practice routine during the summer."

"Some things never change."

"That's the pot calling the kettle black. Manuela tells me you're still single after all these years on that campus with a thousand women to choose from. Finding a wife should be as easy as shootin' fish in a barrel."

Manuela Uprichard taught in the chemistry department and they ran into each other now and again at university functions.

"At my age it would be less like fishin' and more like cradle robbin'. I doubt their East Texas mamas would approve since they expected their daughters to get more out of college than a 'Mrs.' before their name these days."

Coach chuckled and nodded toward the

cages where Sarah's girls were swinging a lot more than they were connecting.

"Since I'm fairly certain they're not yours, what are you doing in here with the three young'uns? And a dog to boot!"

"Something of an experiment," Cullen explained as he stooped to scratch Rocket behind the ears.

Coach Uprichard's brow furrowed, a question in his eyes.

"This little guy is mine but the girls are the daughters of a good friend. I'm hoping that learning a team sport will wear them out a little bit and help ease their constant bickering."

"Would that *friend* happen to be a single female?" Coach nudged his elbow against Cullen's sleeve.

"Yes, she is," Cullen admitted

"Seems you're workin' pretty hard to get into the lady's good graces."

"Scoring brownie points never hurts, but mostly I wanted to see if the girls would take to baseball the same way my brothers and I did at their ages."

"That's an admirable thing for you to do, Temple. As we both know from experience, getting kids involved early can create a love for the game that will last a lifetime."

"That's what I'm hoping, Coach. They're catching on fast, especially for girls."

"Don't underestimate the potential of female ball players. If you end up volunteering in one of their leagues you'll find out they're every bit as aggressive and competitive as the boys."

Cullen conjured up a mental picture of himself as the third base coach waving Meg into home. Or teaching Carrie the fine points of windmill pitching. Or sitting next to Sarah behind home plate, cheering on little Hope as she dashed to beat the tag at first.

"I've never given much consideration to helping out with one of the rec leagues but I have to say the idea is appealing."

"Give these girls a day or two for the muscle aches to set in and then you'll find out whether or not they've got the chops to join a recreational team."

"Insightful point, Coach."

"I still make one occasionally," he joked.

Cullen hadn't considered how sore the girls would be after a long first day of throwing a ball and swinging a bat. A little work-out in the pool would help ease the lactic acid out of their muscles. So they'd stop at the apartment and pick up the girls' swimsuits before heading to his place to cool down. And they'd run by the Malt 'n' Burger for carryout.

The list of details involved in parenting grew by the hour. As did his respect for Sarah and her tireless effort to hold her family together all by herself.

"Will Manuela and I see you at Miss Nancy's wedding?"

"We wouldn't miss it." The invitation was stuck on his refrigerator door alongside a piece of Hope's macaroni artwork.

"We?" Coach Uprichard caught the inference. "Are you and the lady already a couple?"

"I'm testing the waters." Cullen was honest with his old high school coach.

"Is this part of the *experiment* you mentioned before?"

"Sort of. You remember how I operate, Coach. I've got to study things nine ways from Friday before I can make a decision. Remember how long it took me to figure out whether I wanted to play right or center?"

"I sure do. I thought you'd never settle on a spot in the outfield and stay there." Coach laughed. "As you reminded me a minute ago, some things never change."

Coach offered his hand, said he had to

get on with his reconnaissance mission and headed for the practice fields outside.

Cullen stood amid the hubbub of the cages, lost in memories of the past and a few fears for the future, forgetting the time.

"We're tired and hungry," Carrie announced, moving toward him with Meg and Hope right behind.

"If we don't eat soon Hope's blood sugar will drop and she'll get cranky and whiny," Meg added.

"Will not," Hope argued.

"Trust me, Cullen, you don't want to be in charge when this kid morphs into the incredible brat," Meg continued over Hope's objection.

"Hey! I'm right behind you. I can hear everything you say."

"Oh, shut up," Meg taunted.

"That's no way to talk to your baby sister," Carrie admonished Meg. "Show some respect like Cullen says and tell her you're sorry."

"You're right, Carrie." Meg turned to Hope. "I'm sorry you're a cranky, whiny little kid. You can't help it."

"Apology accepted." Hope smiled at her sisters.

It wasn't perfect, but the girls were catching on. More importantly, they were making sincere efforts, giving it their all.

How could Cullen give them back any less?

ON SATURDAY NIGHT, Sarah rushed over to Cullen's to pick up her girls. But instead of the grouchy brood she'd expected, she found a quiet group around the dinner table with Cullen, and a burger was waiting for her.

Meg took a huge bite of cheeseburger, dragged three shoestring fries through the river of ketchup on her paper plate and poked them in an already overloaded mouth.

"Honey, take it easy, you're eating like a starving animal," Sarah cautioned.

"I'm sorry, Mama. I'm hungry," she mumbled.

"If I crammed my mouth that full you'd be lecturing me on the hazards of choking."

Meg swallowed and took a long pull on the straw of her chocolate milk shake.

"I can't help it. I'm so tired that I'm afraid I'll fall asleep in my plate if I don't eat fast."

"Me, too," Carrie agreed.

"Me three," Hope added, a strawberry milk shake mustache on her upper lip.

"Did you play ball with my daughters or make them pull a plow?"

Sarah looked to Cullen for an explanation. His lips curved in a grin over the top of his own burger wrapped in white parchment paper.

"Today I cracked the code on how to wear these three out so well they don't have the energy to argue."

"But they don't have the energy to eat, either."

"They're doing just fine, as you can see from their empty plates. It's the grumbling and name calling that's missing."

Sarah stared from one girl to the next. Three sets of pink cheeks and eyelids at half-mast indicated her brood wasn't in peril but simply bushed from an active day in the sun.

"How can I not love a man who spends his Saturday with three girls who don't belong to him so their mama can go shopping and get her hair done?" Sarah asked.

Had she really brought up *love* for the first time, at the dinner table in front of her girls? Wasn't that normally a private, intimate moment between two people?

Maybe Cullen hadn't noticed.

"Your hair looks especially pretty tonight." He smiled his approval.

At least he'd noticed her cut and highlights, even if he'd missed her mention of love.

"Cullen, may I go lay on your big bed with Rocket?" Carrie asked politely.

"And sleep with the TV on?" Meg pleaded.

"Yeah, we don't have TVs in our bedrooms at the apartment," Hope informed him.

Sarah cut in. "No, let's clean up this mess and then head home, girls."

"It's not even dark outside and it's Saturday night," Cullen reminded her. "Don't dine and dash after I've gone to all the trouble to procure these nutritious meals."

"Cullen, they're not going to last another fifteen minutes. I'll be lucky to get them out of the car when we get to the apartment."

"Then let them go crawl on my bed with Rocket. It's a California king so there's plenty of room. When they wake up you can take them home."

"I don't know…" She really should get them moving while there was still a chance they'd make it to the car under their own steam.

"I was hoping to talk about next week's lectures with you. Otherwise, I won't be prepared."

How could she refuse to help him out when he'd devoted two full days this week to her family? And to tell the truth, there was nowhere she'd rather be, anyway. They were way past the friendship stage, barreling head-long toward emotions that wouldn't be denied and couldn't be hidden.

Sitting beside Cullen on his sofa while he expounded on some bloody battle over ancient relics sounded like the perfect evening.

CHAPTER SEVENTEEN

FROM THE DOORWAY of Cullen's bedroom, Sarah had a perfect view of her three beautiful daughters and one long-legged blond puppy tangled together in a snuggly web. Their breathing had changed as soon as their heads had pressed into the pillows atop the huge pine sleigh bed. Though the girls were fast asleep, Sarah switched on the flat-screen television, tuned it to the country music channel and dialed the volume low.

"They're down for the count," Cullen whispered into her ear. "I bet they don't wiggle before daylight."

"I'm afraid you may be right. How am I going to get them home and into their own beds now?"

"Just leave them here. I'll move Rocket into one of my guest rooms with me later and the girls can sleep over. You can bring them a fresh change of clothes for church in the morning."

"I can't ask you to be responsible for them all night."

He smiled and gestured toward the comatose mound of warm bodies beneath the covers on his bed.

"I don't think you have much choice, my dear."

His hand was warm on the small of Sarah's back as he guided her away from the bedroom and into the kitchen where they'd shared their meal. He'd swept away all signs of the carryout burgers and fries he'd generously provided. She'd been prepared to cook spaghetti, feeling a bit guilty for taking the day for herself. But it had been a relief to arrive at Cullen's house to find he already had dinner covered.

And now he had the girls covered for the night, as well. The man was making himself indispensable and Sarah wasn't sure if that was a good thing or a bad thing.

"What will I do all by myself in a quiet apartment?"

"You can soak in a hot bubble bath with a glass of pink wine while you listen to Michael Bublé. I hear ladies enjoy that activity."

"And where did you pick up such a tidbit?"

"I'm a well-rounded man. I watch *The View*."

"Of course you do." She nodded her head at the mental picture of Cullen watching a panel of women yakking over the top of one another about fashion and food. "Well, I have neither bubble bath nor *pink wine—*" she made a sour face at the idea of the sweet drink "—and I'm more of a Tim McGraw kinda girl, so that whole plan is a no-go. What else have they taught you on *The View?*"

He opened the glass door of the small refrigerator that held his wine collection and pulled out a dark green bottle with a foil-wrapped neck and two chilled crystal flutes.

"That a lady can't refuse a glass of champagne and sunset by the pool."

"Champagne? Are we celebrating something?"

"Peace and quiet for starters. And that pretty new hairdo."

"Thank you for noticing." She made a production of fluffing her auburn waves.

"I heard what you said a little while ago."

"About my hair?"

He set the flutes and the bottle on the countertop. In a motion so fluid and fast that she couldn't possibly resist, he wrapped Sarah in strong arms and pulled her close. His chest was Rock of Gibraltar solid and just as formidable.

He lowered his head until eyes the color of wet slate hovered just above her face.

"I heard what you said about loving a guy like me." His voice was husky with an emotion she'd never heard from Cullen before. "Was that just a figure of speech or do you actually love me, Sarah?"

He asked the question with such need in his voice that it couldn't be disguised.

Her chest tingled where their bodies touched. Blood rushed to her face as her heart pumped double time. Even this soon in their relationship she was sure of the answer to his bold question. Would speaking the words out loud jinx a situation that seemed too perfect to be true?

"You first," she said simply, content to let him lead the way.

"You're right, I should go first. A woman has to be certain she's standing on solid ground with a man before she agrees to take a leap of faith with him."

Her breath seemed to grow still in her lungs as she waited to hear him say the words that would change her world forever. He cupped her chin with his hand, gently but firmly ensuring he had her attention for what he was about to say.

"I love you, Sarah Eason. And I love your

girls. Y'all came at me like a line drive and I never had a chance to get out of the way. Wouldn't have wanted to even if I could have."

Sarah slid her hands into his hair, gripped the curls at the nape of his neck and pulled his lips to hers. She took the lead in a bold kiss, saying what he needed to hear with tenderness and urgency, her mouth hungry for Cullen's. Their sighs mingled as they pressed close, his arms snaking around her body and holding her as if he'd never let her go.

They were breathless when he finally lifted his face from hers. He continued to cradle her close.

"Don't expect that you can distract me with a wanton kiss, woman."

She tilted her head back and laughter burst toward the ceiling. "Wanton kiss? You've gotta stop watching *The View*."

"I read that in one of Alma's romance novels."

"You really are a well-rounded guy, Dr. Temple."

"And how does a guy like me figure into your future?"

"I don't have a crystal ball but I do have a hammering heart and wobbly knees. Those are sure signs of a whirlwind courtship."

"Does that mean you'll agree to let me court you?"

"Yes, sir, it does."

"Because?"

"Because I love you right back."

He kissed her again. This time softly, gently, his lips a promise of what would be, making Sarah all too willing to forget her own warnings about things that seemed too perfect to be true.

Too many changes at once can unsettle children. The success rate is highest when couples wait two years or more instead of piling one drastic family change onto another.

Cullen remembered well the point he'd been studying that very morning. He should go by the book and take things slow. But it was hard to keep a level head when he was holding this amazing woman in his arms and his mind was spinning out of control. Alma said courtship was a lost art, and right now he'd be smart to revive the practice and keep his eager hands to himself.

He could do that; Cullen was nothing if not disciplined. But he'd given his heart and he desperately wanted something in return. Simply had to hear the words again.

"What was that you said? Was it something

important?" He tipped his head to the side as if his hearing was fading.

"When?" she teased.

"Right before you distracted me with that kiss," he reminded her.

Sarah's blue eyes crinkled when she smiled at his silliness.

"I said I love you, too, Cullen."

"Why?"

"You are really fishing for a compliment tonight."

"Kinda, but my mama and Alma are the only women who've ever told me they love me and it wasn't as if they had any choice."

"You're kidding, right?"

"Nope, and as soon as you humor this old boy he'll reward you with a glass of shamefully expensive champagne."

"I love you because you're generous and kind, patient and understanding, all grown up but still a mischievous boy inside, and it doesn't hurt that you're good-lookin' as the Texas sky is high." A soft chuckle deep in her throat held promise for future intimacies. "But mostly, Cullen, I love you because you've accepted the four of us just as we are, without reservations or conditions. I never dared to dream we'd find you, and suddenly here you are. Loving us."

Sarah's words washed over him like a second baptism, cleansing away the fears and insecurities she couldn't see that stained his spirit. His hand slipped through her soft curls and he pressed her head to his chest, hugging her fiercely, determined to hang on to this special woman who was changing his life forever, little by little, day by day.

She raised her face, her eyes shining, a mirror of the happy tears that welled up and spilled over his own lashes. His heart thundered, his palms grew moist, his breathing shuddered. In another lifetime, those would have been dreaded symptoms, and he'd have run and put his head under the covers for sleep and blessed relief. Or much worse, taken a razor blade to his flesh.

But tonight his relief would be holding the hand of the woman who held his heart.

He dared to kiss her waiting lips again and again for long minutes. Slow, deliberate kisses alternating between his hunger and his restraint. In response, Sarah showered him with touch and tenderness, a taste of their life to come.

Later they sat together in the wooden swing on his patio. He pressed her close with his arm around her shoulders and they enjoyed the quiet sunset and their sparkling wine.

"Does it get any better than this?" Cullen murmured.

"I'm sure it must but at the moment this is perfection."

"How about Sunday brunch at Temple Territory after church in the morning? Then you can all come over here, the girls can swim and you can join me to watch the Rangers whip up on the Angels."

"Wouldn't you prefer some downtime away from us ?"

"Darlin', you are my downtime. Before you came along, my days in this house were spent with my nose in a book reading about how life used to be hundreds of years ago. I want to experience how life is right now, and that's what you and the girls have brought to me."

"That's a very kind thing to say."

"It's the simple truth. My brothers will give me the business for waiting this long to catch on to life outside the cover of a book, but it's their job to bust my chops and I suspect I've got it coming."

"Cullen, your academic achievements are nothing short of amazing. All the years of focus and dedication have paid off for you in spades, so I don't understand why they'd be hard on you."

"I never said it was understandable, just

that it was coming. I give as good as I get, so I won't mind."

He reached for the champagne bottle chilling in the bucket of ice on a small table beside the swing.

"No more for me." Sarah handed her half-empty flute to Cullen. "The mosquitoes are starting to bite and that's my cue to go inside."

"You wanna watch a video? It's still kinda early."

He was hopeful she'd stay, but she shook her head and pushed to her feet. Sarah held out her hand and pulled him upright. He took advantage of the chance to pull her close for another lingering kiss.

"Are you sure about letting the girls sleep over?"

"I'm sure. My little buddy and I will be fine in the front guestroom."

Rocket had long since loped outside to find his master. The pup was another delight that had come into his life compliments of Sarah's gaggle of girls.

"Then I'm going to take advantage of what's left of this quiet evening to go over my finances."

"Maybe you should take the rest of the wine with you. That might make the situation seem a little better," he teased, praying she wasn't having problems paying her bills.

"Oh, it's not a bleak picture, just tight since it's about time for school shopping."

"Would you let me help out?"

Her head shake was emphatic.

"I've got it covered. The little ones are still easy to please and Carrie's recently gone green, so the only place she wants to shop is the Goodwill store."

Sarah gathered her purse and keys.

"Recycled clothes have been the trend for college students, too, for a while now. I hear a girl can do a lot of damage at Goodwill with a twenty-dollar bill."

"And when she only wears black it's fairly simple to mix and match."

Monochromatic dress and dark-rimmed eyes had been a common sight on campus for years, but on a thirteen-year-old it was worrisome. He knew from experience how quickly a kid could morph from confused to troubled, from sad to desperate. But Sarah didn't seem concerned.

"How long has Carrie had the Goth thing going on?" Cullen tried to keep the question casual as he walked Sarah to her car.

"Since she started middle school. I'm hoping she'll break out of vampire mode when she goes to high school, but for now I tolerate it as there's no harm in the way she looks. It sure drives my folks nuts that I agreed to let her keep the purple hair and wear eye makeup this summer."

"Will she be able to keep doing that when school starts?"

"No way." Sarah gave him a conspiratorial grin. "But the two of us negotiated an arrangement. I let her do her thing for the summer and over Labor Day weekend she returns Wednesday Addams to the closet and gets Carrie Eason ready for eighth grade. We even put it in writing and taped it to her door so she can't play dumb when the time comes to do her part."

"You're one clever cookie." Cullen admired her approach to what could have been a summer-long argument.

"It helps that I work at a law firm that specializes in arbitration."

Cullen opened Sarah's door but blocked the way as a bid for one more hug. She stepped so easily into his arms, wrapping him in her warmth, that his heart ached for all the years he'd convinced himself he could make it on his own.

Not anymore.

CHAPTER EIGHTEEN

LET THE CHILD set the pace as you do things together—games, sports, activities. Every child is different but given enough time, patience and interest most will come around.

Cullen slipped his 1974 Hank Aaron baseball card into the book, settled it on the nightstand beside the guest bed—that was really too short for his comfort—and flipped off the light. He rolled on his side, scooped Rocket close and considered the wisdom of what he'd just read.

Was he taking things too fast? Had it really only been weeks and not months since they'd knocked his world off its axis and spun him in another direction?

Was it possible to switch his focus so quickly and completely from a life of study to a life of family? His daddy had been a surgeon, spending long hours at the hospital instead of with his sons. What would his father have changed if he'd known his days on earth would be cut short, that his boys would grow older with only his memory instead of his presence? And hadn't that very question been what drove his daddy to go in search of the place where his own father was buried? Pap Temple had set into motion the cycle of loss that his son and grandsons had suffered. And his brothers would likely carry it into their old age if each of them didn't do something to interrupt the pattern.

Joiner and McCarthy were still content as they were, alone, seemingly not knowing any better. But Hunt had found his joy in Gillian. Given the choice, Cullen would follow his twin's lead. A month ago he'd never have guessed that would be the case, but the pages of the calendar couldn't be turned back, and he wouldn't want that, anyway.

Rocket struggled out from under the weight of Cullen's arm, stood on wobbly legs and looked toward the door.

"You wanna go out, buddy?"

Rocket's tail wagged.

Cullen pulled on his T-shirt, slipped his iPhone into the pocket of his pajama pants and the two headed for the door. Cullen settled into the wooden swing while Rocket began his ritual of sniffing every bush in the yard before deciding where to leave his mark. He was more pokey than usual and only half-way around the fence when Cullen pulled out his phone and began surfing the day's scores. Tomorrow Los Angeles would be in town and the rivalry between the Angels and the Rangers would take another turn at bat. There was nothing quite the same as witnessing a major league game in person. The view, even from the nosebleed seats, was like no other.

Cullen's chin popped up from the glow of the small screen. A smile split his face as his bent his head again and tapped in search instructions. Before he could complete his transaction the phone buzzed with a call.

Sarah. The woman who loved him.

The web of scars on his biceps shimmered white in the moonlight. Would she love him, warts and all?

"Hello, beautiful." He meant the greeting with all his heart.

"I hope I didn't wake you," she apologized.

"Nope, just sittin' outside again waiting on Rocket to do his business. Is everything okay?"

"That's what I called to ask you. I can come get my little ones if they wake up and want to go home."

"I peeked in on them not too long ago and, as I suspected, nobody's moved a muscle since they climbed on the bed a few hours ago."

"Probably because their muscles are tired and sore from all you had them doing today."

"They were troopers. Gave it their all at the park and in the batting cages."

"Even Carrie?"

"Especially Carrie. She's a natural leader, just needs a good coach. There could be a team mom position in your future."

"That'll be a challenge since you could put what all four of us know about baseball in a thimble."

"Well, they learned a lot today, and if you don't mind a change of plans for tomorrow I believe a major league lesson is in order."

The chuckle in his ear came from deep in Sarah's throat, causing his insides to stir, his pulse to quicken.

"Cullen, what have you got up your sleeve?"

"I believe I mentioned earlier that the Angels are in town for a double header and there are still seats available for the first game. On the drive over I can give the girls the history of the sport and the basic rules of play so that when we get there they'll be hard-core Rangers fans."

"Shouldn't you be working on your lecture

notes for this week instead of converting kids into supporters for your team?"

"I'm not concerned about the class. Now that I have half the summer term under my belt I've realized Blair was right. Teaching this class is a natural fit for me. I know my subject, and it's just a matter of carving it into small bites so I don't choke the students by ramming it down their throats."

"Does that mean you're going to accept a full-time position in the history department for the fall?"

"I haven't decided yet. I may move in a different direction, but it's too soon to say. At the very least I'll continue to cover Blair's schedule, but I might develop new classes of my own before I accept a contract."

"You're wise to take it slow. If you don't have to rush into a decision, then don't."

"How about you? Are you comfortable enough with this summer's experience that you'll register for a full load in the fall?"

He heard Sarah draw in a deep breath and blow out a resigned sigh.

"I don't have much choice. If I'm going to finish my degree I have to hunker down and get it over with sooner than later. It'll be a juggling act for a couple of years, but the reward at the end of the effort is a better life for my family."

"Very well put. I've never heard of anybody who looked back on their education and said, 'I wish I hadn't bothered with college so I'd have been less qualified for my job and not earned so much money.'"

"You should probably have that printed on a plaque."

"Somebody beat me to it. Miss Nancy sells those plaques in the campus bookstore."

"She works in the bookstore, too?"

"During finals weeks when the student employees need to study."

"Speaking of Miss Nancy, you remember that her wedding's a week from tonight, don't you?" Sarah reminded him.

Cullen never dreamed he'd be excited about a wedding *or* a campus function, but the opportunity to show Sarah off to his geeky colleagues held an excitement he hadn't experienced in years.

"It's on my hectic social calendar," he teased. "Alma's all set to keep the girls overnight so what do you say we drop by the Reo afterward and take a two-step turn around the dance floor?"

"I'm willing to give it a whirl as long as you're patient with me. I'll stop by my folks' house this week and dig out my favorite old pair of Tony Lamas from the closet and have Dad shine them up."

"Bring your boots to me and I'll handle that for you."

"Cullen, you're handling plenty for me already."

"Darlin', learning to take care of ladies has recently become my new field of study and I only just got started. Once I get my OCD on, there's no turning back."

TWELVE MILES AWAY from Cullen's house, Sarah was propped up on her bed pillows smiling at his comment and the pedicure she'd indulged in at the salon. But something about his words and the bright red polish on her toenails was bothersome. Without Cullen's reassuring presence, her doubts crept in again. Was this all too good to be true?

Her daddy said it was. According to her mama, he'd grumbled about what a scoundrel Pap Temple had been and that the apple doesn't fall far from the tree. Mama had reminded Daddy that Pap's son had done well for himself; he'd been a blessing to the folks of Kilgore and raised four fine boys. But Daddy insisted chickens come home to roost and sooner or later another of the Temple men would show their grandfather's true colors.

Sarah respected her daddy's intuition but in this case she was sure she simply knew better.

Yes, the situation seemed like a dream come true. But she and her girls had already suffered unspeakable loss and major upheaval so it was about time their fortunes changed.

By the grace of God, that change had come in the form of a good-lookin' man who was an open book, hiding nothing, giving much more than he got in return. He was the right partner to help her teach her girls about trust and honesty.

"Does that work for you?" Cullen's voice buzzed in her ear. "Sarah, honey, have you fallen asleep over there?"

"I'm still here." She blinked away her daddy's concerns.

"You okay with our new plans for tomorrow? The baseball game? I have to know right now so I can buy the tickets."

"Sure, we'd love to go to the Rangers game with you. But would you mind bringing the girls home tomorrow morning to let them choose their own clothes for the day? If you think Carrie's picky about what she wears, you should see the withering glare I get from

Hope when I buy her an outfit where everything matches. She says, 'Mama, things don't
match anymore, they *'go.'*"

"Now that you mention it, I was under constant criticism today about my favorite old
flannel shirt. Carrie said the Brawny paper
towel guy had called and he wanted his wardrobe back. Meg warned me that wearing flannel in the summer could prevent my body
from cooling properly and it could cause me
to have a heatstroke."

"Oh, Cullen, I'm sorry." Sarah snickered
into the phone.

"Oh, there's more! Your little fashionis-
tas have threatened to nominate me for some
makeover television show where they fly you
to New York City just to throw your whole
wardrobe in a trash can."

She smiled to herself. She knew the show
well and actually had to agree that Cullen
would be a great candidate. But she'd keep
that opinion to herself, for now, anyway

"So, you understand why they ought to
come to the house to get dressed?"

"It'll probably get the day off to a better
start," he agreed. "Shall I stop by the kolache
bakery on the way?"

"No, thanks. I've got a sausage and egg
casserole in the freezer and a can of cinna-

mon rolls in the fridge. I can pop those into the oven and have a hot breakfast ready when you get here."

"You're gonna spoil me with your home cookin'."

Sarah had to laugh out loud since she'd never shown much promise in the kitchen. Thankfully, her mother kept their freezer stocked with quick meals.

"I've eaten Alma's secret recipes and your twin is a celebrity chef. I'm fairly sure your palate is refined far beyond my abilities. You might even ban me from your kitchen the first time you witness the mess I can make of an omelet."

"Don't worry your pretty red head about it, my love. I'm certain nobody will go hungry in our home."

Our home?

Her heart raced beneath her ribs, and she glanced down, certain she'd see evidence of the erratic fluttering. But her summer-weight yellow nightie rose and fell in normal cadence with her breathing that was as sure and steady as the man himself.

Our home.

Well, if Cullen was prepared to go down

that emotional road with Sarah and her girls, they were packed and ready to make the journey with him.

CHAPTER NINETEEN

"WOULD YOU LIKE fries with your hot dog?"
The guy behind the Rangers ballpark concessions counter smiled down at his pint-size
customer.

Hope looked to Cullen, who read the cost
of French fries and mumbled "Freakin' highway robbery." But he smiled and nodded his
approval.

"Yes, please." She practiced the manners
her mama had insisted on during the drive
over from Kilgore.

"While the Rangers are up by five you
should supersize your order and take advantage of your daddy's good mood."

"He's not my daddy," she informed the
man as her bottom lip poked out and began
to quiver.

The guy slanted Cullen a suspicious glance.

"We'd like three more chili cheese dogs
and fries for her mama and sisters who are
waiting at our seats," he pointedly explained
as he handed over four twenties.

"Coming right up, sir."

Cullen gave his attention to Hope, who stood quietly with her gaze downcast and her big foam finger drooping toward the concrete floor. He squatted so he could be eyeball to eyeball with her but she refused to lift her face.

"What is it, baby girl?"

"I don't feel so good anymore."

"Too many peanuts?"

She shook her head.

Cullen touched a finger below her chin and tipped her head up. As Hope's eyes met his, fat tears splashed over her lower lashes and trickled down freckled cheeks.

"I want my daddy back," she blubbered.

Cullen's heart was already over easy where this little one was concerned and at her words it turned to scrambled eggs quicker than he could say "seventh inning stretch." He opened his arms expecting her to rush into his hug. Instead, she inched away, shrinking from his touch as if he were a stranger.

Cullen shivered beneath his flannel shirt at Hope's reaction. In a moment she'd gone from gregarious to wounded, and he was clueless as to how to react. Had he behaved the same in his own teenage way when he'd been orphaned? His mind drew a blank, which was a positive thing since he'd spent a lot of hours in therapy trying to put those painful memories to rest.

When a parent has died, the remarriage of the remaining parent may trigger unfinished grieving in children. Give them space and time to grieve.

He dared to reach forward cautiously and touch her thin shoulder.

"I understand how much it hurts, sweetie. Let's get back to your mama."

"Here ya go, buddy."

Cullen stood as the concessions guy pushed an overloaded cardboard to-go tray across the stainless-steel countertop toward him. Then the man reached over the mound of chili dogs and handed back a few singles and some coins.

"Keep the change," Cullen muttered. Seventy-six bucks for mystery meat and potatoes, for cryin' out loud. Might as well tip the rest.

He struggled to gather up the flimsy carton of overprice food and led Hope to their seats. As the crowd sang "Take Me Out to the Ball Game" he kept a close eye on his sad little shadow as she followed him down the aisle sniffling all the way. When they reached their row she dashed past him and threw herself into Sarah's lap.

"What's wrong with her?" Carrie demanded as the song ended and the crowd waited for the players to return to the field.

Hope blubbered a response but the only discernible word was *Daddy*.

"What about Daddy?" Worry creased Meg's face as she patted her sister's shoulder.

"I want my daddy," she wailed.

"Me, too, Hope. Me, too." Meg's lips twisted to fight the inclination to join in her sister's cries.

"We all want Daddy back," Carrie agreed, sorrow in her words.

Unspoken apology and understanding were communicated in the blue eyes Sarah focused on Cullen.

"The guy behind the counter mistook me for her father," Cullen explained.

"He's not my daddy." Hope continued to whine through tears and hiccups. "I want my real daddy."

Sarah stroked her daughter's hair and murmured soothing sounds, then turned her attention to Cullen again. Based on the sympathetic furrow of her brow his discomfort was obvious.

"It was bound to happen sooner or later,

Cullen. You can't take a family out in public without someone eventually assuming you're part of it."

"But he is," Meg insisted as she pulled her attention away from Hope and slipped a Cracker Jack–sticky hand into Cullen's. "Maybe he's not our forever-daddy, but he's our now-daddy."

The tender comment caused a lump the size of Dallas to lodge in Cullen's throat.

His gut clenched and churned.

There was a burning behind his eyelids and a nervous smile quivered on his lips.

The cardboard tray jiggled, giving visible evidence of the trembling of his hands.

For years he'd done everything possible to avoid this combination of physical symptoms, and here he was putting himself in the position to be drenched by a fire hose of feelings.

There was no doubt it was worth it. The doubt was whether or not he could handle it.

SARAH WATCHED EMOTIONS play out across Cullen's face.

Sadness, confusion, tenderness, guilt and something that seemed a great deal like fear.

Fear?

What could an accomplished scholar such as Cullen Temple possibly have to fear? As far as she knew *failure* was the only thing that worried him and he had certainly been a success with her and the girls. At least until now.

An oblivious passerby bumped Cullen from behind. He lost his footing on the edge of the step and squelched a loud oath as he began to stumble backward. In what seemed like slow motion, the disposable tray that had occupied both of his hands escaped his grasp and launched into the air. All heads jerked toward the commotion as fries rained down on nearby spectators. Cullen twisted in the aisle to recover his balance, but his feet slid out from underneath him and he landed hard on his rear end. Baseball fans gasped as the box filled with open-faced hot dogs flew upward and then plunged toward the ground. But Cullen saved the day by grabbing the cheesy mess, clutching it to his chest and bowing his head over what was left of their meal to shield everyone from chili splatter. The little cups of mustard squashed against his shirt, adding gooey splashes of gold to the blue and red plaid.

"Safe!" shouted a man two rows up, and the crowd around them erupted in applause.

Cullen peered out from under the brim of his Rangers cap to see how many spectators had witnessed the clumsy debacle. Specks of ketchup and chili dotted his cheeks and clung to his chin. Led by Hope, the Eason girls howled with laughter at the silly picture Cullen made sprawled on the steps covered in hot dog fixin's. A Good Samaritan in the aisle behind them extended his hand to pull Cullen to his feet and signaled for an usher.

"That was so funny, Cullen." Hope's woes were forgotten.

"Honey, are you okay?" Sarah jumped from her seat, grabbed her empty popcorn bag and began cleaning up the debris on the steps.

"Our crew will take care of that, ma'am," the usher assured her as he hurried toward the scene. "That was a quite a spill you took. Everybody up on the mezzanine groaned when you hit the deck."

"Oh, great. Half the stadium watched me fall on my keister." He rubbed his tailbone. "At least I didn't make it to the Jumbotron."

"Do you require first aid, sir? We have a station on this level, or I can radio the medics to come down here?" He indicated the walkie-talkie clipped to his belt.

"Nothing's bruised but my ego." Cullen waved away the offer.

"Maybe you better go with him, Cullen,"

Sarah suggested, never expecting him to agree in a million years.

"I'll be right back." He gave a disgusted wag of his head and moved to climb up to the concessions level.

"Should we all go with you in case you want to leave after the EMTs check you out?"

"I don't need medical attention. I'm only going to the men's room to wash off some of this mess and then buy us some more hot dogs."

"Freakin' highway robbery." Hope repeated what she'd heard him say a few minutes earlier.

Sarah arched an eyebrow and glared at her daughter. "Where did you learn that phrase, young lady?"

Hope lifted her eyes to Cullen, reluctant to throw him under the bus.

"From me," he admitted, raising his hand in admission of guilt. "I apologize, Hope. That wasn't a nice thing for me to say and it's not appropriate language for you, either, so please don't repeat that again, okay?"

"Yes, sir."

Sarah mouthed, "Thank you," and gave him a wink.

"You girls sit tight and I'll go wash up. Let's forget about the hot dogs and just head out. With this five-run lead over the Angels we're safe to make a getaway."

"Are you sure you don't mind leaving early?"

"Nope and there's a storm on the way so let's beat it back to Kilgore. As long as you don't mind being seen with a guy covered in mustard and ketchup, we'll find a family restaurant on the way home to get some real food."

Everyone agreed to the plan and fifteen minutes later Sarah and the girls waited for Cullen at the top of the steps by the entrance to their row. Hope proudly held a sack containing a surprise. It had been Meg's idea and they all agreed it was perfect under the circumstances.

Cullen approached with a quizzical look in his eyes and a big wet spot on the front of his shirt.

"This is for you." Meg offered up their treasure.

"What is it?" Cullen accepted it suspiciously.

"Something we wanted our now-daddy to have," Meg announced.

"Yeah, our now-daddy," Hope agreed.

"Cullen, will you be our now-daddy?" Carrie asked.

Sarah watched for his reaction to the nickname the girls had decided should stick. Maybe one day he'd be a forever-daddy but for today *now* was enough.

He dipped his chin, hiding his expression for several seconds. With his right hand Cullen reached to adjust his cap and made a surreptitious swipe of his shirtsleeve across his eyes. He cleared his throat, sniffed and whispered, "I'd be honored."

"Open it." Hope pointed to the bag and gave him a tender, toothless grin.

Cullen did as instructed and spotted the Texas Rangers logo on a summer-weight T-shirt. He rolled the bag closed again, tucked it under his arm and cleared his throat again.

"Thank you, girls. This is the nicest thing anybody ever did for me."

"Put it on!" Hope insisted, dancing on first one foot and then the other.

"Yeah, put it on!" Meg agreed.

"I want to save it for a special occasion."

"This *is* a special occasion. It's our very first baseball game," Carrie reminded him.

"And we figured you might want a clean shirt to put on for the ride home and our dinner date."

"All great points." He seemed to consider

their arguments but for some reason that escaped Sarah, he was hesitant to agree.

"You don't like the shirt we picked out." Meg's voice was deflated, as if all the excitement had leaked out of her.

"That's not it at all. Okay, I'll be back in a minute. Y'all wait right here," Cullen instructed them. Then he strode in the direction of the men's room again.

"Cullen doesn't want to be our now-daddy, does he?" Hope asked Sarah.

"I'd bet my paycheck that he does, but this is all new to Cullen so we have to give him some time to get used to the idea. And it hasn't even been a half hour since he hit the ground like a sack of wet sand in front of all these people, so his behind and his pride will be smarting at least for the rest of the day."

"What if somebody from the university is here and they saw what happened?"

Sarah's hand covered her mouth. "Oh, Carrie, I hadn't even considered that. Well, we'll just hope that's not the case." To the little ones, she said, "And don't either of you bring that possibility up again in front of Cullen. He'd be mortified to think his colleagues or students witnessed his fall."

"But it was funny," Hope insisted, not quite catching on to the embarrassment factor.

Sarah tried to frame it in a way that would make sense to Hope. "If you went to the bathroom at school and came out with the tail of your dress stuck in your underwear and everybody noticed and pointed and laughed at you, would you think it was funny?"

"No, ma'am." The light of understanding dawned in her eyes and she nodded her agreement to keep silent on the subject.

"How do I look?" Cullen asked as he returned to the group.

"The same as you did five minutes ago, like a guy with a big wet spot on the front of his flannel shirt," Sarah answered.

He unfastened the top two snaps and pulled the plaid collar wide to reveal the big "T" logo on a gray background.

"It's close to my heart where it belongs."

"You were supposed to take the dirty shirt off," Meg instructed.

"Yeah, that was the whole point in the gift," Carrie added.

"Was it?" Cullen pretended he hadn't connected the dots. "Well, I'm not wet anymore and the home team's up another run so let's make tracks."

"Make tracks?" Hope crinkled her nose.

"It means let's get moving. My daddy used to say that to us."

"Then it's right that our now-daddy says it, too," she agreed.

Hope's sadness was forgotten as she took Cullen by the hand and made her own little tracks by skipping beside him all the way to the parking lot.

CHAPTER TWENTY

THUNDER RUMBLED IN the distance as rain pelted the window of Sarah's bedroom. Once upon a time she'd loved a good storm at night, but something about this one had her on edge. She rolled to her side, punched her pillow just so and caught sight of the alarm clock— 4:30 a.m.

The ambient noise that came with apartment living had kept her from a deep sleep and she'd pay for it with dark circles beneath her eyes if she didn't drop back off soon.

Then she heard a pounding on the door and jumped to her feet, barely suppressing a startled scream. The glow from the security light in the parking lot filtered through the curtains, giving her just enough visibility to grab her lightweight robe from the foot of the bed. As she slid it over her cotton pajamas and yanked the belt tight, the pounding on the door resumed. She hurried down the short hallway into the family room and pressed her eye against the peephole.

Two of Kilgore Police Department's finest stood on her front step, rivulets of water cascading off their raincoats. And between the tall cops was a smaller figure wrapped in a bright orange rain poncho with an officer's hand on her shoulder. The girl's head tipped forward, a cascade of purple hair shielding her face.

Carrie!

The scream that had threatened moments earlier was in Sarah's throat again as she threw open the dead bolt and yanked the door wide. The officer's hand fell away from Carrie's shoulder and she flung her body against her mother's, sending a spray of water across the linoleum entry and soaking Sarah's clothes.

"Are you Mrs. Sarah Eason?" a familiar voice inquired.

"You know exactly who I am, Stanton. What's this all about?" she asked the man who'd been a lifelong friend of her husband's.

"We spotted your daughter and a young man together outside the Sonic a few blocks from here. When we questioned them about being out so late and in this storm I realized she was Joe's kid and thought it best to give her a ride home."

"Where is this boy you mentioned?" Sarah

gripped Carrie close, unconcerned that her pajamas had soaked through. She needed to get to the bottom of the situation and quickly.

"He's in the squad car. We'll drop him off next," the other officer answered, then he nodded politely to excuse himself and returned to the cruiser parked at the curb.

Sarah pushed Carrie to arm's length, grasped her chin and raised her face so they were eye to eye.

"Go into my room *very quietly* and get out of these wet clothes. *Do not wake your sisters,* do you understand me?"

"Yes, ma'am," Carrie murmured. She shrugged off the poncho and handed it back to the officer before making a soggy escape to Sarah's bedroom and closing the door softly.

"Please come in for a minute, Stanton. The floor's already wet so you won't hurt anything."

She moved aside to make room. He shook off the rain as best he could and stepped across the threshold.

"I can't think what to say besides 'thank you.'" Sarah crossed her arms to cover her clinging night clothes. "I would never have dared to do anything this crazy, and certainly not when I was her age. If I'd slipped out of the house in the middle of the night when I was thirteen I'd *still* be locked in my daddy's woodshed."

Stanton chuckled. "Unfortunately, it happens all the time. We keep an eye out for the young ones and do our best to prevent them from getting into trouble."

"Can you tell me the boy's name, Stanton?"

"Alex Henderson. He's a good kid and I know his parents. They're going through a nasty divorce, so nobody's paying him any attention right now." Sarah suddenly remembered her awkward discussion about sex with the girls—and that it had come up because of information Carrie had gotten from one of her friends. Stanton continued, not noticing Sarah's momentary distraction. "I'll pass this situation on to the coach at the middle school and ask to get Alex added to the list of kids at risk. The athletic department has a program that assigns mentors for the boys and girls who may be struggling socially, and it seems to be changing lives for the better."

"Will there be a record of this incident? Do you have to report Carrie to the school?" Sarah shuddered to think of another weighty issue to deal with and so publicly. Carrie would be mortified, but that might not be a bad thing, considering how she'd behaved.

"No, this is strictly off the record. They weren't breaking any laws, just hanging out in the wrong place at the wrong time. I'm pretty sure a ride in the backseat of a cruiser has put the fear of God in both of them."

"Thanks, Stanton. Joe would appreciate this kindness."

"I promised your husband years ago that he could count on me and I'm a man of my word."

"There aren't many men like you left."

He settled his cap back on his head so she opened the door.

"Oh, sure there are. You'll hook another one when the moment's right." Stanton gave her a kind smile and stepped out into the rain.

Sarah turned the lock and leaned against the wall to steady her pounding heart.

"Actually, I may already have hooked a great guy, but he's gonna spit out the bait if my daughter keeps this up."

Then a disturbing thought struck her. What if this was Carrie's way of rebelling against Sarah's relationship with Cullen? After all, at the baseball game, the kids had used the word *daddy*.

If forced to choose between Cullen and Carrie, Sarah would do what was best for her child. But the very idea of cutting Cullen from her life sent a shiver through her body and her spirit.

Would that be necessary? There was only one way to find out.

Sarah tiptoed down the hall and cracked open the door to the girls' room just enough to reassure herself that Meg and Hope were asleep in their beds. Then she sucked in a deep breath to steel herself for whatever was to come with Carrie and crept into her own bedroom.

She clicked on the night table lamp to find Carrie in the bed, covers pulled up to her chin and her damp purple hair spread across what had once been her daddy's pillow.

"Mamá, I'm so sorry!" Carrie's words were hushed but nonetheless frantic as tears dribbled down both cheeks. "I've screwed up bigtime, haven't I?"

"I'd say that's a fair assessment of the situation," Sarah agreed as she tossed her damp pajamas over a chair and pulled on a soft nightgown.

Sarah flipped the light off, slid beneath the covers and drew her firstborn against her heart. They were silent for long moments, clinging to each other while Carrie's breathing and tears slowed.

"You want to tell me who Alex is and what,

by the name of all that is holy, would possess you to sneak out of the house at all, much less on a night like this?"

"Alex is a guy from school. He texted me to say he couldn't take any more of his parents fighting and being all wrapped up in their own problems. He was going to run away. Or worse, Mama."

The pleading eyes Carrie turned upward told Sarah exactly what "or worse" meant.

"I figured if I could to talk to him in person I could stop him from doing something stupid."

"So you did something stupid yourself instead?"

"I admit I didn't think it through, but it was an emergency and I was trying to help a friend. The Sonic is only a couple of blocks from here. I locked up when I left and figured I'd be back home before you woke up."

"I can understand the situation and I'm even proud of you for having such compassion for a friend. But why didn't you discuss it with me first? What made you take this into your own hands?"

Carrie looked away.

"What? Talk to me, baby," Sarah pleaded softly.

She knew in her heart of hearts that this

was a pivotal moment in their relationship, and maybe in their lives. She sent up a silent prayer for the wisdom to deal with whatever Carrie had to say.

"Please, what's on your mind?" Sarah gave her daughter a tender shake.

"You and Cullen are moving pretty fast. It won't be long before you don't have time left for me. I figured I should start making decisions for myself instead of relying on you for everything."

"Oh, honey," Sarah crooned, and brushed purple strands out of Carrie's eyes. "If you were eighteen I might see the sense in those thoughts. But you're only thirteen and still my little girl, no matter how grown up you seem sometimes."

"Am I right about you and Cullen?"

"Yes and no," Sarah answered. "Yes, things are serious between Cullen and me. But if he stays in our lives it will make us a stronger family. He will never take me away from you and your sisters. I promise."

"Will you tell him what I did?"

"Why do you ask?"

"Because if Cullen knows, then both of you will think I'm dumb, or can't be trusted and need to be treated like a child."

"I don't feel that way and neither will Cullen. In fact, I'm fairly sure he'll be in favor of grown-up punishment since you're mature enough to handle it."

"So you're not going to lock me up in the woodshed like Grandpa claims he did when you were a kid?"

Sarah laughed at her daddy's constant but empty threat.

"He never did any such thing, but mostly because just the idea of that dark, old shed was enough to keep me on the straight and narrow. No, I won't send you to the woodshed, and you're not going to be confined to your room or even the apartment, either. This offense calls for something public."

Carrie's eyes flew wide. "You're not going to make me stand on the corner wearing one of those shaming signs, are you?"

"That's actually not a bad idea, but no. Community service is more along the lines of what I had in mind."

"Community service? Like picking up trash on the side of the road?"

Sarah wished she had a camera handy to capture the expression of distaste on her daughter's face. It was equally charming and horrifying. She had to impose a sentence that would fit the severity of the crime but not scar a thirteen-year-old for life.

"Your service won't be quite that public, but I assure you it will be appropriate and you'll never want to repeat it."

"I realize I don't have any right to ask for a favor at the moment, but could we keep this a secret between you, me and Cullen? Could you *please* not tell Meg and Hope?"

"I wouldn't dream of tarnishing your sterling reputation as their big sister. Besides, I'm sure when the time is right you'll give them the benefit of your lesson learned."

"Because that's what sisters are for?"

"And because you love them almost as much as I love you."

WHILE HE WAITED on his morning coffee to brew, Cullen stood on the patio watching Rocket romp in the wet grass and listened to Sarah as she recounted her past few hours over the phone.

"Girls in general, and your girls in particular, are a constant source of amazement to me," he admitted as he shook his head.

"Well, Carrie is quite concerned over how you'll react to what she did."

"That one is a free spirit but I'd never have expected she'd break out of Shawshank at thirteen."

Sarah's laughter coming from his cell

phone was a morning rainbow after the stormy night that had kept Rocket anxious and whining.

"I wouldn't exactly compare our household to a high-security prison, but after this I may have to install bars on the windows, do a bed check and keep the place locked down till morning."

"Carrie really cares about what I think, huh?"

"It's a fact."

"You're not making that up?"

"No, sir."

"That warms my heart," he confessed as a surge of love for Sarah's daughter coursed through his soul.

"It's interesting that you focused on your warm-fuzzies instead of the fact that my thirteen-year-old was out on the town in the middle of the night."

"I'd hardly call the Kilgore Sonic 'out on the town,' and aren't you glad to know our police are kind enough to pick up young'uns and get them home safely?"

"I am. But what she did was dangerous and she's got to be punished in a way that she will never forget."

"She's already grounded because of last semester's grades, isn't she?"

"Yeah," Sarah snorted. "For all the good that's done. I told her this called for community service. Got any creative ideas?"

Cullen snapped his fingers as an idea struck.

"As a matter of fact I do."

"Let's hear it."

"Miss Nancy is always in need of volunteers for odd jobs on campus. Knowing her she'll drag the library's old card catalog out of the archives, dump it out on the floor and make Carrie reorganize the whole thing."

Sarah's laughter echoed again and his pulse raced in response. The woman was not only in his heart, she was in his blood.

"Can we trust Miss Nancy to keep it to herself if we explain the reason for Carrie's *volunteering?*"

"Miss Nancy doesn't ask questions, she just puts you to work and checks in every couple of hours to make sure you're still breathing."

"And if you're not?"

"Then she throws a sheet over you and calls Merle in to clean up the body."

"Sounds perfect. How much time should Carrie serve for this crime?"

"Hmm... Let's do the math. Slipping out of the house at night. During a thunderstorm. At thirteen. *To meet a boy!* Even with the best of intentions I'd still say that's forty hours of penance."

"Will you talk to Miss Nancy for me today?"

"I'll do better than that. I'll be at your house at nine o'clock to pick up our little purple-haired perpetrator and escort her to the warden myself."

"Cullen Temple, you are too much fun." Sarah giggled. "How did we get along the past couple of years without you?"

"Those are kind words and I appreciate hearing them more than you can possibly know."

"Enjoy them because I'm not sure you'll hear many kind words from Carrie this week."

"Did she happen to say why she made such a big decision on her own?"

"Yes, she did. But I'm going to leave it up to Carrie to tell you that herself."

"Well, we're going to commute together for the next five days so she'll have plenty of opportunity to spill the beans."

"After this week is over she's gonna wish I'd locked her in my daddy's woodshed instead!"

"Given the option, I'd elect that one, too!"

"LET'S GET MOVING, GIRLS," Sarah urged her brood.

"Mama, I just got back to sleep," Carrie grumbled.

"Cullen will be here in twenty minutes, and you need to be dressed so you are ready to go with him."

"Go where?" Her tone was surly, probably for the sake of her sisters, but Carrie threw off the covers and climbed out of her bed just the same.

"To the university. You're going to help him with a project this week."

"Are we going, too?" Meg's face was hopeful.

"Not this time, pumpkin." Sarah ruffled Meg's hair, which was almost the same orange color as her own. "Grandma's expecting you and Hope today."

"I'm bored at Grandma's," Meg complained.

"Me, too," Hope chimed in. "She stinks at cards and she ran out of macaroni and construction paper last week."

"Grandma's not a bad card player, you're just especially good at Crazy Eights."

"That's true," Hope agreed with a grin.

"And if you girls hurry and get ready we can stop on the way and pick up some more art supplies. Before you know it, summer will be over and you'll be back in school, so let's enjoy hanging out with Grandma and Grandpa while we can."

"We? Are you going to stay with us today?"

"No, I'm expected at work later, but I can spare a couple of minutes for a cup of coffee from Grandma's fancy machine."

"What should I wear to the university?"

Carrie returned, fresh faced and looking interested. She probably expected she'd be hanging out with the college girls in the student center. Sarah wished she could be a fly on the wall when Miss Nancy took charge of her new volunteer for the week. She'd have to remind Cullen to call as soon as Carrie was delivered into the hands of Miss Norment the Torment.

"From what I've seen on campus, you can choose anything from your Goodwill wardrobe and you'll fit right in."

"Cool." She selected jeans and a T-shirt and started to turn toward the privacy of the bathroom to dress when she hesitated. "Mama, can I still use my makeup?"

Sarah suppressed a smile. It was enough that the kid was going to be on a chain gang all day. She should at least be allowed the luxury of eyeliner and lipstick.

"Thanks for asking, but we have a deal through the end of the summer and nothing's changed. Go ahead."

Carrie fairly skipped from the room. It would be interesting to see how cooperative she'd be at the same time tomorrow...and the day after and the day after that. Sarah should warn Cullen to expect some arguments, but he was a grown man and he could handle the flip-flop emotions that came with a thirteen-year-old-girl.

Yeah, right.

By nine-thirty, Sarah had waved goodbye to Cullen and Carrie and was at her mother's kitchen table savoring a foamy cup of cappuccino. She sat in the same ladder-back chair at the same oak table where she'd shared meals with her parents for her entire life, which made it hard not to consider just how many years that represented.

"Mama, I can't believe it's almost my fortieth birthday."

"Tell me about it. The only thing worse than turning forty is having a *daughter* who's turning forty," Margaret quipped.

Sarah poked her bottom lip out, pretending to pout.

"Oh, you know I'm just teasing." Her mother plopped a couple of shortbread cookies on a saucer and slid them in front of Sarah. "They say life begins at forty and I think that's gonna be true for you, sweetie."

She reached across the scarred table and rested a warm, soft hand atop Sarah's.

"Cullen Temple is a good man."

"I wish Daddy felt the same."

"Oh, please." Margaret waved away the comment. "Don't pay any attention to that old fool. If he had his druthers it would still be 1960 and Eisenhower would be in the White House. Your daddy wouldn't come into the twenty-first century if I tied him to his John Deere tractor and dragged him."

"Still, it would be nice if he'd get to know Cullen for himself and not for his grandfather's reputation."

"That'll happen soon enough. So what's all this about Carrie going to the university with Cullen today?"

Sarah hated withholding information from her mother but she'd promised Carrie to keep the situation between the two of them and Cullen. Besides, the details would send Margaret Callahan into a ring-tailed hissy fit. Sarah silently swore that if there came a day of payback when one of her girls should make the same decision on her behalf she would understand and let it go.

"Cullen mentioned that with the wedding next weekend Miss Nancy could use a hand. So Carrie's going to spend the week helping out in the office."

"That's admirable. Our girl is becoming a young woman and it's good she's thinking of others now because pretty soon she'll be all wrapped up in herself."

"It's not exactly an altruistic situation. When Carrie agreed to help out all week at the university she didn't know she'd be Miss Nancy's minion."

"Oh, well, that's different." Margaret chuckled. "You better hope that by Friday she's only a minion and not a flying monkey."

THAT AFTERNOON, CARRIE climbed into Cullen's SUV and slammed the door.

"How was your first day of community service?" Cullen asked, preparing for a teenage outburst.

Instead of the grimace he was expecting Carrie graced him with a charming smile.

"Actually, not too bad. Miss Nancy's pretty cool."

"Seriously?" He stopped short, his hand still poised to put the key in the ignition. "The two of you didn't butt heads?"

"Not at all." The girl's charcoal-rimmed

eyes glowed with confidence and accomplishment. "We got along great and she even asked me if I wanted a part-time job when school starts again. She's going to retire next year and there are a lot of loose ends that have to be tied up before she and Merle can set sail."

"Set sail?"

"Yes! They're planning one of those world cruises that stops in London, Athens, Singapore, Sydney, you name it. How awesome is that?"

Cullen leaned his head against the seat. He needed a moment to digest this news. In all these years, nobody had gotten the inside scoop on Miss Nancy—himself included. But in one day this girl had come away with more details than he'd gleaned after a dozen years on campus with the cantankerous woman.

"Miss Nancy also told me all about the wedding plans for this weekend and showed me the list of things she still has to do before Saturday. She said I was a blessing in disguise and she has you to thank."

"My goodness," was the best response Cullen had to offer in his bewildered state.

Maybe when he finished his research on family dynamics he'd study adolescent behavior. He hadn't been one himself for a very long time, but he didn't remember having the skills back then to charm the likes of a Miss Nancy Norment. Then again, she was one of a kind, and he'd never known anyone of any age, other than Merle, who could lay claim to such a talent.

"I'm extremely proud of you," he complimented Carrie.

"For reals?" Her brows furrowed together.

"For reals. You spent the day in the lion's den and lived to tell the story."

"Oh, please." She scrunched up her face. "Miss Nancy is a sweetheart and I can't wait to come back tomorrow and get to work on her wedding details."

"You remember your mother and I are invited to the ceremony, right?"

"Of course. Miss Nancy said I could come if I wanted to, but we already have plans with Nana Alma and the wedding party is really for older people like you and Mama."

"Ugh!" Cullen clutched at his chest with both hands. "For such a low blow that shot went straight to the heart."

Carrie's cheeks flushed pink.

"You're not *old*-old, like Grandma, just *older*-old, like my teachers." She tried to apologize. "You know what I mean."

"I'm afraid I do and I resemble that remark."

Cullen started the engine, navigated the busy parking lot and turned the SUV toward home.

"Can I ask you a question?" Cullen tried to sound nonchalant, though his armpits were nervously damp as he approached an important subject.

"Sure."

"Are you okay with us? With me and your mama? That we're dating? Getting so close and all, if you know what I mean?"

"I get it, Cullen. I'm not stupid, despite what I did last night."

"Not to change the subject, because I want to talk about it some more, but since you brought last night up... Why did you go off like that without talking to your mother?"

"She didn't tell you?"

He shook his head. "She said that was up to you."

Carrie stared at the road before them and seemed to consider that news. He hoped she appreciated hearing that her mother had kept a confidence, even from him.

"I figured it was time I started making decisions on my own."

"Independence is good, but you're only

thirteen. Why would you want to cut the apron strings so soon?"

"Meg and Hope were so little when our daddy died that I'm not even sure they remember him." She turned glistening eyes to Cullen. "I remember everything. Mama looks at you the way she used to look at him. But it's different. There's no sadness."

"I love your mama, Carrie."

"She loves you, too, I can tell. So I figured I had to grow up and take care of myself so she'd have more time for you. I don't want her to be sad anymore."

Cullen felt a lump of emotion the size of Dallas form in his throat. He glanced in the rearview mirror, switched on his emergency flashers and pulled to the side of the road. He held his right arm out in invitation. Carrie moved in and hugged him as tightly as her seat belt would allow.

"Honey, I will never take your mama away from you and your sisters. You've suffered enough loss, we all have. If I'm fortunate enough to be a part of your life, then I intend to bless you, not steal from you."

"Do you really mean that?"

"With all my heart. But I'm new at this family stuff and I'm gonna need lots of help. Will you be my coach?"

"If you'll keep coaching me in baseball, I'll coach you in fatherhood." She extended her hand to shake on it.

"It's a deal." He gave her his hand.

She already had his heart.

CHAPTER TWENTY-ONE

"IT'S A PERFECT evening for a wedding," Sarah murmured to the summer sky as they stepped out Cullen's front door on Saturday and headed for his SUV.

As she admired the ocean of blue above their heads, he took full advantage of the opportunity to admire the beautiful picture she made in her colorful, calf-length sundress with the skinny straps across her bare shoulders. The ruffled skirt brushed the tops of the tall, oxblood leather classics that Cullen had buffed to a gloss, an accomplishment considering the mileage on the pair of boots.

"What are you doing back there?" she asked, realizing he hadn't left the front step.

"Sarah, darlin', I'm enjoying the view of you in that dress," he drawled.

She made a full twirl that caused her skirt to flare and then settle softly against her legs. He loved the fact that she was curved in all the right places and comfortable in her fair skin, never fretting because she wasn't rail-thin or the color of a tanned deer hide.

"The girls agreed that my boots go well with this prairie skirt, but I'm a little worried I'm done up like a thirty-nine-year-old Taylor Swift wannabe."

"Every inch of you is amazing and original, and those old Tony Lamas are the perfect touch."

"I'm glad Mama kept them for me all these years."

"Your mama's a smart lady and she understands that fine wine and well made cowboy boots increase in value with age."

"I hope you have the same opinion about women. You might take a little heat from your friends tonight for dating a decade above you when you're surrounded all day by females half my age."

"Six years is not a decade, and those girls can't stand in your shade. Why, you've forgotten more than those college kids have even learned. And here's something you'll appreciate about hanging out with a bunch of academics—their measuring stick is what's up here." He tapped her lightly on the temple. "If you pass that test you'll be tenured with my peeps."

"Peeps?" Her lips curved invitingly. "Did you really say 'peeps'?"

"Hey, I keep up. I'm hip to pop culture. I only *appear to be* an East Texas redneck."

"Wearing that sport coat and expensive straw hat, you resemble a Texas Ranger more than a redneck."

"A Ranger, huh?" He stretched an inch taller in his boots.

"The kind that wears a star, not cleats."

"Either way it's a compliment and I thank you, ma'am." He dipped his head and touched the brim of his hat.

Cullen's face warmed from her praise. He'd taken extra care to iron a white dress shirt and press a smart crease in his jeans. When he'd settled the summer-weight straw hat—custom-made for him by Texas Hatters over in Austin—on his head, Cullen had felt more like Hunt's twin than he had in years. His persnickety brother would approve. From the clean shave on his jaw, to the spit-shined toes of his boots, he was a man out to impress the woman he loved.

He moved close to slide his arm around her shoulders and give them a squeeze.

"I can't wait to get you on the dance floor at the Reo tonight."

"Can't you teach me somewhere less public, such as your living room?"

"Sarah, honey, back in the day, Jerry Lee and Elvis played the Reo Palm Isle. Why, it's a Texas landmark."

"Exactly! You wouldn't teach me to rollerblade in front of the Alamo, would you? So why let me make a fool of myself at the Reo where any country music legend passing through East Texas might drop by for a set?"

Cullen caught Sarah by the hand and pulled her into a sweetheart dance hold. The surprise in her wide eyes made his pulse skip with delight. He glanced left and right for other signs of life on his quiet street.

"We're all alone. My driveway will do just fine for your first lesson."

"Won't we be late for the wedding?" She caught her lower lip between her teeth.

"Stop makin' excuses. Just follow my lead and keep your eyes on mine."

As they began the basics he called the cadence to her softly. "Quick, quick, slow, slow. Quick, quick, slow, slow."

He talked out the steps while she caught on to the simple rhythm of the dance that had a tangle of roots from Europe and Mexico.

"It seems easy enough," she commented while concentrating on mirroring his footwork. "But it doesn't seem that way when I watch couples on the dance floor."

"That's because doing the two-step is like making chili or margaritas. People use the same basic ingredients, but there are endless combinations."

Cullen hummed "Amarillo by Morning" as he navigated a careful circle, heart to heart with his beloved. To end their first experience with flair, he smoothly led Sarah through a turn, caught her to his chest and gently dipped her backward over his arm, tightening his hold.

She rewarded him with a giggle that reminded him of Hope as he pulled her upright and stood her steady on both feet, her shoulders in the crook of his right arm.

"That was fun," Sarah admitted, brushing waves of auburn hair from her eyes.

"See? You were working yourself into a tizzy over nothing."

"I wasn't even close to a tizzy, but I will admit to a minor dither."

"Call it what you want but you were about to gnaw a hole in your lip." He bent to examine her mouth. "Here, let me kiss it for you."

SARAH MELTED INTO Cullen's kiss as if her life depended upon it. And maybe it did. She'd regained the joy of being a woman again in the weeks since he'd blessed her life. Wrapped in his strong arms right now, she'd never felt so alive. Their sighs mingled with their breathing as they gave and took control of the intimate moment.

A door slammed and footsteps slapped the sidewalk somewhere nearby. There was no chance it was her girls since she'd dropped them at Alma's before meeting Cullen at his house. Still, it was time to bring the sweet kiss to a reluctant end.

Cullen lifted his face, his gray eyes smiling down.

"I guess we'd better get going…unless you wouldn't mind being late to the ceremony?"

"And incur the wrath of Miss Nancy? Norment the Torment?" Sarah was still nervous when she encountered the woman. She didn't have Carrie's skill with the older woman— but then, as Cullen had already observed, nobody had that skill aside from Merle.

"Excellent point."

Cullen guided her to his freshly washed vehicle, opened the door and took her hand as she stepped up into the passenger's seat. Once she was seated, she flipped the visor down to check her hair and makeup and a woman she hadn't seen in ages peered back.

The blue eyes reflected the evening ahead of her, bright with pleasure and promise.

"THIS MUST BE the student Nancy caught you kissing in the lecture hall." The groom's comment could be heard by everyone in the receiving line. The guests snickered in response.

"Guilty as charged," Sarah admitted. There was no way to navigate around the truth so she might as well own up to it and laugh it off. She dared to glance at Cullen, who appeared unaffected, so she returned her attention to the groom.

"It's true, I'm taking one of Cullen's classes but, as you can see, I'm hardly the typical coed."

"Is there a chance for anything serious between you two, or are you participating in another one of his research efforts, like everybody claims?"

Research?

"I beg your pardon!" Cullen feigned offense. "How am I supposed to get valid data if the subject is aware of the blind study?"

Both men chuckled and Cullen waved away the exchange, then turned back to Sarah. "Pay him no mind, darlin'. He's been hitting the wedding punch."

"I'm sober as a judge," Merle insisted. "I'm just nosin' for a little insider information. I bought five squares on the pot Lanier drew up for how long it would take for you to finish dabbling in psychology and get down to business in the history department where you belong."

Miss Nancy jabbed a pointy elbow into her new husband's ribs hard enough to make him grunt.

"Ignore this big fool." Miss Nancy apologized to Sarah before saying to Merle, "If you poke that subject again it'll be the only thing you poke tonight, old man." She spoke the threat loud enough to crack up nearby listeners.

Then Miss Nancy smiled kindly at Sarah.

"I want you to know that your daughter was a life saver this week. I couldn't have gotten everything done without that girl. I hope you'll consider letting her take on a few hours with me in the fall."

"So she wasn't exaggerating? You really offered Carrie a job?"

"You better believe I did. She's got potential, reminds me of myself at her age, a diamond in the rough. Why, Carrie accomplished more in a few days than this boyfriend of yours probably has all summer."

"I can see this conversation is not going to end in my favor, so let's get something to eat."

Cullen took Sarah's hand and pulled her away from the receiving line and toward the tent set up for the reception.

"How nice to hear such kind words from Miss Nancy," Sarah enthused.

"It was certainly a new experience for me."

"What did Merle mean when he said I was part of your research?" She tried to sound casual, irritated by the older man's insinuation but not wanting to make an issue of the comment when his bride had been so good to Carrie.

"Search me. He's an eccentric old guy with a strange sense of humor. I suppose he was trying to be funny."

While they filled their plates with pulled pork and potato salad, other wedding guests approached and greeted Cullen. He was a perfect gentleman, hovering and solicitous, but introducing Sarah to his colleagues as his *good friend*. She squashed down a niggling instinct to be offended and resolved to put herself in his position, but it was a struggle. Did he think he was doing her a favor by not making a big deal out of their relationship?

They probably should have discussed the situation before they arrived.

He held out her chair and seated her at a table of folks she'd only just met and went to get them some cold drinks.

"So, I hear you have three daughters," a woman named Manuela commented. She was seated beside her husband, David, whom Cullen had introduced as his high school baseball coach.

"Indeed I do."

"How old are they?"

"Hope is seven, Meg is ten and Carrie will be fourteen in September."

"I met them when they were with Cullen at the batting cages," David interjected.

Sarah had to laugh at the memory of the girls' aches and pains after their first day of baseball.

"Cullen's taken my daughters under his wing to teach them about team sports."

"You couldn't have a better coach for your girls. Both he and Hunt had professional potential, but college didn't interest Hunt, and Cullen was always more of a bookworm than a hot corner."

"Hot corner?"

"That's baseball slang for third baseman," Manuela translated.

"The Temple twins were five tool players."

Sarah looked to his wife for another explanation.

"He means they had exceptional running and fielding skills, strong throwing arms and could hit for power and average."

"We're always recruiting coaching talent for the rec leagues. I'm glad to see Cullen experiment with the idea of working with kids."

Experiment? Was this college-speak or did these folks know something she didn't?

Sarah recalled something she'd heard earlier at Alma's when she'd gone inside with the girls to get them settled for the night. Alma had greeted each with a hug and called them Cullen's *pequeño proyectos*.

Little projects.

At the time Sarah had thought it was an odd thing to say but she'd chalked it up to being lost in translation.

Now she wasn't so sure.

CHAPTER TWENTY-TWO

CULLEN REJOINED THE TABLE, smiled at her as he placed a frosty glass of iced tea beside each of their plates and settled into his chair. He reached for the plastic squeeze bottle of barbecue sauce, gave it a shake and tipped it over his pulled pork.

"Hey, Temple, we heard you took a dive at the Rangers doubleheader last Sunday!" a male voice shouted from several tables away.

"Thanks for announcing it, Lanier." Cullen winked at Sarah and gave a wag of his neatly groomed head. "It was only a matter of time before that secret got out."

"So give us the color commentary," Lanier called out, obviously determined to have a laugh at Cullen's expense.

"That big goon has been heckling you since middle school," Coach Uprichard recollected. "Who would've guessed he'd parlay his years as a flyboy into a campus recruiter position?"

Cullen must have been imagining he had

Lanier's throat in his grasp instead of the sauce bottle, he squeezed it so tightly.

Too tightly.

The plastic lid popped off and a mixture of tomato paste, honey and vinegar erupted from the neck of the bottle with the force of Old Faithful and then flew in every direction, but mostly toward Cullen. His pristine white shirt, camel sport coat and starched jeans took the brunt of the gusher.

Wedding guests sucked in a collective gasp as Cullen jumped to his feet. Paper napkins were passed to him from around the table. He grabbed the nearest handful and sopped at the mess, smearing the sauce and spreading the stains.

The embarrassing moment of silence was shattered as Lanier called, "Way to go, Temple! That was better than instant replay of the game on the Jumbotron!" Applause broke out beneath the tent.

"What is the deal with people cheering for a guy who's just made a fool of himself?"

"We're glad it's you and not us," Lanier pointed out. The laughter that followed said the crowd agreed.

Sarah remained in her seat, stunned by his spate of public misfortune and certain that anything she did would only draw more attention and make the situation worse. There was no area of his body she could blot that wouldn't bring catcalls and suggestive comments from these people that Cullen would have to face again on Monday. So she simply dipped a cloth napkin into her water glass and offered it like a porter offering beach towels on the *Titanic*.

Cullen eventually gave up the effort and dropped into his seat. He recovered the plastic bottle and poured what was left of the sauce on his serving of pork.

"No point in letting good food go to waste." He licked his fingers and raised a thumbs-up sign for the onlookers, who gave a final round of applause.

"Well, Temple, if that performance doesn't send this pretty lady running for the hills, I'd say dabbling in a new field may be working out for you." Coach Uprichard patted Cullen on the shoulder.

There it was again. Another comment that made Sarah feel like some kind of lab animal.

Cullen gave her an apologetic glance and said, "I realize it's in the opposite direction, but unless you want to go out with me resembling a bus boy at the rib shack, we're going to have to go back to my house so I can change."

"You two kids got plans for later this evening?"

"Sure do, Coach. I'm taking this lovely lady dancin' at the Reo Palm Isle."

"Gosh, we haven't been there in years." Manuela stared pointedly at her husband.

"And we're not going to end my streak of luck tonight," Coach responded. "As soon they cut the cake we're making our getaway so I can catch the new episode of *Duck Dynasty.*"

"We'll give you a rain check," Sarah offered. "That is, if Cullen isn't afraid to be near me after I've trampled his boots on the dance floor."

"Temple's got stick-to-it in spades. He managed to see those other degrees through to the end and he'll make it through this new one, too."

A short while later, as an ensemble from the university stage band took their seats beside the dance floor, Cullen leaned close to Manuela. "Do you think Miss Nancy will understand if Sarah and I slip away before the music starts? Besides being a walking crime scene, the dampness has worked its way through my clothes and I've become a wet, sticky mess."

"You were here for the 'I do's' and made

it to the front of the receiving line. I'm sure Miss Nancy will forgive you, considering the circumstances." Manuela angled her eyes toward the pile of barbecue-sauce-splattered napkins beside his plate.

"Can we go, too?" The coach's voice was hopeful.

"You just keep your seat and come up with something nice to say about the happy couple when our table has to offer a toast," she instructed her husband.

"Actually," Cullen said. "I was wondering if you two would mind walking over to the bar with us while the waiter clears away this mess. Then it won't be too obvious that we're leaving."

"When did you sprout a social protocol gene?" Coach cocked an eyebrow at Cullen.

"When a beautiful woman became his primary subject matter, the same as with you thirty years ago," Manuela reminded her husband. "Now, let's escort these kids to the bar and you can buy me a glass of wine."

On the drive to Cullen's house, he seemed to be in a great mood in spite of his stained clothing. He hummed along with country tunes on the radio, which Sarah would normally find charming. But she couldn't help but turn the odd remarks that had been made at the wedding over and over in her mind.

Research.

Experiment.

Dabbling in a new field.

Subject matter.

Maybe people who worked at a university naturally spoke in such terms, but intuition said there was more to it than that. Something had given a number of people the same impression. Should she mention it to Cullen and risk upsetting the special evening ahead of them?

No. She was making much ado about nothing. Cullen was an open book, not a confidential file. As her mother had recently reminded her, she couldn't let Joe's decision to withhold the facts of his cancer make Sarah suspicious of another man's true intentions.

At the house Cullen unlocked his front door and bent to share a greeting with Rocket, who was very interested in his master's hickory-smoked scent.

"I'll jump in the shower and pull together a fresh set of clothes. I hope you won't mind making yourself at home for fifteen minutes."

"Of course not," she answered.

Cullen used the bootjack he kept by the door to shrug off his cowboy boots and then he and Rocket headed down the hallway. Moments later the door to the master bedroom thumped closed behind them.

Sarah followed Cullen's lead and used the wooden device to anchor the heel of her boot while she pulled her foot free of the snug-fitting leather. She padded into the kitchen, filled a glass with ice, poured herself a soda and headed to Cullen's cozy study.

She settled on the sofa with her feet drawn up beneath her flowing skirt and reached for the television remote on the end table. As she lifted the remote, she read the title of the book Cullen had evidently been reading.

Blended Family Dynamics: A Study in the Psychology of Starting Over.

She leafed through the text, noting the many pages Cullen had apparently streaked with yellow highlighter, his handwritten notes in the margins, the Post-it tabs that he'd applied in a dozen places. As she perused the information in the book her pulse stirred and then raced. But it was the legal pad underneath that caused her heart to skitter into an erratic beat. He'd written a to-do list of activities. As each event had occurred, it was checked off as completed, reviewed and then given a grade.

At-home activity: pool party, Grade D
First outing: amusement park, Grade D
Second outing: park and batting cages,
Grade C.
Third outing: Rangers game, Grade F
Fourth outing: Wedding…

As Sarah read the list, her curiosity turned to shock and then anger. She grabbed the book and looked at the title again. She had been feeling like a guinea pig with good reason. She was being used for Cullen's study, for his research! And even worse, her *children* were being used. He'd charmed them, made them all care about him, and all for what? Another degree?

Sarah dropped down on the sofa to think. There had to be a simple explanation. Cullen had seemed so sincere, always showing them consideration and thoughtfulness. Always giving them the benefit of the doubt and erring on the side of what would make them happy.

"These Temple boys know how to turn on the charm when it suits them, so watch out for their ulterior motives."

Sarah recalled Alma's warning.

Had she walked blindly into a snare and

led her daughters along behind her? The very idea chilled her to the bone on this hot summer evening.

CULLEN TOPPED HIS comfortable jeans with one of his many plaid flannels and moved down the hall silently in stocking feet. He'd left the ironing board up but had to switch on the steam iron to press another dress shirt.

"You need anything, darlin'?" he asked as he passed through his den and continued toward the laundry room.

Sarah was silent.

He stopped in midstride.

"Sarah? Are you okay?"

Angry eyes flashed up at him. An expression he'd never seen on her face told Cullen very little other than something was terribly wrong. She lifted her hand and held out his yellow legal pad. The one he'd used to track his progress with Sarah and her girls.

"What is this, Cullen?"

Her tone was flat. Her words an accusation.

"My private notes."

"It's too bad you didn't keep them in a private place."

"My den is my sanctuary. I didn't think I needed to hide my work."

"Your work? *Your work?*" Her voice crescendoed as she rose to her feet. "Is that what we've been to you, Cullen? Work?" Her voice broke on the last word.

"Yes, but…" He stopped.

How could he explain to her that structure was his comfort zone? That he required the safety of a process in order to have a relationship, otherwise he risked a setback in his PTSD recovery? Even to him it sounded crazy. And at one time he had believed he was sliding into that pit, behaving in a crazy way. He'd begun to fear how Sarah would react when she found out about the therapy. About the attacks.

And about the cutting.

She wouldn't want him around her girls anymore. She wouldn't want him around, period. And he couldn't blame her.

"But what?" she demanded. She lifted the book he'd been studying and brandished it like a sword. "Is analyzing people really more important to you than the people themselves?"

"Of course not, but that book is a means to an end."

"Well, you've come to this end sooner than you planned, Dr. Temple."

Sarah slung the strap of her purse over

her shoulder and stomped in stocking feet into the foyer. There she grabbed her boots in one hand and gripped the doorknob with the other. She paused with her back to him, as if giving him a chance to stop her from leaving. But what could he say that would change things?

Nothing.

Cullen Temple was damaged goods. Sarah Eason and her girls had already been dealt a tough hand. They didn't deserve to go through more hard times.

"You'll have to find yourself some new subjects to examine and evaluate." She turned to stare him down one last time. "You gave us *grades,* for crying out loud."

"No, I didn't," he defended himself softly.

"And now you're going to lie about it right to my face. I hate to admit it but my daddy was right. The fruit doesn't fall far from the tree. Sure enough, you've proven to be Pap Temple's grandson, after all."

She yanked the door open, stepped out of Cullen's home and out of his life.

CHAPTER TWENTY-THREE

WHEN THE SUN came up, Cullen didn't stir from the spot on the sofa where he'd sat all night. He didn't move when the Sunday paper thumped against the driveway, nor when the timer turned on the coffeemaker or when Rocket climbed up beside him, poked his long nose into his master's face and licked the tear streaks from his cheeks.

He sat still and waited for the inevitable moment when the anxiety he'd dreaded for so many years would wash over him and drown out the profound sadness in his heart.

It was Alma's voice on the old-fashioned answering machine that finally caught his attention.

"Cullen, *mi chico,* I know you're there. Pick up the phone *este minuto!*" This minute, Alma demanded. After several seconds without a response she continued. "We're on our way over, and if you don't let us in, Felix will chop a hole in your nice front door."

Still he kept his seat, his spirit as cold as

the dark side of the moon. Speechless since the moment Sarah had accused him of being just like his grandfather.

A liar.

The line disconnected, the buzz of the dial tone echoed in the room and Rocket whimpered for attention. Cullen pushed to his feet and followed his sweet pup across the room to the sliding glass door. He shoved it wide, stepped out into his yard and resumed his quiet stupor on the swing. The very place where he'd declared his love for a woman who now believed him to be dishonest, a user, a fraud.

Car doors slammed somewhere in the distance. Voices called out as fists pounded on wood. Rocket raced inside again and barked loudly at the intruders as Cullen followed.

"Cullen!" McCarthy shouted.

"Open this door, you big idiot," Joiner insisted.

"Don't make me beat you over the head with a wooden spoon." Hunt was only half joking since he'd done it once before.

"I'm coming!" Cullen hollered in response.

The moment he turned the dead bolt the door burst open and his brothers poured inside followed by Alma and Felix.

"What is this all about?" he asked his family.

"Sarah came to get the girls this morning and told me she was sorry but they wouldn't be staying with me again. She cried and said she'd learned some stuff about you last night that changed everything and you could no longer be friends." Poor Alma wrung her hands as she spoke, already attached to Hope, Meg and Carrie.

"What happened, little brother? She find out you still wear Underoos?" Joiner tried to make light of the moment.

"Hey, those will eventually come back into style. He's just ahead of the curve." Hunt wrapped his twin in a side embrace and refused to let go.

"I smell coffee. Let's go into the kitchen," Mac suggested.

Alma led the way, filled cups and set them on the counter along with sugar and cream, and the men helped themselves. Cullen allowed her to put his favorite mug in his hand and forced a few sips past his lips.

"Sit," Mac instructed everyone as he took the spot at the head of the table that had once been their daddy's seat. "What's this all about? I'm pretty sure Sarah is smitten with you. Did you have to break the news to her that you don't feel the same?"

"I love her." Cullen spoke into his coffee mug.

"What?" the table chorused.

"I said, I love her. I love Sarah," he replied sadly, realizing that now his emotions for her were wasted.

"Then what's the problem?" Mac demanded.

Cullen sent pleading eyes to Alma, who sat beside him, praying she'd understand and intervene. Spare him more pain than he was already in.

"Tell them," she said simply.

His heart stalled in his chest. Losing Sarah was almost more than he could bear. Losing the respect of his brothers would surely kill him.

"Tell us what?" Mac asked.

Cullen pushed his coffee cup away, dropped his gaze and then his hands into his lap. He was certain they would be trembling. But when he looked at them, his hands were steady, his palms dry. He curled his fingers into fists, and let his nails bite into his flesh so deeply that one pierced the tender skin. As he continued to stare, a tiny drop of blood appeared, bright red.

There had been a time when Cullen had associated that sight with a sense of control. As blood seeped from his body, a sense of relief would spread along with it. But those days when he'd been so helpless and hopeless that he'd taken a knife to his own flesh were long ago. He'd overcome the worst nightmare of his life. At least he'd thought so until today.

What would his brothers say if they learned the truth?

What would Sarah say?

"Tell them," Alma repeated.

On the other side of Cullen, Hunt pushed his chair away from the table and dropped to one knee so he could gaze up into his twin's face. Oblivious to the blood on Cullen's palm, Hunt took hold of his brother's hands and squeezed them tightly.

Cullen felt a single tear seep past his lower lashes and then watched as it splashed on the spot where their hands clasped.

Hunt quickly swiped the place with his thumb to hide it from the others.

Gray eyes sought gray eyes.

"Whatever it is, buddy, we'll deal with it together. We always have." Hunt's voice was sure and strong.

Between the two, there was an unbreakable bond that had carried them through great loss. It would see them through this, too, Cullen was certain of it. And he'd rely on it again to get through whatever lay ahead.

"I should have trusted all of you years ago." Cullen glanced around the table at his family.

"You're right." Hunt moved back into his seat. "But it's never too late, trust us now."

Cullen closed his eyes, dipped his chin. He sucked his lungs full of oxygen, drawing the strength to push the story out. He shook his head, ashamed to admit his weakness.

Maybe withholding the truth made him a liar, after all.

"Is this about you cutting yourself?" Joiner was matter-of-fact.

Cullen's head snapped up, expecting to see judgment, but finding understanding in the faces of his brothers.

He stared at Alma. "You told them?"

Her loving smile was sad. "They told me."

"But how did you know?" He'd been so careful to hide the signs.

"How could we not know?" Mac's voice sounded so much like their father's. "We lived under the same roof, shared a bathroom."

"Heck, I shared a *bedroom* with you," Hunt reminded him. "Did you think I was so self-involved that I wouldn't notice the cuts on your arms or the way you tried to hide them by covering up the evidence with long sleeves, even in the summer?"

"Now that you mention it, between girls, baseball and cast-iron skillets you were fairly distracted in those days," Cullen responded. "I guess I figured that since you never said anything, it meant you hadn't noticed."

"We figured out what you were doing, and we understood why," Mac assured Cullen. "All four of us were devastated when we lost Daddy and Mama, but we each handled it in a different way. Hunt took to camping out over at Pap's. Joiner took to horses and I took to numbers. Your way was the only one that was scary. So we told Alma."

She laid a gentle hand on Cullen's bare forearm where his sleeve was rolled up.

"That's when I took you to see Dr. Dermer. She saved your sanity and maybe your life."

Again, nods of agreement.

It was true. If Alma hadn't gotten him into therapy, he might be in a padded cell today, or worse.

"You knew about that, too?" Cullen looked to his brothers for a response.

"Alma agreed to keep us posted as long as we kept our mouths shut and let the doctor guide you through the anxiety in a healthy way," Joiner explained. "It's a shame you still believe you have to hide the scars from us after all these years, but we understand."

"So you didn't find my flannel shirts fashion-forward, after all?" Cullen joked as the silent, heavy burden he'd carried for so long began to lift.

"Even I'm aware that *flannel* and *fashion* have no place in the same sentence," Joiner responded.

"And that's why you were so quick to get in the pool with Sarah's girls the first weekend they came over."

"I realized you couldn't do it and they were dying for some horseplay."

"Thank you, Joiner." Cullen's voice was husky as he realized once more how much his brothers meant to him.

"No need to thank me. A dip in your pool on a hot summer day isn't exactly a hardship."

"Speaking of Sarah, what happened last night that caused this fallout?" Mac ventured into the other dark place.

"She found out I was studying family dynamics and drew the conclusion that I was just using her and the girls to test my interest in pursuing a psychology degree."

"Were you?" Alma asked.

"Of course not. But Sarah caught me off guard and before I could explain myself she started talking about her daddy and how he'd said the fruit doesn't fall far from the tree and that sooner or later I'd turn out like Pap."

"You wait till the next time I see that *viejo chisme* at the farmer's market. I'm gonna give him something to gossip about," Alma fumed, her arms crossed over her bosom to block out the idea of anyone disrespecting her Temple boys.

"Maybe there's something to what Sarah said. I've been lying to all of you for years, and creating a safe little world for myself where I wouldn't have to deal with the truth."

"That's hardly reason to equate you with a guy who stole a few million barrels of oil," Mac insisted.

"And now that you've admitted what you've been holding inside, it changes nothing about how much we love you, little brother," Joiner added. "And if Sarah loves you, too, it won't change what she feels, either."

"Cullen, you're the one who encouraged me to go for it with Gillian," Hunt reminded his twin. "Now let me do the same for you. Sarah's a special lady with adorable daughters. If you love them, then do more than study a family. Go be a family."

CHAPTER TWENTY-FOUR

It was a good thing Cullen had been able to nap after Alma made them all a big family breakfast on Sunday, because he didn't sleep a wink that night. By five o'clock Monday morning he was showered, shaved and resolved to catch Sarah before she left for work and explain everything face-to-face. If she didn't want him in their lives, at least he'd be sure. But he'd prayed throughout the night that she'd listen and maybe give him the benefit of the doubt.

The sun had only been up for a few minutes when he grabbed his keys and headed to the foyer. Rocket was already sitting at the door, his nose sniffing at the crack. An excited whimper and wag of his tail indicated there was something on the porch. The neighbor's cat probably, as he knew Cullen was an easy mark for a handout.

"Scat!" Cullen hissed as he pulled the door wide.

But instead of a pesky, yellow tabby there

was an auburn-haired beauty on his door-step. Her bluebonnet eyes were puffy and red-rimmed, matching his own.

"Sounds like I've come at a bad time," Sarah responded. "I realize it's early but I wanted to catch you first thing."

He watched for some sign that she'd be agreeable to the hug that would be so natural, but decided it was best to keep his instincts to himself.

"I was just about to leave." He rattled his keys.

"Can you give me a few minutes? I won't stay long."

"Actually, I had the same goal, to talk to you before you left for work. Please, come inside."

He stepped into the foyer and opened the door wide. As he watched Sarah pass, Cullen was aware of how small and fragile she seemed. Her carriage was normally confident and proud, but this morning her shoulders were slumped and her eyes were downcast. Whatever she had to say would only take a short while. His gut twisted; this couldn't end well.

"I have coffee," he offered as he followed her into his study.

"No, thanks." Her reply was sad.

He blinked hard, willing himself to remain in control. Whatever the outcome, he would not break down, he would not fall apart.

Not again.

His family would get him through whatever lay ahead.

He saw Sarah glance toward the table where his notepad and textbook had been the night before, but those things were gone. The book was in back in the stack belonging to Blair and the legal pad had been tossed in the trash along with the Sunday newspaper. Some things shouldn't be learned from books, shouldn't be studied. Some things were meant to be experienced hands-on, up close and personal.

He'd been a fool to believe he could treat a family as if it were a class called Fatherhood 101. Families didn't come with a syllabus made of paper. They came with hearts that could be broken, emotions that could be damaged and bodies that could be scarred.

"I've come to apologize," Sarah said softly.

"If anybody should apologize, it's me," he disagreed.

"That's not true. Cullen, whatever your reasons were for doing what you were doing, they were your own and it was not for me to judge. I just wish you'd been up-front with me from the first."

"Wait—"

She held up her hand to stop him. "Let me get through this, please." Her voice broke.

He nodded, the thumping of his heart resounding in his ears.

"When I repeated what my daddy said to Mama, I was completely out of line. I don't believe those words for a moment and he really doesn't believe them, either, especially now that my mama's worked his clock over for spreading fifty-year-old gossip."

"Then why did you say it?"

"I was hurting. I was hurting and I wanted you to hurt, too. Maybe I was never truly close to your heart, but I knew your family was everything to you. So I lashed out at them and I've been ashamed of myself ever since. If one of my girls said something so ugly I'd ground her for a month."

"Is there more?" He wanted to make sure she had her say, wanted to make sure they covered everything since he may never get another chance.

"Almost." Sarah hesitated as if uncertain whether or not to go on. She squared her shoulders and continued. " Joe learned his diagnosis months before he confided it to me. I understand he meant to spare me the grief for as long as he could, but deep inside it felt like a betrayal to me. As if he didn't completely trust me with the weight of his fear. Mama says I shouldn't let that color the way I view other men, but I can't seem to help it. And what you've done sure didn't improve the situation." She bowed her head, swiped away a tear.

"Mama also says forgiveness is something you do for yourself, not for the other person. You had your reasons, just as Joe did. I forgave him long ago but I never told him so. I can't have that on my conscience again so I want you to know I forgive you, Cullen. It's a lot to ask, but can you forgive me in return?"

"You were forgiven the moment you walked out the door and I realized there was more truth to your accusation than you even realized."

Auburn brows pulled together over puzzled eyes the color of a summer morning sky. Cullen slowly extended one arm and offered Sarah his hand, praying all the while that she'd take it and never let go.

Especially after he revealed the secrets he'd kept for too long.

SARAH PRESSED HER palm to Cullen's and her pulse raced as if their very hearts had reconnected. She wanted desperately to wrap her arms around his waist and lay her cheek against his chest, draw strength from him on whatever level he was willing to offer it. She should be ashamed to love him so unconditionally, but wasn't that what giving your heart was all about?

He tugged her to the sofa, sat and pulled her down beside him.

"I have to show you something. Until you see this, nothing I have to say will make sense."

He released her hand. The loss of his touch was painful.

He reached for the collar of his shirt and unfastened the top button. Then the second button. Then the third. But there was nothing sensual about this undressing. His dark eyes were intense as he stared at her hard, telegraphing a fear she'd never seen in his face before this moment.

With all the buttons unfastened he pulled the front of his shirt open wide.

"Ta-da!" He voiced the classic fanfare as he revealed the Rangers shirt the girls had bought him underneath his flannel.

The chuckle they shared dulled the intensity of the moment, and they both took a breath.

"Is that what was so important?"

"No. But as long as I was doing show-and-tell I figured I'd better start with something positive. Something special."

"You did well. Buying that shirt for you was entirely Meg's idea. Hope helped her pick it out and Carrie used her savings to pay for it. They wanted a gift for their now-daddy."

The glint of tears in his eyes made Sarah regret using the nickname, but there had to be complete honesty between them, even if they would only remain friends.

"Let's see the rest," she encouraged him.

Cullen stood, shrugged out of his shirt and then sat down beside her. He pushed the sleeves of his T-shirt up to his shoulders and stretched out his bare arms. Even in the dim light of the room she was able to appreciate his fine, strong athletic build for the first time.

He waited.

"What?" she asked.

"Look closer."

She focused on his hands, tanned from hours outdoors with the girls. Her eyes roamed up to his wrists where the dusting of dark hair began. His forearms were defined from years of working out, the muscles that connected the two bones evident and strong.

Her gaze scanned upward to his biceps, triceps and deltoids, the chisel of his body obvious even without the tan on his forearms. There was clearly something there he wanted her to notice. She reached out her hand, placed it on his arm just above the elbow and smoothed it upward over his warm skin.

When she encountered the web of lines her hand stopped and so did her heart.

"What in the world?" Sarah muttered.

She stood, caught Cullen by the hand and pulled him out the patio door. In the morning sunshine there was no mistaking the healed but always present marks.

Scars.

From cutting.

She recognized the sight from evidence photos she'd seen at their law firm. They'd defended a man arrested for harm to a child and proven to the court that his son's scars were not from abuse but from cutting. At work, she'd recoiled from the sickening, still-fresh images.

Sarah was unable to grasp a kid making such a bizarre cry for help, but had to accept that it was very real and could happen to any of her daughters if she was not vigilant about their mental health.

But Cullen…?

"How? When?" She could hardly get the words out, couldn't stop staring at the secret Cullen had hidden. Was there more?

Cullen took her hand again and led her to the swing where they'd been sitting the moment he'd claimed to love her. They settled close on the wooden slats and she sat quietly as he spoke.

"Within weeks of losing my folks, I started to experience anxiety attacks. I didn't understand what was happening at first, I just assumed I was nervous and jumpy from not getting enough sleep. I had horrible nightmares about the plane crash. I couldn't shut my eyes without imagining what Mama and Daddy must have gone through in those last moments. So, I avoided my bed at night. I'd sit in Daddy's favorite chair in front of the television or with a book, fighting sleep until I passed out. I would stay awake for so many hours that I'd get shaky and dizzy. When the world would spin from exhaustion, my only choice was to go to bed and sleep it off. But burying my head under the covers came with its own set of problems and I couldn't keep it to myself or make my fears go away."

Sarah watched Cullen's freshly shaved face as he verbalized the painful memories, the creases around his eyes deepening as he squinted against the mental images.

"Where were your brothers when this was going on?"

"They were dealing with grief, too, but in different ways."

She nodded, understanding. After Joe's death she'd become keenly aware that each girl's suffering was personal and individual. She'd kept a close eye on her daughters, especially Carrie. Self-injury seemed to be an expression of the Goth culture, one of the reasons Sarah let Carrie use hair color and makeup to demonstrate her individuality.

"How about Alma and Felix?"

"They moved in with us so we could stay in our home, but we were all teenagers by then so they gave us our space. On the surface we seemed to be handling our new normal, but each of us had to find a way to cope."

"And you found this way?" She placed her hand on his arm, touching the marks on his exposed skin as if she was touching the hidden scars on his heart.

"I could sense when an attack was coming on. I learned the signs—my pulse would race for no reason, my palms would sweat, my attention span would evaporate so that I couldn't concentrate on my studies or baseball practice. It was a chain reaction that had to be broken before it got out of control. One day at school the symptoms hit and it felt like my skin was crawling. I dug my nails in deep and the pain helped ease the panic."

He crossed his arms and gripped his biceps tightly to show what he meant.

"I focused on the pain and the jitters, and the pounding of my heart got better. I thought I'd beaten the attack, but when I got home that afternoon everything started again. I was desperate for relief."

Cullen dropped his chin and closed his eyes. Sarah watched and waited as he collected himself. He sucked in strength and opened his eyes but kept them fixed on his hands.

"I was the only one at the house and I considered getting into the expensive bottle of Scotch that Daddy kept for special occasions. But the seal had never been broken on the bottle, and even though he was gone, it still seemed like stealing. I couldn't do it. I went to their bathroom and poked around in Daddy's side of the medicine cabinet, wondering if he kept any narcotics that would help."

Cullen clenched and unclenched his fists,

seemed to struggle for breath. Sarah reached for his hand, entwined her fingers with his and held on tightly, willing into him the little bit of peace she'd been able to hold on to over the past thirty-six hours.

"Fishing through the nasal spray and hair tonic, I came across his old double-edged safety razor, the kind that opened when you twisted the handle. Next to it was a little packet of blades. I unfolded the paper cover and ran my finger across the edge, pressing just hard enough to break the skin and release a drop of blood."

He raised his eyes to hers, pleading forgiveness without words. Sarah desperately wanted to stop him from sharing more, to tell him it was okay, to tell him it didn't matter. But that wasn't true. What Cullen had been through mattered almost more than anything in his life. His struggle deserved to be told and, in his way, he was sharing his deepest heart with her.

"Go ahead." She encouraged him to continue.

"You can look at my arms and figure out the rest. That day I found a distraction, a fascination that was more real than all the strange symptoms I was experiencing. But I was aware from the very first cut that it was wrong and it could only be temporary, something I had to hide from my brothers."

"But they figured it out?"

He laughed to himself as if finding humor in the question.

"I never thought so but it seems they deserved more credit than I gave them. Hunt knew all along and eventually said something to Alma. The jig was up one day when she sat me down and explained she'd made an appointment for me with a therapist. I've learned a great deal since then about posttraumatic stress disorder. Dr. Sue not only saved my hide, she saved my life."

He rotated his arm and exposed a wide scar on the soft inside of his bicep.

"Another incident like that and I might have bled to death. It probably should have had stitches but I was too ashamed to show anybody. I bandaged it myself with butterfly closures from our first aid kit and prayed it would heal."

"How long did this go on, Cullen?"

"A couple of years. Even with therapy I'd still cut occasionally. It took a while for me to be able to recognize and avoid my stressors. Plus, they're right when they say that time heals all wounds. I was finally able to stop cutting when I started college and began to focus my mind on new studies. Going from one degree to another became my coping mechanism. I've learned to keep my mind so crowded with historical facts that there's no room for fear. It's what worked for me, but it may be something completely different for another PTSD survivor."

Post traumatic stress disorder.

"Is that why you've decided to study psychology now?" Sarah approached the subject that had to be discussed before she could begin to find healing for this new break in her heart.

Cullen shook his head, adamant.

"You totally misunderstood the deal with the book and my notes the other night."

"Why didn't you say so right there and then?"

"I was caught off guard. And frankly, I was embarrassed to look like such an idiot. And second, because I knew that before you could understand why I needed to approach you and the girls that way, that I'd have to explain this." He held out his arm, once again calling her attention to the crisscross of thin, white lines. "I wasn't prepared to expose my secret and risk losing you all."

"So you weren't studying us? You weren't

experimenting with different situations and grading the outcome?"

"Yes, I suppose that's all true. Sarah, I've forgotten what a family feels like. I don't know anything about little girls, and girls who've lost their daddy at that. In my defense I learn from reading, making notes, exploring. How else could I find a way to fit in permanently with a ready-made family?"

"*Permanently?* So we're not just a short-term project for you?"

Cullen shifted in the swing to place a gentle hand on either side of Sarah's jaw, drawing her face to his.

"Darlin', listen to me." His voice was husky and thick with emotion, his eyes brimming with tears, just like the ones that shimmered on her own lashes. "I love you. I love your girls. I want to build a life with the four of you. I want us to be a family."

"But you gave us such poor grades," she whispered.

"Those grades weren't for you. *They were for me.* I know my progress report seems grim right now, but I'm willing to bring the scores up, stay after class, do extra credit, anything it takes."

They shared a smile at the silly metaphor,

but then he sobered again and pulled her face closer.

"I don't want to be a now-daddy. I want to be a forever-daddy—if you and the girls will give me the chance."

Sarah's heart beat erratically as she slid her hands up to grasp Cullen's wrists. She turned her eyes to first one of his arms and then the other, pausing to kiss the scars he'd inflicted on himself, then suffered through alone. And as she touched her lips to the faded marks, Sarah vowed silently that he'd never be alone again.

She wrapped her hands around his neck, twined her fingers behind his head and pulled his mouth to hers as their kisses, tears, hearts and lives melted together.

In an instant, the difficult years of the past were overcome and they became a forever-family.

CHAPTER TWENTY-FIVE

CULLEN OPENED THE door of the jewelry store and let all his girls step through first, just as Alma had reminded him to do when they'd conspired over the shopping trip weeks earlier. Sarah's fortieth birthday was a special occasion and deserved a gift she would treasure forever.

"Good afternoon," the woman behind the counter greeted them. "May I help you folks?"

"We're going to look around for a bit," Cullen replied. "These young ladies want to buy their mother a gift."

"Certainly. Just wave if you want me to show you something."

"Go ahead, girls." He swept his palm outward, indicating they were free to roam. "Help your mama find something pretty from me, too. There's no rush. I'm gonna check out a new wristwatch for myself."

The jeweler behind the counter nodded at Cullen to note their arrival and then disappeared into the workshop where custom designs were created by hand.

"Let's see some bracelets," Carrie insisted as she pulled her mother in the direction of the sparkling glass cases.

"Yeah, maybe the kind that has charms," Hope suggested, unable to keep their secret any longer.

"Shush!" Meg gave her baby sister a stern warning.

Sarah bent forward to peer through the countertop as the girls pointed out first one style of sterling link chain and then another.

"Are you ladies shopping for anything in particular?" the woman behind the counter asked.

"A bracelet for Mama," Carrie explained.

"It's her fortieth birthday," Hope announced.

"You're not supposed to tell people she's so old," Meg admonished her sister.

The saleswoman's brows shot up and she grinned. "Out of the mouths of babes."

"You got that right." Sarah returned the smile. "And now that the cow is out of the barn, I guess there's no point in trying to close the gate. Yes, today's my big 4-0 and my daughters want to get me something special."

The store owner reappeared with a slender, rectangular box in his hand and moved toward them.

"I just happen to have something special right here. Would you like to see it?"

"Yes!" the girls shouted, and danced. Even Carrie bounced up and down on her toes, every bit as excited as her siblings that their surprise was going to be revealed.

The owner removed a black velvet case from the box and placed it atop a jeweler's display tray. The girls gathered around their mama, and Cullen moved behind her and placed his hands on her shoulders.

"Open it, Mama," Meg pleaded. "Too much suspense isn't good for an older person's blood pressure."

"Oh, great." Sarah glanced over her shoulder at Cullen. "Now she has age issues to be concerned about. A whole new world of worries just opened up and swallowed us whole."

"Just open the box, darlin'," he encouraged her, every bit as excited for the surprises to come.

Sarah lifted the box and flipped open the velvet lid. Nestled on a bed of white satin lay an antique curb-link bracelet molded from the finest sterling silver the mines near El Paso, Texas, had once produced. At Cullen's

request, the jeweler had polished the chain
to restore its luster and updated the bracelet with four button charms, each encrusted
with colored stones on one side, and names
engraved on the other. Amethyst for Carrie,
emerald for Meg, sapphire for Hope and ruby
for Cullen.

"Happy birthday to you," they broke into
song as Cullen fastened the dazzling piece
around Sarah's slender wrist.

"Wait a minute." The store owner snapped
his fingers. "I just remembered there's more."

All eyes followed as he produced a key
from his pocket and fitted it into a locked
cabinet built into the counter behind him.
Reaching inside he found a small red velvet
bag that closed with a drawstring.

"Sir, I believe this is also part of your special order."

As the manager poured the contents of the
bag into Cullen's hand, his heart thumped
hard against his ribs and his palms grew
moist. But with excitement, not fear.

He dropped to one knee in front of God
and Sarah's three daughters and offered them
signs of his unending love. He slipped a tiny
circle of diamonds on the ring finger of each
girl's left hand, and informed them it was to
be worn until it was replaced by an engage-

ment ring one day from a boy that Cullen himself would approve.

Then he reached for Sarah's hand.

"My sweet Sarah, I'm not so much of an East Texas redneck that I didn't realize I needed to get your daddy's permission before asking you to be my wife. He didn't exactly give his blessing, but he said he'd be honored to walk you down the aisle whenever you're ready to say 'I do.'"

Cullen didn't dare look in the direction of the sniffling group of girls or he'd forget everything else he'd practiced that morning in front of the mirror.

Sarah's mama and Alma had helped him pick out the platinum-and-diamond ring, and they'd both agreed it was magnificent. Now, he slipped the ring onto Sarah's hand.

"Will you marry me, darlin'?"

She nodded, unable to speak. He stood and folded her in his arms, her tears hot against his shoulder.

"Are those happy tears?"

"Yes," she whispered. "Cullen, you've done so much to put our family back together. How can I ever show you how much I love you in return?"

"One more little girl should do the trick,"

he replied from the bottom of his mushy heart.

And he meant it.

What could be more fun than a house filled with female laughter, squabbling, worries and wonder?

As long as the good Lord was willin' and the creek didn't rise, Cullen Temple was about to find out.

EPILOGUE

"A‍RE YOU SURE you want to share the spotlight with us? There's still time to change your mind." Sarah gave Gillian one last chance to say she wanted to be the only bride at the ceremony on her wedding day.

"I wouldn't dream of it," Gillian insisted. "We're marrying identical twin brothers and I'm fairly sure that means we're going to be sharing for the rest of our lives. This is the perfect start for all of us."

"You are stunning in that Vera Wang ball gown. It must have cost a fortune." Sarah had browsed the couture designer's site just for fun and the price of a one-of-a-kind dress would purchase a three-bedroom home in Kilgore.

"It probably did, but it was a present and I never dared to look this gift horse in its mouth."

"A present?"

"Last year when the celebrity couple who were going to get married at Temple Territory called off their wedding, the bride refused to take the dress. It couldn't be returned and she didn't want any part of it so she told me I could keep it."

"That's amazing! The grand staircase of Temple Territory is going to look like a scene from *Gone with the Wind* when you glide down those steps on your father's arm, Gillian."

"I wish you'd enter by the stairs, too."

Sarah shook her head. "Nope, that spotlight is yours alone. I'd probably stop, drop and roll—not quite what either of us intend for our guests' entertainment today."

The two brides shared a laugh and a sip of champagne.

"You're beautiful, too, Sarah. That vintage lace gown your mother made is breathtaking."

Sarah slid her left hand down the bodice of the mermaid-style dress and admired the lace that had belonged to her grandmother.

"I'll share a secret with you. Mama took my first wedding gown apart and used the layers of lace to sew this one. It's meaningful on so many levels."

"Does Cullen know?"

"It was his idea. Mama pulled it out of her cedar closet the night of our engagement dinner, and Cullen said it was a shame to let such intricate handiwork go to waste. The dress was horribly out of style, though, so Mama and I had no qualms about ripping it apart to be repurposed." Sarah's voice fell to a whisper. "It felt as if the dress was going through the same thing I'd gone through, so we all agreed it was fitting and right."

Emotion swelled in the eyes of both brides and they dabbed at the corners with blue hankies that had once belonged to the twins' mother. Alma had given one to each bride at the rehearsal the night before, asking them to carry it with their bouquet as a sign of what would surely be her blessing on their marriages.

A soft knock on the door brought them out of the private moment and back to the present.

"Ladies, are you ready?" Gillian's father asked.

"Come in, Daddy."

Sarah's father followed on James Moore's heels. The fathers of the brides were never more handsome than this moment in their black tuxedo jackets with tails and top hats.

"I feel like a Barnum and Bailey ring leader in this thing," Sarah's daddy complained. "But if my baby girl asked me to dress up as Bozo the Clown that would be okay, too."

"I must say I appreciate you ladies choosing black tuxes instead of the powder blue my wife made me wear at our own wedding," James said.

Roger Callaghan burst out laughing and slapped James on the back.

"The lengths a man will go to make his womenfolk happy would try the patience of Job."

"Do you think we should warn our future sons-in-law?" Gillian's father asked.

Sarah's daddy wagged his gray head. "Heck, no. We had to figure it out on our own and they should, too. It shapes a man's character in ways nothing else can, not even the military."

Music could be heard from downstairs, their two-minute warning cue.

Sarah took her father by the hand. "Remember, Daddy, we're taking the elevator down to the first floor so we can go through the back hallway and enter from the terrace."

"I was here for the rehearsal, missy, and I'm not so forgetful that you have to remind me what happened last night."

"I, on the other hand, am quite feeble-minded," Gillian's daddy admitted as she took him by the elbow. "Tell me when to step off and pinch me if I go too fast."

The brides wished each other good luck and Sarah tugged her father toward the elevator. As they found their marks downstairs and the glass doors were about to be swept wide, Sarah caught a glimpse of Cullen under the archway made of yellow calla lilies. He'd chosen her favorite flower! The thoughtfulness and insight of the man who would share the rest of her life caused Sarah to gasp with joy.

"Honey, I need to tell you something." Her father forced her eyes away from her beloved.

"Can't it wait, Daddy? We're kinda busy here."

"It won't take long and you should hear what I have to say before you tie the knot with that boy."

Oh, please Lord, no lectures on the history of the Temple family right now!

"Daddy, Cullen's not a boy. He's a grown man. Accomplished, respected and successful. He loves me and adores my girls, so how could this possibly be wrong?"

Bushy eyebrows knitted together in a scowl.

"Who said anything about this being wrong?"

"You did every time you brought up Cullen's grandfather."

"Has your mother been repeating gossip again? I swear that woman couldn't keep a secret to herself if it was sewn inside her brassiere."

Sara snickered in spite of the seriousness of the moment.

"Cullen Temple is a fine man. Actually, Pap Temple was, too, only he had a greedy streak in him two ax handles wide. What I wanted to say before we walk down this aisle together is that this union has more than my approval. It has my blessing."

"Thank you, Daddy. I love you." Sarah kissed his freshly shaved cheek. She almost raised her blue hanky to wipe away the scarlet lip prints but decided he should be wearing that badge of surrender when he handed his only daughter over to her groom.

CULLEN'S HEART THUMPED hard beneath the black onyx studs of his tuxedo shirt. The white bow tie cinched tighter around his neck. His breathing became difficult, like two fists had reached into his chest and squeezed his lungs without mercy. His pulse surged a message through his amygdala.

Danger! Danger! Danger! the fear center of his brain warned him over and over again.

Cullen felt the corners of his mouth lift in a lovesick grin as he experienced the fight or flight sensation he'd been looking forward to since Sarah and the girls had accepted his proposal. It was more intense than his worst panic attack and more fun than his first free fall in the Tower of Power at Six Flags.

He couldn't wait to experience life with four females!

He was certain he looked good on this most special of all days because his mirror image stood six feet away beneath his own arch of flowers. Hunt had chosen violet orchids because he said they matched Gillian's eyes.

The string quartet began Pachelbel's *Canon in D Major*. Joiner escorted Gillian's mother to her seat and McCarthy walked Sarah's mother through the guests and to her front row seat, as well. The two older brothers took their positions of honor beside the grooms as best men, Joiner with Cullen and McCarthy with Hunt.

Next down the aisle marched the precious girls Cullen would make his legal daughters as soon as he and Sarah returned from their honeymoon in Ireland. Then he'd officially be their forever-daddy. He stepped down from the archway to give each girl a loud and silly kiss on the cheek as they passed before him on the way to their seats.

During the final strains of the classic processional, Cullen took a moment to seek out and remember special faces in the crowded room. Alma and Felix, beaming as proudly as any two natural parents. Blair and Ailean, back from Italy for the occasion. Coach Uprichard and his wife, Manuela, who would mentor the girls' baseball team Cullen had signed up to manage. High school friends and university colleagues had come to support the Temple brothers, and Cullen was reminded that God is good, all the time.

The quartet moved effortlessly into Wagner's *Bridal Chorus,* the terrace doors were opened, the guests stood and all heads swiveled toward the stunning red-haired bride in a white lace gown that hugged her curves and showed off her fair skin to perfection. When Sarah and her father stopped before Cullen, he struggled with the desire to take her in his arms and kiss her before the vows were said.

But true to their promise to Hunt and Gillian, Cullen and Sarah turned with the guests and gave their attention to the grand staircase as the second bride floated down twenty-five steps on the arm of her father.

Over the next hour, vows and rings were exchanged, heads were bowed for prayers, unity candles were lit and somewhere in the back of the room Rocket barked his approval when Cullen and Hunt kissed their wives for the first time.

Temple Territory was finally a place filled with great joy and family celebration, just as Mason Dixon Temple had hoped it would be all those years ago.

* * * * *

USA TODAY Bestselling Author

Ingrid Weaver

Finders Keepers

INGRID WEAVER

began her writing career by propping an old manual
typewriter on her children's play table. Twenty years
later she is a *USA TODAY* bestselling author of thirty
books and the recipient of a Romance Writers of
America RITA® Award. She currently resides on a farm
near Frankford, Ontario, with her family and a varying
collection of critters.

Other books by Ingrid Weaver

HARLEQUIN HEARTWARMING

WINNING AMELIA

CHAPTER ONE

IT WAS THE Harley she noticed first. A bike like that was hard to miss in a sleepy, small town like Port Hope, Ontario. Sunlight flashed from the chrome, momentarily blinding Brittany Barton as she carried two orders of fries to the teenage girls at the front table. She squinted through the window. Several adolescent boys had noticed the bike, too. They clustered on the curb, trying to act cool as they postured for the girls who pretended not to be watching them.

What was it about a motorcycle, especially an in-your-face, old-school machine like a Harley-Davidson, that conjured up images of rebellion and adventure? Even a twenty-four-year-old woman who had been there, done that, and should know better wasn't immune to the mystique, that lure of the open road. Brittany hated the way her pulse danced, and her breathing wasn't quite steady, because of course it wasn't the bike she reacted to, it was the memory of a particular boy who used to ride one.

It had been nearly eight years since she had seen Jesse Koostra. He'd been everything her mother had warned her about, the quintessential bad boy: tall, tough and wickedly handsome. He had a voice as sensual as dark chocolate that fuelled her dreams like the rumble of his Harley.

Countless summer nights she would lie awake in her bedroom under the eaves, restless and sweaty, listening to the crickets and the hum of mosquitoes on the screen while she waited to hear the distinctive echo of the engine as Jesse made his way home. His family lived a mile down the road from the Barton farm on a piece of land that was mostly swamp. Their yard and barns were crammed with vehicles in various states of disrepair. Old, rusted-out cars seemed to be the only crop his father raised. As for Jesse and his sister, they were allowed to grow wild.

Brittany had longed to be free like them, but she hadn't had the nerve. Instead, she dutifully did her homework, weeded the garden and tended the chickens. She tried her best to live up to everyone's expectations, all the while secretly yearning for the next time she would see Jesse.

Pathetic, wasn't it? What was worse, the unrequited crush of her childhood years had so warped her mind that she later searched for a bad-boy like Jesse in every man she met.

Apparently, she was still doing it, because the longer she looked, the more it appeared as if the bike parked in front of the restaurant didn't simply resemble Jesse's, it was *precisely* like his, right down to the hand-painted wolf adorning the blue gas tank.

No. It couldn't be his. He'd disappeared right after the trial.

The bell above the front entrance tinkled. Sunshine streamed past the man who stepped into the doorway, hiding his features in shadow.

But Brittany didn't need to see his face. Her heart had already felt his presence.

CHAPTER TWO

"HELLO-OO?" THE sing-song question came from one of the girls at the window table. It was followed by a quick succession of finger-snaps and muffled giggles. "Those fries are for us, right?"

Brittany realized she was still holding the plates. Speechless. Frozen in place. Like an idiot. And all because Jesse Koostra stood less than six feet away.

Terrific. And here she'd believed that she'd come a long way in eight years.

She deposited the plates and pasted on a smile for the teenagers, but she could have saved the effort. They were no longer looking at her, or at their cooling French fries. Their attention had shifted to a point just past her shoulder. One of the girls was actually blushing.

Okay, so evidently idiocy was contagious. Or maybe no female, regardless of age, was resistant to whatever it was that Jesse exuded.

Brittany wiped her hands on her apron. She

hated the fact that his mere presence could make her palms damp. She also hated the frilly, pea-green apron her Aunt Mae insisted all the waitresses wear. This wasn't how she'd fantasized being dressed when she saw Jesse again....

Stop it! she told herself. *He's just a man. A customer. Who'll likely tip better than the rude girls. Besides, he probably doesn't even recognize you.*

Buoyed by that thought, she kept her smile firmly in place as she turned. "Hi. Welcome to Mae B's. Table for one?"

"I'm supposed to meet someone here, but it looks like I'm early."

Oh, great. How could she pretend to be professional when his voice was the same as she remembered, deep and rich and unhurried, as if there was nothing he would rather be doing than talking to her. She kept her gaze on his chest, which was easy to do since the top of her head scarcely reached his shoulders. If she thought that would minimize his effect on her, she was wrong. His battered leather motorcycle jacket hung open over a white T-shirt that clung to every muscular contour. She caught a whiff of fresh air, sunshine and designer cologne.

Designer cologne? On a trouble-making bad-boy like Jesse?

But people could change. Heaven knows she had. She lifted her gaze.

It should have been impossible for him to get better-looking, but he had. His jaw was squarer, his cheeks leaner. The dimples beside his mouth had elongated and deepened. His distinctive, ice-blue eyes were more enthralling than ever. And his hair, oh, that lovely, fine blond hair that he used to keep tied back in a dashingly romantic ponytail a decade ago was cut short, the perfect length to run her fingers through. Her hands tingled with the urge....

"Okay if I sit at the booth in the back?"

She caught herself before she could dry her palms again. "Sure. Go ahead and sit anywhere. Would you like something cool to drink while you're waiting?"

"Thanks. Iced tea would be great."

Iced tea? Jesse? "Uh, coming right up."

Rather than moving away, he tilted his head to study her. "Don't I know you?"

CHAPTER THREE

DON'T I KNOW *YOU*?

At least a dozen responses sprang to Brittany's mind. No, Jesse had never really known her. To him she would have been the chubby kid next door, his quiet and clumsy friend. At least, she hoped it was friendship he felt, though it could have been pity. He wouldn't have a clue how fervently she had adored him, or how many lovesick glances she'd hidden behind the curtain of her hair.

She remembered well the day she'd cut her hair short. She'd been sixteen, and it had hung almost to her waist. She dared to think it was pretty, until one of the kids on the school bus called her Cousin Itt, the short, hairy creature from *The Addams Family*. The other names they called her, like stumpy or porko, didn't hurt as much as being ridiculed for her beautiful hair. She'd lopped it off with her sewing shears that night.

Jesse had already disappeared by then. She hadn't realized it would be for good. She as-

sumed he would come back once the public-
ity stirred up by the trial ran its course, and
the sightseers and treasure hunters stopped
traipsing around the Koostra place. Jesse
wasn't shy or ugly or awkward like her. He
was strong and fearless. He wouldn't care
what people said or thought. Besides, it was
his father who had been convicted, not him.

But the family never returned. Sometimes at night, Brittany glimpsed a light at
the house or moving around the yard or flick-
ering through the trees, and her pulse would
do the little dance it always did at the thought
of seeing Jesse. Yet the property remained
vacant, even during the years she'd been on
the road herself.

Then how could he recognize her now?
Her hair was short and streaked with purple.
It couldn't hide anything, including the metal
studs on the rims of her ears. And her waist
was so small, she had to make a double bow
with the strings from Aunt Mae's frilly apron
so the ends wouldn't hang past her knees. On
the outside, she wasn't the same person. She
believed she'd changed on the inside, too.

Jesse smiled. "You're Brittany Barton,
aren't you?"

Oh, great. Whatever progress she might
have made just evaporated. His smile had

the same effect it always did. It made her feel special, warm, cherished....

And idiotic. She dipped her chin once in what she hoped was a casual nod. "Yes, that's me."

"I'm Jesse." He thrust out his right hand. "Jesse Koostra. My family used to live down the road from yours. Don't you remember me?"

The question was so absurd, it brought out an answering smile. She took his hand without thinking.

CHAPTER FOUR

THE HAND THAT enclosed Brittany's was warm and gentle. She thrilled at the contact. For an instant, the restaurant smells and sounds disappeared and she was once more an eight-year-old girl with skinned elbows and knees, sitting on the side of the road, staring through her tears at the mangled bicycle in the ditch.

Her parents had repeatedly cautioned her not to ride her bike on the hill to the north of the farm, because the road curved sharply, the gravel was loose and they worried she might fall. But they cautioned her about everything, so she did it anyway. With the sun warm on her face and the breeze ripe with the smell of freshly cut hay, she pedaled faster and faster, leaning low over the handlebars as the world blurred around her. The sensation of speed was intoxicating, her recklessness empowering.

Naturally, she crashed. The new bicycle she'd begged her parents to buy her was ruined. Her sweater was torn. Her scrapes stung like crazy. She had never felt more miserable, because she knew she would get in trouble, and that simply wasn't like her. When she heard the rumble in the distance, she thought it was thunder, but it turned out to be Jesse's Harley.

That was how they met. He was only fourteen, far too young to have a driver's license, yet he was big for his age and capable of handling the large machine. It was an old, rebuilt bike of questionable ownership that he cruised around the back roads where the cops seldom patrolled.

Brittany didn't care how many laws he was breaking. In her mind, he was the proverbial knight in shining armor, arriving on his flashy steed to rescue her.

His touch was gentle then, too. He didn't make fun of her for falling off her bicycle or for crying like a baby. He didn't comment on how she was too fat to ride it in the first place. Instead, he helped her onto the seat behind him and took her home on his Harley.

How could she help falling in love with him? He was the epitome of cool. Gorgeous, too. The six-year gap in their ages only made him more fascinating. Each time she saw him, she found more to love about him. He was kind. Funny. Smart. Sensitive. He wasn't bad, like everyone in town said.

Or so she'd fantasized.

She'd been a fool. Her naive longing for an imaginary love was the reason she'd nearly ruined her life.

Cutlery clinked against a stoneware plate, snapping Brittany out of her trance. She dropped her hand to her side, finally breaking the contact with Jesse. "Yes, of course I remember you," she said. "What brings you back to Port Hope?"

His smile faded. His features firmed into an expression every bit as tough as his reputation. "I'm looking for something."

CHAPTER FIVE

BEFORE BRITTANY COULD ask Jesse to explain what he was seeking, the bell over the restaurant door signalled the arrival of another customer. It was Ian Taylor, a local real estate agent, who turned out to be the man Jesse was waiting for. She ushered them to the booth against the back wall next to a plastic philodendron. By the time she returned with their glasses of iced tea, they were deep in discussion. It wasn't hard to deduce the topic. One not-very-subtle glance at the documents that were spread on the table between them confirmed her guess.

Jesse was selling his family home.

Well, it was bound to happen. She was surprised he had hung on to the property as long as he had. The land was poor, and the house had been badly neglected even before the family had abandoned it. This was no concern of hers, anyway. Her relationship with Jesse had been mostly in her mind. She should be pleased that she and her parents would be getting some new neighbors. She had absolutely no reason to feel sad. Maybe now she could close that disastrous chapter of her life for good.

Yet her crush on Jesse hadn't been all bad. Sure, it had led her into making some serious mistakes, but she'd learned from them, hadn't she? She wasn't waiting for anyone to rescue her. She began taking control of her life the day she forced herself to stop hiding behind her hair. She *had* changed.

Apparently, so had Jesse. The distinctive Harley and the leather jacket had thrown her at first. Now that she could observe him more thoroughly, she saw other differences in addition to the ones she'd noticed earlier. He used to work at a garage in town, and he regularly tinkered with his father's cars, but there was no trace of grease or motor oil on his hands now, not even along the cuticles. The expensive-looking gold watch that circled his wrist was at odds with the plain white T-shirt he wore. His demeanor as he spoke to Ian was businesslike, as if he was no stranger to dealing with legal contracts. The tough-guy image was further eroded when he put on a pair of reading glasses to scrutinize the fine print.

Whatever he'd been doing in the years

since he left town, he hadn't followed the same criminal career path as his father.

Or else he was much better at it.

No, she still couldn't believe Jesse was guilty. The police had arrested him primarily because of his reputation, which was totally unfair. He had a solid alibi. The garage records proved he had been fixing the brakes on the mayor's Monte Carlo during the time his father had been hijacking an armored car in Toronto. There was no evidence to connect Jesse with the crime.

But that didn't stop the whispers. The loot from the robbery was never found. Rumor had it, there was more than three million in cash hidden somewhere on the Koostra property.

I'm looking for something....

No. That couldn't be what he'd meant.

Or could it?

CHAPTER SIX

JESSE SHUT OFF the engine at the top of the driveway and let the bike coast the rest of the distance into the Bartons' yard. A few of the chickens that had been wandering around the grass flapped toward the lilac hedge in a panic. He remained motionless until they calmed, then set the kickstand. The day promised to be another hot one, yet the air was still cool in the shadow of the house. Pale curtains fluttered at windows that were wide open to catch the morning breeze. The lilting song of a robin drifted from the big maple at the edge of the lawn. Dew glistened on the flowers beside the steps. Soft tinkling came from the wind chimes that dangled beneath the veranda roof.

This was how Jesse remembered it. Clean. Neat. Peaceful. This house was more than a house, it was a home.

He used to wish he lived here. Every winter the Bartons decorated the veranda eaves with strings of Christmas lights. He could see them from his bedroom. The colors twinkled across the snowy fields as invitingly as traces of distant laughter. In the summer, the family planted marigolds around their mailbox. The flowers were whimsical, an unexpected patch of blooms amid the roadside weeds, and they made him smile whenever he went past.

The first time he came as far as the house was the day Brittany fell off her bicycle. He was naive enough to think the Bartons would thank him for helping their kid and maybe even ask him inside. Yeah, right. Emma Barton took one look at him and his Harley and snatched her daughter away as if *he* had caused her tears and skinned knees. Then to make sure he got the message, John Barton drove to the Koostra farm that night and had a talk with Jesse's father. Teenage boys had no business messing around with innocent, eight-year-old girls.

The old man went ballistic. Not because he cared whether or not Jesse might have done something wrong. No, Emile Koostra didn't like the implication that the neighbor's goody-two-shoes kid was too good for his son. He threw the man out, speeding him on his way by hurling a beer bottle after his car. Then he yelled at Jesse for getting involved in the first place. His exact words were, "I didn't raise no bleeding-heart pansy!"

Jesse knew better than to tell his father that he went back and got Brittany's bicycle out of the ditch, or that he repaired the frame, straightened the wheels and put on new tires. After he made sure it was safe to ride, he carried it to the Barton farm one night, when all the windows in the house were dark and the chickens were in their coop. He left it beside the veranda steps.

He wasn't sure if she got the bike, because he never saw her ride it again. He suspected her parents spotted it first, guessed it was from him and threw it out.

CHAPTER SEVEN

JESSE'S STOMACH CHURNED as he climbed the steps to the Bartons' veranda. That bothered him. He shouldn't need to remind himself he was no longer a kid. He was a thirty-year-old man who did business all over the world. The prejudices and petty gossip of his hometown could no longer hurt him. His childhood yearning for a home like this one shouldn't sting anymore, either. He'd grown out of that years ago.

Brittany's voice came through the screen door before he reached it. "Why would you want to come home, Mom? You and Dad haven't taken a holiday in ages. I thought you were enjoying yourselves."

Jesse raised his hand to knock.

"Yes, I know he's back. I saw him at the restaurant yesterday. Why would you say that's alarming?"

He hesitated. Was she talking about him?

"Mom, you're being unfair. He came back because he's selling the farm, that's all. He's a good person. He wouldn't want anything to do with his father's stolen money."

Great. He should have known that Emma Barton's attitude wouldn't change, even after eight years. The story of the loot hadn't died, either. At least Brittany sounded as if she still had faith in him.

"No, I'm not going to stay with Uncle Ronnie and Aunt Mae. Yes, I promise to call the police if I see anything suspicious, even though I think you're being ridiculous."

His lips twitched. It was good to hear Brittany stand up for herself. That was one thing that *had* changed. He rapped lightly on the door frame.

"I've got to go, Mom. Someone's at the door. Yes, I love you, too. Enjoy the beach, and stop worrying!" Footsteps padded across hardwood. A second later, Brittany appeared on the other side of the screen. Her eyes widened when she saw him. "Uh, hi."

He smiled as he returned her regard. The girl he remembered often avoided meeting his gaze. It was a shame, because her eyes were a striking shade of green. She'd been painfully shy, and probably self-conscious about her weight, but to him she'd seemed as adorable as a cherub. In spite of her parents' concerns, his feelings for Brittany had been nothing but brotherly.

Man, he'd been pathetic. Not only had he wished he could live in a house like hers, he'd wished that she was his little sister. Someone to love without fear of being mocked and called soft would have made life with Emile more bearable. His own sister was two years older than him and as tough as their father. She left home at seventeen, shortly after their mother died, and she never came back. She lost herself so thoroughly that he'd had to hire a private detective to find her so she could sign off on the house sale.

But it was just as well that Jesse never got his wish, because the feelings the grown-up Brittany evoked were definitely not brotherly.

CHAPTER EIGHT

"Um, this is a surprise."

Jesse smiled. Oh yeah, Brittany had grown up. Her once cherubic face now sported cheekbones and a delicately pointed chin, and the chestnut hair that used to flow way past her shoulders was cut short, yet her beautiful green eyes hadn't changed. Neither had the way she looked at him as if she cared....

Get real. He held out a tractor company magazine. "I found this in my mailbox. It's addressed to your father."

"Thanks. I'll give it to him when he gets back." She pushed open the door and took the magazine. "My parents are on vacation. So's our regular mail lady. Someone else is doing her route and this is the second time something went astray. It was nice of you to bring it over."

"No problem. I wanted to talk to you, anyway. We didn't get a chance yesterday at the restaurant."

"Uh…"

Easy there, he told himself. It had been eight years since they'd spoken. That was a long time for any friendship to endure. To her, he would be the guy who used to live in the junkyard next door. The jailbird's son. She wouldn't know how important she had been to him. "I sold the farm," he said. "I thought you and your folks would want to know. Is this a bad time?"

"No, I've been up for hours. Come on in."

He'd known she was up, because he had seen her bedroom light go on before dawn. She was an early riser when she was a kid, too. He used to imagine her mother calling her downstairs for breakfast. It wouldn't consist of leftover pizza or a spoonful of peanut butter straight from the jar. It would be something wholesome, maybe hot oatmeal or scrambled eggs.

The screen door squeaked behind him and sprang closed with a thunk. He followed Brittany the few steps into the kitchen. The room was large and homey, stretching from one side of the house to the other. The table in the center of the floor was big and wooden, but it didn't hold any food. Instead it held a sewing machine and a pile of shiny, red fabric. Colorful drawings of dresses on stick figures were taped to the cupboards and a large sketchbook lay across the sink.

Brittany swept fabric scraps off one of the chairs and motioned for him to sit down. "Sorry about the mess. I work in here because this room has a good cross draft and stays cool the longest. Would you like some coffee? There's another cup left in the pot. Or I could make up some iced tea."

He shook his head as he moved closer to one of the drawings. "Did you do these?"

"Those are just some ideas I scribbled this morning."

"They're very impressive. You're a fashion designer."

"So far I'm just a student. I work at Mae B's to pay my tuition, but yes, eventually I want to design professionally."

"Seems to me that you've already started."

"It took me a while to figure out that's what I want to do with my life. Actually, it's because of you that I did."

CHAPTER NINE

"ME? HOW DID I influence you?"

Brittany hesitated, as if she regretted her blurted admission, but then she lifted her chin, wiped her palms on her shorts and gave him a crooked smile. "This might sound strange, because you probably don't realize how big an impact you made on me when I was a kid. I didn't have the nerve to tell you then, but I envied you."

Of all the things Brittany might have said, that was the last one Jesse expected. "*You* envied *me?*"

She nodded. "You were so brave. You did whatever you pleased, and no one pushed you around."

He restrained himself from snorting. She'd never observed his father in action.

"When I saw you on your motorcycle, I used to wish I could ride away like that. I wanted adventure, and freedom, and—" She halted. "I'm sorry. That sounds really lame when I say it aloud."

Not as pathetic as his old fantasies about her. He gestured toward a sketch of a long, red dress. "I don't recall wearing stuff like that when I rode my Harley, so how did I steer you into fashion design?"

She laughed the same quick way she did as a child when he employed humor to draw her out, as if she was startled that anyone wanted to listen to her. "That's not what I meant," she said. "I set out to search for what I saw in you. Along the way, I happened to find what I really wanted."

He took the chair she'd cleared off earlier, turned it around and straddled it. He folded his arms across the back. "What were you looking for? The adventure and freedom thing?"

"Yes, but we've gotten way off topic." She pulled out another chair and sat facing him. "You came over to talk about selling the farm."

Right. That was the excuse he'd given her. "The couple who bought it are retirees from Toronto. They're not farmers but they're not deadbeats, either. They shouldn't cause you any trouble."

"A lot of retirees from the city end up out here. They want the country lifestyle."

"Which doesn't include a junkyard. The

buyers made cleaning the place up one of the conditions of the sale. A scrap metal dealer's coming out tomorrow, and I've already started on the house."

"When's the closing date?"

"The end of the month."

"So soon? That's less than two weeks."

When he'd agreed to the sale, he felt the date couldn't come soon enough. He believed it would give him plenty of time to find what he was looking for and end that period of his life for good. He didn't feel in such a hurry now. "Tell me about your adventure, Brittany. You still haven't explained how you got into fashion design."

"It doesn't matter."

"Hey, it does to me."

"Funny. You still sound as if you mean it. That's why I used to love talking to you."

"Well?"

CHAPTER TEN

BRITTANY SIGHED, BRACED her elbow on the edge of the table and leaned her head on her hand.

"Okay, fine, it's no secret. You'll probably hear the gossip anyway if you're here for two weeks. The day after I finished high school, I ran away from home."

It was a morning for surprises. So far, this was the biggest one. "You ran away from home? *This* home?"

"Why is that so hard to believe?"

"A lot of people would do anything to have a home like this and a family like yours."

"Don't you remember my mom and dad? They were the original helicopter parents even before the term was invented. I know they love me and I love them, but their constant hovering made me too afraid of making mistakes to try anything new. You were different. You treated me as if my opinion counted."

"You were a good kid. I liked you."

She pursed her lips. "That's nice of you to say, but you didn't really know me."

"I think I did. I realize there was an age gap, but we had a connection. I considered us friends. I enjoyed every one of our conversations."

"I did, too."

"Even though you used to talk through your hair a lot?"

She laughed, keeping her gaze steady on his face. "There, is that better?"

Not exactly. His attention shifted to her mouth. Her lips were plump and moist and as inviting as the raspberries that grew along the south boundary of the Barton place. He used to climb over the fence to steal them. What would she do if he stole a kiss?

He wrenched his thoughts back on track. "So, did you run away to an art school?" he asked. "Montreal? Milan?"

"No, I hooked up with a drummer in a heavy metal band and went on tour with them."

Jesse's first impulse was to laugh, because he assumed she must be joking. His sweet, little cherub, touring with a rock band? But her tone was matter-of-fact, and there were those studs in her ears, and purple streaks in her hair. There was also a flash of pain in her eyes. She was dead serious. He took her hand between his, wishing he could kiss away the bad memory. "What happened?" he asked.

"I started managing the band's wardrobe. I got pretty good at designing costumes. By the time the drummer dumped me, I realized I had been sticking around for the work, not for him." Her expression grew wistful as she focused on their joined hands. "He wasn't who I thought he was."

Neither am I, Jesse thought. *She deserves to know....*

Heavy footsteps sounded on the veranda. He glanced over his shoulder just as a large man appeared outside the screen door. A uniformed man with a holster on his belt.

Terrific.

There were plenty of reasons Jesse didn't like cops. Now he could add bad timing to the list.

CHAPTER ELEVEN

THERE HAD BEEN few occasions in Brittany's life when she'd been irritated enough to consider violence. This was one of them. She balled her fists and followed her cousin across the yard.

"What are you doing here, Arty? Did Mom call you?"

He lengthened his stride as he walked to his patrol car. "Keep out of this, Britt."

"No, I will not keep out of it. You have no grounds for coming to my house and harassing my guest. Jesse's not obligated to go anywhere with you."

"It's okay, Brittany," Jesse said. "He's only doing his job. We'll finish our conversation later, all right?" He swung his leg over his Harley and dug into his jeans for the key. "I assume you know where I live, Constable Reid?"

"Lead the way. I'll be right behind you."

The big engine rumbled to life. Jesse lifted

a hand to her in farewell and eased the bike down the driveway.

Brittany blinked hard, struck by a pang of loss at the sight of Jesse leaving. Which was absurd. If they were going to his place, he would only be a mile away.

"Go back inside," Arty said. "This doesn't concern you."

She darted in front of him to block his way to the car. "Mom did ask you to check up on me, didn't she? Why else would you show up here like this?"

"She did call, but I was on my way to see Koostra anyway."

"Why?"

"I just need to ask him a few questions. Police business."

"Arty…"

Without further explanation, he stepped around her, got into his car and drove off. Dust swirled across the lawn. The chickens squawked and retreated to the lilacs. Brittany shaded her eyes with her hand and watched until the vehicles turned down the road toward the Koostra place.

This was so frustrating. Her family was being overprotective, and they were still treating Jesse like a criminal. They were also treating her like an idiot. Which she had been, and still was a lot of the time, but not in this case. Jesse was a good man. Was she the only one who saw it? He had dropped in here to be neighborly. He didn't deserve his reputation. He couldn't choose which family he was born into any more than she could.

Just like she couldn't choose which man she fell in love with....

Her hands curled into fists again, but this time her frustration was directed at herself. She had to think logically. What she felt couldn't be love. It was the remnant of her childhood crush mixed together with a very adult reaction to an incredibly good-looking man. She hadn't seen Jesse for eight years. She couldn't possibly fall in love with him again in less than a day.

Nevertheless, the sense of loss that had been triggered by Jesse's departure was rapidly deepening into panic.

Brittany wasn't aware of making a decision, yet somehow she found herself behind the wheel of her car and barrelling down the driveway.

CHAPTER TWELVE

BRUSH GREW UNCHECKED at the sides of the gravel lane, narrowing it to the point that some of the branches scraped along Brittany's car. She slowed as she neared the Koostra house. A rusty pick-up truck with no wheels sat in the center of what once might have been a lawn. Weeds swallowed what was left of a picket fence. More rusted-out car carcasses lay haphazardly around the barn. Jesse's Harley was angled near a large and relatively new-looking Dumpster. There was no sign of Arty's black-and-white cruiser, which meant her cousin had already finished his "chat" with Jesse.

Or else he'd taken Jesse to the station with him....

Seized by the same sense of urgency that had brought her here, Brittany left her car beside the motorcycle and picked her way through the weeds to the house. It was a clapboard two-story, similar in design to her family's farmhouse since it was built around the turn of the last century like theirs, but it showed every one of its years. Moss had taken hold on the roof shingles and paint flaked from the siding. The screen door at the front stood ajar, propped open by a bucket with a mop in it. Before she reached the steps, Jesse emerged from the doorway carrying two bulging plastic garbage bags. He halted when he saw her. "Brittany! What are you doing here?"

That was a complex question. She gave the simplest answer. "I was worried about you."

He dropped the bags on the porch and brushed off his hands. He seemed more surprised by her admission than by her arrival. "You were worried about me?"

"I'm sorry my cousin hassled you. It wasn't your fault. Ever since he got that badge he likes to throw his weight around."

"Don't blame him. It wasn't personal."

"How can you say that? This whole town has never been fair to you. If people had only given you a chance and gotten to know you the way I did, you wouldn't have felt the need to disappear after the trial. You would have stayed here and…"…*and let me love you.* Thankfully, she stopped before she completed the sentence aloud. "It wasn't fair," she repeated, starting up the stairs.

"Maybe not, but that isn't what's going on now." He grasped her hand to help her past a step where the wood had rotted away. "Your cousin wanted to talk to me about my father, that's all."

"Your father? Why? The police know you weren't an accomplice. You proved your innocence. The case was closed years ago."

"Not entirely."

"But—"

"Emile gets out of the penitentiary in November. The cops assume he'll come after the money."

"You mean the loot from the robbery? I thought that was just a legend."

Jesse tightened his grasp on her hand to lead her into the house. "Let me show you something."

CHAPTER THIRTEEN

THE AIR INSIDE the Koostra house was heavy with the scent of pine cleanser—Jesse had evidently been busy—but eight years of accumulated dust wasn't the only problem he faced. There were holes in the walls. And in the floor. They didn't appear to be from rot, like the hole on the step outside. Brittany followed Jesse down a short hall to a small room that the original builders had likely intended as a parlor. The destruction was worse here. One lathe-and-plaster wall had been ripped apart entirely, exposing aged wooden studs and part of the kitchen beyond them.

She remembered the occasional lights she had seen in the abandoned house. It was easy to guess what had happened. "This must have been done by treasure hunters."

"Uh-huh. It sure wasn't mice. My real estate agent downplayed the extent of the damage when he listed the place. I hadn't realized how bad it was until I got here. It's a wonder anyone would agree to buy it." He snorted a laugh. "On the other hand, maybe those retirees who bought it are counting on finding the money themselves."

"Then the story about the loot is true?"

"Between the cops and the jerks who trashed this house, the whole property was gone over dozens of times. If the money was ever here, chances are it's not anymore."

"*If* it was here? You don't know for sure?"

"My father didn't confide in me." He stooped to pick up a chunk of plaster from the floor and dropped it in an open garbage bag. "But I know my old man. He had two months between the robbery and his arrest. It wouldn't surprise me if he lost every penny of what he stole."

"It was more than three million, wasn't it?"

"Three million, six hundred and seventy thousand plus change, but he liked to gamble. He wasn't much good at it. Every dollar he got hold of went to feed his habit."

"I'm sorry, Jesse. That must have been so hard on you."

"The only reason we didn't end up living in one of his junked cars was because this farm belonged to my mother, not him. She knew how he was. She willed it directly to my sister and me so we'd at least have a roof over our heads when she was gone." He took a deep breath, rubbed his face hard, then dropped his hands and looked at her. "I didn't mean to go on like that. It's this place. I'll be glad to be rid of it."

"I shouldn't have complained about my own family to you. What you went through… I can't even imagine." Yet that wasn't true, because she could all too readily imagine the deep scars Jesse carried from his childhood. It was a testament to his character that he'd grown into such a strong and sensitive man.

"We were some pair, weren't we, Brittany? You envying me, and me envying you."

She started. Had she heard him right? "*You* envied *me?*"

CHAPTER FOURTEEN

"YOU'RE BIG ON FAIRNESS," Jesse said. "After the way you told me about your stint with the rock band, it's only fair if I come clean with you."

But Brittany hadn't told him everything. She'd omitted the fact that the drummer she'd run off with had blue eyes and blond hair. He also had a motorcycle that he clamped to the back of the band's bus to transport between gigs. She'd been a fool to think his superficial resemblance to Jesse extended any deeper. No one compared to the man who stood in front of her.

Jesse hesitated, then lifted her hand and brushed his mouth over her fingers. "You weren't the only one who left town in search of something, Brittany. I wanted what you had."

The sensation of his lips against her skin made it hard to concentrate on his words. The contact felt more than good, it felt natural. Right. She longed to tell him that *this* was

what she'd been searching for. Him. Jesse.
And the way he made her feel. But all that
came out was, "What?"

"There's nothing exciting or free about
being a grease monkey and living in a junkyard," he said. "I wanted respectability and
a real home like yours. Nobody forced me to
leave town, I was happy to go. After the trial,
I went out to Calgary to get a fresh start."

Calgary? "That's so far."

"It wasn't far enough. No matter what I
did, I couldn't seem to shake off the taint of
where I came from."

"Don't say that. You've always been a
good person. Besides, this place isn't so bad.
There's nothing that some paint and a truck-
load of new lumber wouldn't fix."

He smiled. "My sweet, little Brittany. You
see good in anything."

"Only when it's there, Jesse. And don't
talk to me as if I'm still a child. I'm a grown
woman, in case you haven't noticed."

His smile broadened. "Believe me, I've noticed."

Brittany had always loved Jesse's smile.
She'd dreamed of it often when she was
younger. It didn't merely deepen his dimples
and crinkle the skin around his eyes, it gave
her a glimpse of the kind, gentle young man

she adored. He smiled like a friend who was happy to see her, who wanted to comfort her over the silliest of her worries or celebrate the most trivial accomplishment.

But she had never seen him smile this particular smile before. He hadn't needed to be reminded she had grown up, because he clearly wasn't regarding her as a child. She was old enough to realize that his gaze was focused on her mouth as if he wanted to...

Yes! *Yes! Kiss me, Jesse.*

He raised his hand to her temple and tunneled his fingers through her hair. "It looks good short."

"So does yours."

He followed the curve of her ear, rubbing his thumb along the studs on the rim. "These suit you."

"Really?"

"Yeah. Somehow they make you look even sweeter." He paused. "I have a confession to make."

CHAPTER FIFTEEN

WHAT CONFESSION? THAT you want to kiss me? I know. I see that. Go ahead. Please.

"I knew who you were before I came into the restaurant yesterday," Jesse said.

"I don't understand."

He dropped his hand to her shoulder. "I was trying to act cool because I didn't want to scare you off, but I was eager to see you. I recognized you through the window. You were looking at my bike."

"It's a unique bike."

"And that's something else I should come clean about. I'm not the guy you think I am."

"Jesse…"

"You've been quick to defend me, because it must seem as if I haven't changed, but I have."

There had been changes to the outside, like his shorter hair, and the other differences she had noticed, but nothing he could say would convince her that he wasn't still her Jesse.

"I haven't ridden that bike in almost eight

years," he said. "I got rid of it before I went out west. I traded it to a friend in exchange for his car."

"Why…?"

"Harleys are great for making a statement, but not so great for making a trip across the country."

"No, I mean why do you have it now?"

"I stopped by my friend's place on my way here from the airport and he agreed to loan it back to me. Like I said, it makes a statement. I thought if I returned to town the same way I left, it would help me get over my past. That's the main reason I came home. It's why I'm taking the time to clean up the house myself before I leave. It wasn't just to sell this farm. I hope to break its hold on me for good so I can get on with my life."

Hearing him talk about leaving should have doused her feelings. It didn't. It only made the urge to kiss him stronger. In another two weeks at the most, he would disappear again. Was she going to spend the rest of her life wondering what might have happened if only she'd had more courage? She placed her palms on his chest and swayed closer. "Are all your memories of this place bad ones, Jesse?" she asked.

"No, Brittany. Not my memories of you."

They fell silent, their gazes locked on each other. She wasn't sure how long they stood there, and she never knew who moved first. What happened next seemed inevitable. She was already lifting herself up on her toes to reach him when he lowered his head.

Their lips met.

Her breath caught.

Her pulse skipped and launched into a sprint.

When her balance deserted her, it didn't matter because her hands had somehow anchored themselves in Jesse's T-shirt and his arms were locked around her back.

Yes, *yes!* This was better than she had dreamed. No fantasy could compare to the flood of pleasure from Jesse's kiss. It was empowering. Exhilarating.

And it was as reckless as racing down a gravel hill on a bicycle.

CHAPTER SIXTEEN

AIR BRAKES HISSED as the truck from the scrap dealer backed to a stop. Jesse glanced out the window, then hit the key to send the invoice, turned off his laptop and walked out to the porch. Regardless of how many more business details needed his attention, there was no way he would miss seeing this. He had looked forward to shedding the weight of his father's lifestyle for eight years.

The guys he'd hired worked smoothly and efficiently. One operated the crane on the back of the truck while the other looped the chains around the wrecks. By noon, they'd secured the first load to the truck bed and maneuvered it down the driveway. Though plenty of junk remained in the barn, apart from the lingering smells of rusty metal and diesel exhaust, the yard was clear.

So where was the satisfaction he'd expected to feel? Had the anger, the resentment and the shame dissipated? He still didn't see his past in an entirely new way. He just saw a lawn that needed mowing, and a fence that needed painting.

Are all your memories of this place bad ones, Jesse?

Brittany's voice stole into his thoughts, drawing out the ghost of a smile. She had a knack for making him view things from a different angle. She'd definitely left him with a good memory of the front parlor. He wasn't certain how their kiss happened, because he tried all day to resist it. He should have told her the rest of the truth about himself first. Instead, he'd given in to...

To what? An urge? A passing fancy? She meant more to him than that. So did the kiss. Remembering it had kept him up most of the night. Across the field, her bedroom had been dark, but he sensed she was awake, too, maybe listening to the mosquitoes on the screen, and relishing the touch of the cool breeze on her hot skin, and thinking about him the way he was thinking about her.

A sharp buzz interrupted Jesse's musings. He laughed softly and slipped his cell phone from his pocket. He'd only been home for three days and already he was reverting to a love-starved kid.

"Mr. Koostra?"

The man's voice was familiar, but Jesse couldn't place it. "Yes?"

"This is Constable Reid. We spoke yesterday concerning your father's case."

Right. Brittany's cousin. "What can I do for you, officer?"

"Your father was released from prison this morning."

It took a few seconds for the words to sink in. Jesse staggered, bracing his free hand against the side of the house. He fought to keep his voice level. "There must be some mistake. He wasn't due to be released until November."

"There were special circumstances."

His gut clenched with concern. It was a reflex reaction, and it surprised him. "What happened? Is he sick? Is he in a hospital?"

"No. He's headed your way. I'll explain more later. We have units moving into place to secure the perimeter. Can we count on your cooperation?"

CHAPTER SEVENTEEN

THE AFTERNOON DRAGGED ON. Nothing stirred in the yard except an occasional barn swallow swooping after a fly. When Jesse saw movement in the brush near the property line, he assumed it was one of the cops who were posted around the farm. He was wrong. The branches parted to reveal a petite woman with purple-streaked hair.

"Brittany!" He ran to meet her. "What are you doing here?"

That made twice in two days he'd asked the same question. Her reply was the same this time, too. "I was worried about you."

He grasped her arms to steady her. Her face was damp and she was breathing hard. She must have run all the way across the field from the Barton place. "I'm fine," he said. "Why—"

"Arty called me at work. He told me to stay in town. He said there was a police operation at your place, but he wouldn't tell me any more, so I came to see for myself. What's going on? Where are the cops?"

Jesse looped his arm over her shoulders and guided her to the house. Her cousin should have known better than to give Brittany orders. "They're waiting for my father." He handed her a bottle of water and filled her in on the morning's developments while she drank. "You should have listened to your cousin," he said.

"I'm glad I didn't." She finished the water, set the bottle aside and caught his hands. "Whatever happens, I want to be here for you, Jesse."

They were such simple words. Other people probably heard them all the time, but this was a first for Jesse. He had no doubt Brittany meant what she said, too. Her gaze brimmed with concern. It moved him as deeply as her kiss, only on a different level. He squeezed her fingers. "You would be better off at your place."

"You don't think your father would hurt anyone, do you?"

"He had a temper, but he wasn't violent. He didn't hurt anyone during that robbery, either. Still, it's been eight years."

"Eight years? You mean you never visited him?"

He experienced an unfamiliar twinge of guilt. "The last time I saw him, he was being driven away in the back of a police car. I hadn't planned to meet him now, either. The sale of the farm was supposed to close months before he got out. I should have been on the other side of the country before he set one foot outside the pen."

She stretched to bring her face closer to his. "Now for sure I'm not going home. I'm staying right here."

"Why?"

"I already told you. I don't want you to be alone." Her lips trembled. "I care about you, Jesse. I always have. To be honest, I…"

He put his finger against her lips. "Wait, Brittany. I need to be honest, too."

CHAPTER EIGHTEEN

THE FLUSH THAT Brittany's run across the field had brought to her cheeks slowly faded. She pulled back. "You're married, aren't you? I should have known. You're so gorgeous and sexy and I'm an idiot for not guessing—"

"I'm not married. Never even got close."

She paused. "No?"

"No," he said firmly. "There's no one."

"What's wrong with the women out west? Are they blind? Not that I wish you were in a relationship, because that would make me feel even more of an idiot, but..." She waved her hand in front of her face in an erasing motion. "I'm babbling. I'll stop now."

His gaze dropped to her mouth. He could think of a more enjoyable way to stop her words. "You think I'm sexy?"

"Do they not have mirrors in Calgary, either?" She made another erasing motion. "What did you want to tell me, Jesse?"

He shoved his hands in the pockets of his jeans to prevent himself from reaching for her. "You couldn't know how good it makes me feel every time you show your faith in me, Brittany. You were the one person in this town who treated me as if I was worth something."

"I know you, Jesse. I—"

"Please, I need to finish. You said you envied me, and you thought my motorcycle represented adventure and freedom. You ran off with a rock band because you were searching for some kind of idealized, romantic picture of what I had."

She seemed about to speak, then pressed her lips together and nodded.

"I already told you I no longer own that Harley. What I didn't tell you is that I'm about as exciting as a bank statement. I drive a sedan and wear a suit to work. I prefer classical music to rock. I pay my taxes on time every year. I'm no rebel, Brittany. I'm a salesman for a company that manufactures drill bits."

Her teeth dug into her lower lip.

"You don't need to come to my defense with the police, either. I don't like them, but I have nothing to fear from them. I'm an upstanding, law-abiding citizen. So upstanding I'm downright boring."

She covered her mouth with her hand. Her shoulders shook.

"I'm sorry if that disappoints you, but I felt you should know."

"Oh, Jesse." She dropped her hand, revealing her grin. It was laughter she had been suppressing, not distress. "The women out west might have problems with their vision, but there's nothing wrong with mine. I already noticed your manicure. And the reading glasses, and the expensive watch and cologne. It was nice of you to explain, but you didn't have to. I've loved you too long to stop now. Whatever you do, you'll always be my Jesse."

Love. She said *love*. To *him*. He couldn't reply. He couldn't even breathe.

Into the silence came the crunch of tires on gravel. Jesse glanced out the window just as a police car rolled into the yard.

CHAPTER NINETEEN

THOUGH JESSE'S FATHER was sixty-two, his hair was still thick and free of gray, and he kept his back straight, his chin out and his shoulders squared as he walked. He was a large man, the same height as Jesse, and yet… somehow he looked smaller than he used to.

The police officers who had brought him home remained beside the patrol car. Emile climbed the steps to the porch where Jesse waited and dipped his chin in a curt nod. "Hello, Jesse."

No handshake, and no hug, even after eight years, but Jesse hadn't expected either one. Their family had never been big on touching. He crossed his arms. "Hello, Dad."

"You been doing some clean-up in the yard."

"Yes."

"Hope you got a good price for the scrap."

"Sure did. Congratulations on your early release."

"Guess the cops told you I made a deal?"

"They said you agreed to show them where you left the money."

"That's why they let me out."

"You only had three more months to serve. You could have waited and gotten the money on your own. Why make the deal now?"

"I heard you came home to sell the farm."

"How'd you hear that?"

"Believe it or not, your sister told me right after you got her to sign the papers."

That stunned him. Then again, he never knew what to expect from Annie. "Were you worried the new owners would get your stash?"

"No, I had to get out before you disappeared again."

"I don't understand."

"I don't want the money, son, I came to see you. That's worth more than a few million to me."

There had been no change in Emile's expression, but his voice had roughened with emotion to the point it was almost unrecognizable.

The screen door squeaked open behind Jesse. A moment later, he felt Brittany move to his side. Without uttering a word, she slipped her arm around his waist. She was a head shorter than him and half his weight, but it wasn't physical support that she offered. He draped his arm over her shoulders gratefully, his mind reeling.

"I can't blame you for cutting me loose when I got arrested," Emile continued. "You stuck it out with me years longer than your sister did. Your mother...you take after her. She had a good soul." He coughed, then used his sleeve to wipe his eyes. "She hated my gambling, and I just didn't see how bad it dragged me down until it was too late. I hit bottom when I pulled that heist. Just about went crazy after I heard they arrested you, too. But that was the kick in the butt I needed. I got help, Jesse. I went through a program they had at the pen. I've got a job lined up too, an honest job. I..." He sighed. "That's why I had to see you. I want you to know I'm sorry."

Jesse was unable to speak past the lump in his throat. He reached out his free hand to grasp his father's shoulder.

Emile clamped his hand over Jesse's to keep it in place. His gaze shifted to Brittany. "So, who're you?"

"I'm Brittany Barton, Mr. Koostra. I live next door."

"Barton?" Emile laughed suddenly and

turned his head to yell at the police officers in the yard.

"You don't need me. She can show you where the money is."

CHAPTER TWENTY

IT WAS AFTER midnight by the time the legendary Koostra loot was found. By then, television crews from three networks were parked at the foot of the Bartons' driveway. Police vehicles crowded the yard. Under the glare of portable floodlights, Brittany's cousin Arty tossed down his shovel as one of the Tyvek-suited crime scene specialists emerged from the hole that the cops had dug beneath the Bartons' chicken coop. A dirt-streaked canvas sack was clutched triumphantly in his hand.

"I still can't believe this," Brittany muttered, slapping at a mosquito. She and Jesse stood near the big maple by the house, beyond the ring of light yet close enough to have a good view of the action. "All these years. Three and a half million dollars. Right under our noses."

Jesse crossed his arms in front of her waist to pull her back against his chest. He'd been smiling so much, his cheeks ached. "I'd say 'noses' is the operative word."

She laughed and leaned her head on his shoulder. "Poor Arty. He never did like our chickens."

"My father chose a good spot."

"I'll say. No one would expect to find a fortune here."

"Well, you never know. Sometimes you go out searching for what you think you want only to find what you truly want along the way."

"Mmm. That sounds familiar."

"It should. That's what you told me." He rubbed his chin over her hair, marveling at how natural, how right, it felt to hold her like this. Marveling at how Fate worked. "I decided to cancel the sale of the farm."

She inhaled sharply. A tremor went through her body. "You did? Why?"

"My father needs a place to live."

"Oh. That's great. He'll appreciate it."

"Yeah. I realized something today. I do care about him. I guess that's why I stayed with him as long as I did."

"I hope you give him a chance. He seems sincere about wanting to improve things between you."

"We'll get plenty of opportunity for that, since I'll be living here, too."

She twisted to face him. "You're moving back home?"

"Not right away. I'll need to sell my condo, and if I can't get my job transferred to my company's Toronto office, I'll have to find a new one. It's going to take more than lumber and paint to fix up that old house, but it's got a great location, and terrific neighbors."

Her back was to the floodlights so he couldn't see her expression clearly, yet he did catch the gleam of her eyes. Beautiful, green eyes, that always made him feel strong, special, good…

Good enough to be loved.

And just like that, the weight of Jesse's past crumbled and fell away. He placed his hands on Brittany's cheeks, cradling her with the gentleness that a treasure like her deserved. "Remember the love and the not-being-alone stuff you talked about this afternoon?"

She nodded.

"I could get used to that."

* * * * *

REQUEST YOUR FREE BOOKS!

2 FREE INSPIRATIONAL NOVELS
PLUS 2
FREE
MYSTERY GIFTS

Love Inspired

LIDIR13R